RIDE TO THE BULLET

ALSO BY WAYNE D DUNDEE

RIDE TO THE BULLET

A LONE MCGANTRY WESTERN

WAYNE D DUNDEE

WOLFPACK
PUBLISHING
— EST 2013 —

RIDE TO THE BULLET

CHAPTER ONE

THE TINY SETTLEMENT OF SARBEN WAS LOCATED ON THE southern fringes of Nebraska's fabled Sandhills, a dozen miles above the north branch of the Platte River. This also placed it some thirty miles west of the railroad town of North Platte and an equal distance east of the cow town of Ogallala. Sarben boasted only fifty or so residents, roughly half of them retired Army personnel —old soldiers and their wives or, in a few cases, the remaining widows of soldiers—once stationed at Fort McPherson when it operated off to the east for the purpose of guarding immigrant on the Oregon Trail, and then as an important post during the Great Plains Indian Wars.

At Sarben's hub was a combination general store/saloon. There was also a blacksmith shop and a barber who pulled teeth as a sideline. The latter offered nothing in the way of dental *care*, mind you, only the service of yanking out problem choppers—even if it took two or three tries to get the right one. Additionally, there was a small non-denominational church with services held in a converted tool shed out behind the home of Pastor Isaac Potter and his wife Eliza. Three mornings a week, Eliza taught school classes in the same building for children and adults alike who sought to gain a little bit of rudimentary education.

In short, Sarben was the sort of place some might scoff at as being a mighty poor excuse for anything resembling a town. However, to those who saw it for what it attempted to be and succeeded at—a gathering spot for its residents and surrounding ranch folk, and the place where a few basic needs and supplies could be acquired without making the long trip to either North Platte or Ogallala—it was well appreciated.

Former Army scout Lone McGantry fit in the latter category. He'd spent some brief time in and around Sarben in the past, back when he and his partner, one-legged, old mountain man Peg O'Malley, had started a small horse ranch called the Busted Spur in the nearby Sandhills. That undertaking ended when Peg was killed by a gang of marauding horse thieves while Lone was away earning some side money to buy more stock. The ensuing months were eaten up by Lone taking Peg's body to a final resting place in his beloved mountains and then running down the curs who killed him. After that, Lone had gone on the drift once again, pursuing scattered interests the way he'd done when his scouting days were first over—but none of them included an attempt at resurrecting the Busted Spur.

This changed the previous year when, right on the heels of finding and then tragically losing the love of his life, Lone learned how a slick-talking con man by the name of Swain had jilted his oldest and dearest remaining friend in the world; about the closest thing he ever had to a family. Adeline "Ma" Sharples had been an Army wife at Fort McPherson who played a major role in raising Lone after he was orphaned by an Indian raid that killed his parents. Thanks to Swain, she was tricked out of her life savings as well as the boarding house that she, an elderly widow now, had run in North Platte for a decade and a half. Lone went after the conniving skunk and was able to regain enough of Ma's money to set her back on her feet again, though not enough for her to re-open a new boarding house. Declaring herself weary of running a business anyway and wanting to get out of North Platte where she felt humiliated and embarrassed by allowing herself to be swindled the way she had, Ma opted to relocate to Sarben where she would share a house with another Army widow already living there. The process of helping Ma get moved and settled into her new digs had rekindled in Lone, thoughts of maybe doing some settling down himself and taking another stab at making a go of the Busted Spur.

And so it was on this fine spring day of a new year that Lone rode into Sarben looking to pick up some supplies for his ranch. He was a big man, tall in the saddle, thick through the chest and shoulders. His face was a squarish, weathered slab built around a prominent nose and set with alert blue eyes. His features plainly showed his nearly forty years of life, etched to a large extent by exposure to the harsh sun and biting winds. It was a face men tended to eye warily, and though it would seldom, if ever, be called handsome, one the gazes of women often lingered on. His attire of a flat-crowned Stetson, buckskin vest worn over a collarless, boiled white shirt, and faded denim britches giving way to dusty, well-worn boots further marked him as a man of the frontier. The Colt .44 riding easy in a holster on his right hip and the bone-handled Bowie with its ten-inch blade sheathed on his left gave added silent testimony that at times, both in and out of his Army scouting years, he'd dealt with violence and continued to be prepared should any more come his way.

Lone had endured an obligingly mild winter upon his return to the Busted Spur. In the course of it, he'd made necessary repairs after leaving things abandoned for so long and then got started on a list of additional modifications and improvements. He'd also acquired a starter string of a dozen sturdy, if not spectacular horses, three of them mares due to foal in a few weeks.

It all felt good, felt right. Like the decision to take up the ranch again was something it had been the proper time and circumstance for. The one-man operation still gave Lone the stretches of solitude he craved, those periods that not only fit his name but also his nature, the part of him honed by all those years of scouting and drifting across the frontier on his own. But the visits to small, simple Sarben every four or five weeks—to stop in and see Ma, to pick up a few supplies, maybe grab a couple beers, and do a little chin wagging with the regulars at the saloon—gave him just the right doses of mingling with others, too. That was something he'd surprisingly grown to feel more a need for of late. Ever since losing Velda. Those alone times that had always before suited him well enough in and of themselves now contained odd moments of feeling empty in a way he'd never known until she came into his life and then was torn so cruelly out of it. So today's trip to the settlement was for the purpose of re-stocking supplies, true enough, but it was also aimed at filling some of that emptiness.

A big chunk of the latter was promptly taken care of by having lunch with Ma and her housemate, Mabel Kromier. Mabel had also been at Fort McPherson when Ma and Lone were there, though she showed up later, when Lone was old enough to begin serving his hitch in uniform before moving on to the role of civilian scout. But except for appearance—Mabel was an energetic wisp of a gal, whereas Ma was the stouter, more methodical type—the two were cut from very similar cloth. And since each had been married to a hearty-eating man, it worked to Lone's benefit that whenever he stopped by for one of his intermittent visits, they were all too eager to serve up a heaping, delicious meal for him.

It crossed Lone's mind now and then that maybe he ought to feel guilty for showing up unannounced and expecting such grand treatment, but then he would have an internal argument and manage to convince himself the ladies got as much enjoyment out of the routine as he did. After all, he didn't want to risk hurting their feelings by *not* chowing down in a proper display of appreciation. Further undermining his willpower to do otherwise was the fact that, in addition to the fine fare placed before him at the table, he also was invariably sent on his way with a sack of vittles that would feed him for another couple days once he got back to the Busted Spur.

To help erase any lingering guilt about taking advantage, and by way of compensation for what he gained from his visits, Lone had an arrangement—strictly unknown to Ma and Mabel—with Hans

Gottlieb at the general store. Lone always overpaid a bit on any of his purchases and Hans would, in turn, covertly apply these amounts as bits of price shaving on goods bought by the widows. "You know," the proprietor often lamented in his thick German accent, "if either of those prideful, wonderful old *frauleins* ever catch on to this, they will have both of our scalps."

To which Lone's standard reply was to point to Hans' bald dome and say, "Since you got nothing left to lose, what are you so worried about? Besides, don't tell me you don't get a kick out of livin' a little dangerously."

No such conversation took place today, however. When Lone finished his visit with Ma and Mabel and made his swing by the general store, he found Hans was laid up with a severe attack of gout that kept him confined to the second-floor living quarters above the business, unable to navigate the stairs. This information was related by Gerta, Hans' stern-faced wife, who was clerking and taking care of things in his absence with the help of their nephew Rudy. Asking that his sympathy and best wishes for a speedy recovery be conveyed to the patient, Lone handed over the list of supplies he needed and then moseyed on over to the adjacent saloon to have a couple of drinks while the items were being gathered up.

Though trees, and therefore lumber, were scarce throughout the Sandhills, somebody at some point had scavenged enough material to build the tall, rectangular, two-story wood frame building which now housed Gottlieb's store, saloon, and living quarters. The store took up three-quarters of the structure's length, and the saloon occupied the remaining quarter on the west end. The drinking establishment could be accessed either directly from the outside via a set of standard batwing doors or, on the inside, by passing over from the store by means of a short hallway and a flimsy door meant to help keep a lid on the noise level in case the discourse among drinkers got a bit too spirited.

Stepping through the inside door this afternoon, Lone found the noise level in the barroom a long way from posing any threat to tranquility. Hell, he'd attended noisier church services—and not even the fire and brimstone kind. At one end of the bar—an actual, for-real slab of polished, handcrafted cherrywood complete with a brass foot rail and a strip of padded leather for a body to lean his elbows on, not the one-by-twelve planks nailed across the tops of upended wooden barrels too commonly found in small town watering holes—two men were hunched intently over a chessboard.

The gent leaning from the back side of the bar was Walt Barnstable, the Gottliebs' barkeep. He was a transplant from New York City. Average height, trim, always nattily dressed and groomed, right down to a black silk vest and bowtie and black hair perfectly parted down the middle and slicked back so tight and so heavily greased that it, too, glistened almost like silk. On the other side of the bar was a tall, almost painfully thin-looking stick figure of a fellow, also well dressed in good quality dark trousers and a starched white shirt with wide suspenders riding on bony shoulders. He, too, had dark hair parted in the middle, but in his case, strands of it kept falling loose and spilling down around the angular features of his face. This was Jerome Dooley, Sarben's barber-cum-dentist who ran his business out of a small building next door. Since, in the gaps of time when he had no one in his chair either for barbering or a tooth extraction, he could almost always be found here engaged in chess warfare with Walt, the running joke was that Dooley had only two signs printed for display in his front window. One that read CLOSED and one that read NEXT DOOR PLAYING CHESS; the latter being the closest he came to signaling he was open for business, providing his would-be customer was willing to go over and fetch him.

Lone moved up along the front of the bar, saying, "'Lo, Walt...Dooley."

The faces of the chess warriors turned to look at him, and both quickly displayed smiles. "Hey, Lone," the barkeep greeted. "I was saying just the other day it seemed about time for you to be coming 'round."

"Nobody's ever sorry to see Lone McGantry come to town," Dooley agreed.

Lone grinned. "Been past places where some folks didn't necessarily feel that way. But it's good to hear this ain't one of 'em."

"Can I set you up a drink?" Walt asked.

"Sure can. The usual, a nice cold beer," Lone told him.

"We serve the coldest in town," came the automatic reply. Another running joke since this was the only place in town that served beer.

While Walt filled a tall glass, Dooley inquired of Lone, "Been to see the widows yet?"

"Yep. Just came from there."

Placing Lone's beer in front of him, Walt cocked a brow. "You lucky dog. Me and Dooley had liverwurst and swiss cheese sandwiches on sourdough bread for our lunch. The way those old gals pamper you, I bet you got practically a Thanksgiving feast, didn't you?"

"Came close," Lone drawled. Then, his grin taking on a sly twist as he raised his glass, he added, "I was barely able to save room for this. I won't go into any more detail on what all was dished up; it might make you plumb break down and cry."

Dooley cackled. "You might as well go ahead and tell him. I'm about two moves away from winning this game —making it three in a row—so when I do, this sore loser is apt to break down anyway."

"In the first place, I ain't no sore loser," Walt grumbled, bellying back up to the chessboard. "In the second place, I'm a long way from losing this game. I got moves ain't been invented yet!"

Dooley cackled some more. "That means they probably ain't legal. Thanks for the warning. Now I know to keep a closer eye on you than ever."

Lone sipped his beer and smiled at this exchange. It was the kind of banter that went on regularly between the two old friends.

CHAPTER TWO

WHILE HE NURSED HIS DRINK AND HALF-LISTENED TO Walt and Dooley continue bickering over their game, Lone turned a hip to the bar and let his gaze sweep again over the rest of the room. Out of habit, he'd given it a quick once over from the doorway. Satisfied at that juncture, he'd gone on in. Now, he was taking a more leisurely, thorough look. There were only three other customers in the place, three men seated at a table toward the back. A deck of cards sat in the middle of the table but there was no game underway, and the men were just chewing the fat and sipping from glasses of beer poured out of a pitcher also occupying the table-top. Lone knew each of the men—which was to say, he knew their names and was familiar enough to exchange nods in passing. Not much more than that.

One of them was Les Varble, a leathery, wiry old veteran puncher who rode for the Circle L, a good-sized spread north of Lone's Busted Spur. The other two were both from Asa Hallam's Slash H, a smaller outfit bordering Lone's property to the west. The youngest of the pair, in fact, was Asa's son, Harold. The remaining gent was called Red Smith, something of a newcomer to the area, and somebody Lone didn't know much about.

In truth, nobody really knew much about Smith. Not even Smith himself. It was a curious damn thing that young Doc Hurlbert out of North Platte called *amnesia*. Late the previous summer, just before Lone began helping Ma Sharples get re-situated to Sarben, this Smith hombre apparently got caught in a sudden thunderstorm while crossing the Slash H range. The way folks pieced it together afterward, he must have foolishly taken shelter under a tree—the only one anywhere close, and therefore, the tallest point on a grassy meadow. Its height drew a bolt of lightning, a strong enough blast to split the tree, kill the man's horse, and leave its rider sprawled half-dead on the ground. Riding out the next morning to check for any cattle damage the storm might have caused, Harold spotted the body and took him back home.

Once there, he wasn't given much chance to live. Despite no burns or any other outward signs of injury, he lay unconscious for three days. Then, abruptly, he came out of it. He seemed alert and physically okay, except for being understandably confused and shaky at first. That passed quickly enough, but next came the full revelation of what his experience had done to him—the bizarre and unsettling discovery that he had no memory of who he was. Not his name, nothing about his past, no idea where he'd come from, or why he'd been traveling through this part of the country when he got caught in the storm. Nor did his personal effects yield anything that helped.

The only thing Dr. Hurlbert could offer about the

condition was to share his limited knowledge on amnesia. How it could sometimes be caused by certain illnesses or more commonly by a severe blow or sudden trauma, which surely made getting hit by lightning qualify. The doctor said the memory blanks might start to fill in gradually, or perhaps all in a rush. Or maybe not at all. Beyond that, the doc wasn't willing to speculate and knew of nothing that could be done to help or hurry the healing process.

That had been a little over six months ago. Knowing no other place where he might belong, nor having any clue where to go to try searching for his past, the stranger opted to remain in the Sarben area. Because he had to be called something, he was dubbed "Red Smith," combining his fiery shock of hair with the common name of Smith. Since the Hallams—Asa, his wife Livvy, and their grown children Harold and Judith—were good, charitable people, and the Slash H had grown big enough to be a handful for just Asa and Harold; they made Smith an offer to stay on with them and earn his keep by helping out until such time as his memory returned or he simply felt ready to move on. Smith had accepted, and so far, nothing had happened to change the arrangement.

All of this passed quickly through Lone's mind as his gaze touched on the three men at the rear table and once again, he reflected how Smith's tale was one of the darnedest things he'd ever heard. No doubt there were others who felt the same, yet in the relatively short time he'd been around, Smith had proven to be so amiable and easygoing—nor did it hurt the way he remained closely associated with the well-liked Hallams—that his foggy past seemed hardly a thought in most folks' minds anymore.

Apparently thirstier than he thought, Lone realized he'd already drained his glass of beer. Turning back around and placing the empty glass on the bar, he was just about to call for a refill when the squeak of the front entrance batwings announced someone coming in. Lone cut a glance over his shoulder to have a look at who it was. What he saw wasn't much to his liking.

Sarben didn't get many strangers passing through. Located as it was, well above the Platte and thereby off-kilter from the natural east–west route forged by the river—the Great Platte River Road, as it was called, a course followed for decades by travelers ranging from nomadic Indians to mountain men and pioneers, even the Pony Express and eventually the railroad—it was too out of the way to attract hardly anyone besides those from the surrounding ranches or the freight haulers who came and went as part of delivering goods. None of which was viewed as a bad thing by most residents. Their semi-isolated status was fine by them. It kept the riff-raff out and kept their settlement the quiet, peaceful place they wanted it to remain.

The three hombres who now crowded their way through the batwings were definitely not good additions to Sarben, nor anywhere else they showed their ugly mugs. This wasn't just speculation on Lone's part due to their roughshod appearance. It went deeper. Two of these sorry specimens he had the misfortune of knowing from past encounters—and not encounters that had been particularly pleasant for any of them.

The man at the center of the trio was Granger Weems. He was roughly Lone's age, not much over six feet in height, hard-faced and hard-bodied, with prematurely gray hair as demonstrated by the bushy sideburns running down to the hinge of each jaw. At one time, he, like Lone, had been a civilian scout for the Army. And a fairly decent one for a while. As the Indian Wars came to a close though, laziness and greed had corrupted him and tugged him off into some bad pursuits. Selling illegal moonshine to reservation Indians, for starters. Hunting scalps for a while, at a time when there was money to be made off such—even stooping low enough, it was rumored, to in some cases lift the hair off poor dumb bastards he'd first taken payment from for his rotgut then waited until they passed out drunk and made easier pickings for lifting their hair. From there, it was a steady downward spiral into rustling, general thievery, thug work for moneyed men not wanting to dirty their own hands, and reported association with a handful of different ragtag gangs suspected of bank and stagecoach robberies. Last Lone had heard of him, Weems was said to be raising hell with some such outfit up Montana way. Too bad he hadn't stayed there.

On Weems' right as he started into the barroom was Milt Bossner, a horse thief, card cheat, and backshooter who'd squirted out ahead of the law from just about any town you could name up and down the eastern boundaries of Nebraska and Kansas. He was a rat-faced, half-assed albino runt with stringy, milk-colored hair, permanently bloodshot eyes, and sickly-looking, fish-belly white skin. What kink in the Devil's tail caused the likes of Weems and Bossner to be thrown together, Lone had no idea. But it was a certainty that the good of their fellow man was damn sure not part of the plan.

The third member of the group Lone had never seen before. He was a pot-bellied, bow-legged Mexican with gimlet eyes, a drooping mustache, and one gold tooth in front that protruded down over his bottom lip even when his mouth was closed. Whoever he was, Lone was willing to bet good money he *wasn't* a spiritual savior on a mission to rescue the damaged souls of the other two.

All three were heeled. Weems and Bossner wore six-guns, prominently displayed in holsters riding low on their hips. Additionally, as if to help compensate for his runt size and overall anemic appearance, Bossner had a Henry repeating rifle cradled in the crook of one arm. The nameless Mexican was putting on an even showier display with a pair of converted Navy Colts worn for the cross draw by having them jammed in behind a wide red sash, though somewhat faded and food-stained, cinched tight around his bulbous middle. If that wasn't enough, he also had a bandolier hanging from one shoulder and draped at an angle down across his sunken chest.

One look at this motley collection was enough to tighten Lone's gut and put a sour taste in his mouth. He wished he didn't have the recent feast dished out by Ma and Mabel riding so heavy in him. He had a hunch that once Weems and Bossner got a good look at him, and old animosities flared to mind—stoked even hotter by a numbers advantage and especially if they discovered they *both* had raw feelings toward him—he might need to move fast and could ill afford even a trace of slug-gishness.

Lone swiveled slowly to face them full-on, bracing himself as he watched the three pause for a moment to scan the room—exactly as he had done—before coming all the way in. When those sweeping gazes came to rest on him, Lone figured things were apt to turn real interesting real quick.

He was half right.

Things did turn interesting mighty quick. But not due to any recognition or acknowledgment of Lone. Rather, it was Weems' eyes landing on Red Smith that ignited everything that came next.

"You! You lousy sonofabitch!"

There was raw, vicious hatred behind those words. Hatred intense enough to explode instantly into more than merely an epithet hurled across a smoky room. Even as he was spitting out the curse, Weems was lunging forward and simultaneously clawing for the gun on his hip.

At that point, it was already too late. Bad things were going to happen. There was no stopping it, even though Lone felt compelled to try. Only his sharply honed natural reflexes and the fact he'd been primed for the possibility of trouble from the new arrivals—albeit trouble aimed *his* way, not toward somebody else—gave him any chance at all.

Nor did it hurt that Granger Weems, while certainly no stranger to gun work, wasn't considered a particularly fast draw. Neither was Lone, for that matter, but a single clock tick of time and a cooler, less enraged focus could add up to key differences when it came to throwing lead. And, in that vein, one more thing compelling Lone to take action was the knowledge that Red Smith never packed a sidearm. Which meant that any lead-throwing between *just* him and Weems would be decidedly lopsided.

Dropping low and pressing tight to the front of the bar as he reached to unleather his Colt, Lone shouted, "Weems!" His intent was to distract the man, even if only for a second, and hopefully gain the unarmed Smith that much time to somehow react, to at least duck or maybe try making a run for it.

But the attempted distraction didn't work worth a damn. Weems' hate-filled eyes stayed totally locked on Smith, and his gun hand, now filled with unholstered iron, was starting its upward swing without wavering one bit.

That didn't mean Lone's shout didn't draw *any* attention, though. It came from Milt Bossner, positioned beside Weems with his Henry rifle held at the ready—and, it would soon become evident, with a round already chambered. The bleached-out little bastard was quicker than Lone would have ever guessed. His red-rimmed eyes sliced over and down, pinning Lone with a hard glare, and an instant later, the gaping bore of the Henry's muzzle was glaring at him, too. Then flame and smoke roared out of the bore, and a slug went ripping above Lone's head. Yeah, Bossner had reacted quick—but too quick to take proper aim. His bullet screamed down the length of the bar and blew the hell out of the chessboard and its pieces set up on the far end, sending Walt and Dooley spinning away to either side.

Before Bossner could jack home a fresh cartridge, Lone had his Colt drawn and extended, angled up at the rifleman. The cutter bucked in his hand. The aim was accurate, and the .44 caliber slug licked out by a red-gold tongue, sizzled through the air and punched a thumb-sized hole just above Bossner's left eyebrow. The milky-haired runt was knocked backward out through the batwings, his outflung arms sending the Henry spinning end over end until it dropped flat onto the dusty street several feet beyond where Bossner himself fell equally flat and motionless.

While this was taking place, Lone was aware that another shooting had also broken out inside the barroom. Between the reports of Bossner's Henry and Lone's Colt, Granger Weems had begun triggering rounds at Red Smith. Dropping to one elbow and flattening his back against the front of the bar, Lone twisted around and frantically swept his gaze to determine how that was playing out. What he saw was that Smith and the men sitting with him had managed to flip their table up on edge and get hunkered down behind it before Weems cut loose.

The smart, desperate move had succeeded in buying them a few precious seconds of cover. But the flimsy tabletop was never meant to withstand the kind of punishment Weems was now bringing to bear with his relentless barrage. Bullet after bullet punched into the cheap wood, gouging away splinters that burst out into the air and mixed with the roils of thickening powder smoke. And, on the other side of Weems, Lone saw the pot-bellied Mexican drawing his twin Navy Colts with a flourish and thrusting them forward, getting ready to add to the hail of lead. Neither he nor Weems seemed to have noticed the sudden departure of Bossner.

Steadying himself on his left elbow, Lone thrust out his own Colt, fisted in his right hand, and got ready to add another dose of his own lead to the mix. Only, his wouldn't be aimed at the tipped-up table, and this time, he didn't intend to shout any kind of warning.

But then, suddenly, right before Lone's trigger finger

squeezed again, a figure sprang out from behind the upturned table. It was Red Smith. He went into a diving roll that carried him five feet toward the opposite side of the room. All in a single, smooth motion, he came out of the roll and rose up on one knee, partially behind a chair hitched up to a neighboring table. In his right hand, held at chest level, was a six-gun. It would later be revealed he had snatched the weapon from the holster of the old wrangler Les Varble, the only man at Smith's table who was heeled. In a continuation of fluid, almost blindingly fast motion, Smith's left palm blurred above the hammer of the gun, and he fanned three shots so tightly spaced that the individual reports sounded like one elongated roar.

Almost as tightly spaced were the three slugs that pounded into the center of Weems' chest. The scalp hunter's entire body shuddered under the impacts. His shoulders hunched forward, his chin dropped down onto his chest, and his feet did a ragged backward shuffle. He stood teetering for a moment, powder smoke writhing about him until his right knee abruptly buckled and he tipped to that side, twisting slightly before toppling face down like a felled tree.

If the nameless Mexican had taken that moment to throw down his guns and raise his hands, he could have lived. But he was too stupid. Stupidity was the only allowance Lone would make—he refused to honor it as boldness or bravery—for the action the Mex took instead. The pistolero's eyes darted around like a trapped wild animal. Then, peeling back his lips and hissing, "Bastardos," he swung his arms wide and brought one pistol in line with Red Smith, the other at Lone.

Lone and Smith responded before he got any farther. Their guns spoke simultaneously, the double blast once again sounding like a single roar. Smith's bullet hit high in the chest, just above the slanting bandolier; Lone's drilled into the man's temple. The Mexican's head was knocked to one side like it was on a hinge, and his body was driven back to slam hard against the door frame. The Navy Colts slipped from lifeless fingers, clattering to the floor as he slid down and collapsed in a heap between them.

CHAPTER THREE

SHOOTOUTS WERE RARE ENOUGH IN QUIET LITTLE SARBEN, so the gunning of the three lowlifes that afternoon at Gottlieb's was guaranteed to generate excited talk for a long time to come. And the gun skills demonstrated by Lone and the mysterious Red Smith would only add to the widespread re-telling and embellishments of the incident. But in the immediate aftermath, for all in and around Sarben, a tragic reality of the shooting took precedence over any tale spinning. Barely had the powder smoke begun to clear before a fourth victim was discovered. One of Weems' bullets had punched through the upturned tabletop and hit young Harold Hallam. With its force greatly reduced by penetrating the wood, had the slug struck him almost anywhere else, it might have amounted to a relatively minor wound. But it caught Harold in the soft tissue of his throat.

Despite frantic efforts to administer aid, the lad bled out before enough could be done to stanch the flow from the punctured artery.

The death cast a pall over the settlement and the whole surrounding area. All of the Hallams were well-liked and highly regarded, but none more than Harold. At only twenty years of age, he was friendly, hardworking, devoted to his family and his god, and showed the promise of growing into the kind of man who would make a positive mark in the years to come.

The scum responsible for cutting him down were buried in unmarked plots well outside the boundaries of the settlement. Pastor Isaac felt obligated to say some words over the graves, but the only one there to hear them was his wife, Eliza. Not even the dour-faced gravediggers who grudgingly agreed to do the planting —after considerable arm-twisting by blacksmith Burl Ketchum, who served as the sort of default constable for Sarben and pitched in himself to do part of the shoveling—stuck around once the holes were covered over.

Two days later, however, when Harold Hallam was laid to rest, the turnout of mourners numbered nearly a hundred. The town basically emptied out, and its residents were joined by families and wranglers from several surrounding ranches. The gravesite was on the crest of a low hill overlooking the Hallam house, and though the day was sunny, every heart there was heavy and dark, and scarcely a dry eye was in evidence by the time Pastor Isaac finished his service and called for the singing of "Yes, We Will Gather At The River."

Lone was there for all of it. He brought Ma and Mabel out from town in a buckboard and took them home when it was over. In spite of them urging him to stay the night because it was growing late, Lone stubbornly headed home after he dropped the widows off.

The part of him who lived up to his name badly needed to do so right then. His eyes were dry, but his heart was plenty dark and heavy. Times like this, he told himself bitterly, were when being a loner had its advantages. The farther away you stayed from the inevitable highs and lows of others, the fewer sad valleys and dark clouds you had to stand in and under with them.

———

"THE BURYING and the heartfelt send-off are done. But that doesn't mean it's over, does it?"

So went the question posed by Red Smith when Lone found the man waiting for him upon his return home. There was an early moonrise in a clear sky, making the horse hitched up in front of the house clearly visible from a good distance off. Drawing cautiously closer, Lone then spotted Smith parked in the chair placed to one side of the front door, where Lone often sat enjoying the sunset with a post-supper cup of coffee.

The former scout nosed Ironsides, his big gray stallion, up alongside Smith's gelding and swung down from the saddle. In response to the query that had greeted him, he said, "Plenty of things in this ol' world that ain't over, friend. Afraid you'll have to chew your meanin' a little finer."

Smith rose from the chair. He was a man of thirty or so, an inch over six feet, solid through the chest and shoulders. His eyes were bright green and alert-looking under a ledge of brows colored the same fiery red as his hair. Despite possessing these strong physical features,

Lone had always before sensed a faint air of discomfort and uncertainty about him. Probably not surprising for anybody who'd had their whole past and memory of who they were wiped clean and then left to wander around knowing *things* without understanding how or where they'd been learned and none of them traceable to an identity. But now, suddenly, as Smith stepped out into the full wash of moonlight, no sense of discomfort or uncertainty seemed present. It was like they had been replaced by something else, a diamond-hard focus. Another notable difference was the silver-trimmed, tooled leather gun belt strapped around his waist with a newer model Colt .45 riding in its holster.

"I think you've probably got a pretty good hunch about my meaning," he told Lone, demonstrating some of that newfound assuredness. "Those three hard cases we tangled with the other day are the kind who carry trouble around with them like the stink of a cheap cigar. Even after you stub it out, its stink has a way of not going away so easy."

A corner of Lone's mouth quirked up. "Which is a roundabout way of sayin' you expect we might be due some additional trouble from other varmints friendly to those we put in the ground. That it?"

"It is. Haven't you had any similar thoughts?"

"Matter of fact, I have. Then again, I got a long line of scoundrels who'd love to do me harm if given half a chance. Any newcomers, if they was to take their proper turn, would have to hold off for quite a spell."

"Unfortunately," Smith said, "I doubt the kind of scoundrels we're talking about are big on following any rules like waiting their proper turn."

"Expect you're right," Lone grunted. "Come in inside. I'll make a pot of mud, we can talk."

Like many dwellings across the treeless great plains and particularly in the Sandhills, Lone's home was a sod house with some wood framing and reinforcements. Its interior was tidy, ruggedly simple, and everything was efficiently arranged. After a wall-mounted coal oil lamp was lighted for them to see by, Smith was motioned into a wooden chair hitched up to a varnished plank table. While Lone got some coffee brewing, they continued to talk.

"I take it," Lone said, "your concern over some friends of the recently departed trio showin' up is why you're packin' the new hardware?"

"You're half right," Smith answered. "Yeah, my concern is why I'm packing it—but the rig isn't new. I was wearing it when I shook hands with that lightning bolt last summer. After I agreed to ride for the Slash H, Asa Hallam convinced me that going around heeled all the time wasn't necessary. Said a saddle gun to deal with snakes and coyotes out on the range was sufficient. So I stowed this rig away and never brought it out again, until today, after the funeral service was over."

"Never?" Lone prodded with a sly smile.

Smith couldn't hold back a sheepish grin. "Okay, you caught me. Yeah, I snuck it out every once in a while. Took it to where nobody was around and did some practice shooting in order to stay reasonably sharp. You know...just in case."

"Uh-huh. From what I saw the other day at Gottlieb's, the staying reasonably sharp part appears to have worked out pretty good," Lone remarked. "And now you figure things have gone past the 'just in case' stage?"

Smith's expression went tight. "They went there that day at Gottlieb's. Had I been wearing this then, Weems never would have gotten off a shot and Harold Hallam would still be alive."

"Come on. You can't blame yourself for that."

"Can't I? Who was it Weems opened fire on?" Smith insisted.

"That's exactly the point. *Weems* did the trigger pullin' that killed the boy. Not you."

Smith shook his head determinedly. "I'm not going to argue the point. I've already been through it with Asa. My mind is made up about what I'm going to do, and it involves more than just strapping on this .45."

Lone frowned. "What's that supposed to mean?"

"It means," Smith replied, "I'm going to backtrack Weems and those other two skunks. Find out where they came from, what they were last involved in, and what sent them down this way. Marshal Overstreet said he got some reports a while back of Weems being part of a gang operating up in Montana. Even though it's dated information, it's all I got to go on. It's at least a start, a direction to head."

Keith Overstreet was the town marshal of North Platte. Sarben and the vicinity was well out of his official jurisdiction, but because he was familiar with many from the area who did much of their trading in North Platte, and due to there being no closer legal authority without calling in a US Marshal, he had agreed to come when requested for the sake of filing a proper report on the shooting at Gottlieb's. Since it was clearly a matter of self-defense and both Weems and Bossner had known criminal records—no one was able to come up with an identity for their Mexican comrade—it was a pretty standard bit of documentation. The marshal was also present for Harold Hallam's funeral service.

Lone had a high opinion of Overstreet, counting him as a friend of sorts dating back to Ma's many years spent living in North Platte and Lone's frequent visits to her there. Now, in response to Smith's statement, he said, "Keith keeps a pretty sharp eye on the fliers and notices that come through. If there was anything more recent on Weems, not likely he would've missed spottin' it. But Good God, man. Montana—not to mention everything between here and there—makes a mighty big chunk of real estate for you to try backtrackin' through."

"Like I said, it's all I got," Smith repeated stubbornly. "You saw how Weems reacted to the sight of me. It wasn't simply like somebody spotting an old enemy or some past score left unsettled. It was raw, gut-level hatred that made him instantly want to kill me. That kind of hate can only come from having been terribly wronged or betrayed in some deeply personal way. Can you imagine what kind of questions that sends screaming through my mind? How, in the past, I can no longer remember, was I connected with the likes of scum such as Weems? It strikes me that in order for anybody to feel so badly wronged or betrayed, there must have initially been some kind of bond that got broken. So what does that make me—what or who was I to have ever had a bond with somebody like Weems?"

"Maybe that's something better left unanswered," Lone suggested.

"But I can't do that. Now that those three polecats

have shown up, I can't just leave it hanging." Smith's mouth twisted wryly. "Before then, that's exactly what I was ready to do. Ready to quit wondering and worrying about my lost past and accept how things were now. In fact, I'd decided I was pretty damned content with how things were in the present. So much so I'd even..."

The coffee had begun to bubble and send its aroma wafting through the room. Lone took the opportunity of Smith's words trailing off to rise up and fill a couple of large mugs. He returned to the table and placed one of them in front of the red-haired man.

Smith took a cautious sip and then continued. "We hadn't made any kind of announcement outside the family, but Judith Hallam and I have fallen in love. Asa and Livvy gave us their full blessing. Harold, too. It was Judith's practical side that wanted to hold off saying anything more for a little while longer. Until we were sure our feelings were truly sincere and strong, she said..." He paused, his mouth again taking on a rueful twist. "I guess she has pretty good instincts. Suddenly discovering the mystery man you just married is some kind of desperado, maybe wanted by the law or maybe even a killer, would sure take the edge off a honeymoon, wouldn't it?"

"Seems to me you're tryin' awful hard to think the worst," said Lone.

"But none of it's impossible, is it? That's why I've got to *know*. No matter how bad it turns out to be, I can no longer leave it just twisting in the wind. I not only can't let the doubt fester in my own mind, but neither can I ask it of Judith. Not to mention the risk I might be putting her to."

Lone cocked a brow. "Risk?"

"Come on. Stop and think," Smith said impatiently. "You figure that shooting show you and me put on at Gottlieb's isn't going to get talked up all through the territory? Wranglers from the surrounding ranches regularly go into North Platte and Ogallala to do their drinking and carousing, don't they? Hell, half of them will probably end up claiming they were there to see it firsthand. No offense, but you and your adventures are already pretty well known hereabouts, so your part may not generate that much added attention. But me—the red-haired stranger with the blank past—you think that won't set jaws to jacking double time? And the more they jack and the more the tale gets embellished, the wider it will spread."

"Until," Lone picked up, starting to see where Smith was headed, "it might spread far enough to reach some compadres of Weems who possibly share his hard feelin's toward you."

"Bingo," declared Smith. "And if their feelings, based on whatever the hell I did, are anywhere close to his, then they'll come hunting for blood. Mine, for sure. But—as was proven by what happened to Harold—they won't be too fussy about anybody else's getting spilled in the process. You think I *want* to turn away from Judith, or leave Asa in a lurch running the ranch with Harold already gone? But I can't stick around and let anyone close to me be put in danger. Not until I get things figured out."

"Reckon that's one way of lookin' at it," Lone allowed. "But that still don't mean you have to charge straight into the teeth of the thing. What's more, a big chunk of what you're thinkin' is only speculation. For whatever reason, Weems' hatred for you could have been strictly his."

"That nonetheless leaves me needing to find out for sure." Smith took a drink of his coffee and glared down into the remaining black pool after he lowered his cup. "If there are others out there who have it in for me like Weems did, then that means there's a bullet somewhere with my name on it. I don't like that feeling, waiting for it to be delivered when somebody else is ready. To hell with that. If that's the case, then I mean to ride to that goddamn bullet and turn it back on whoever figures to send it my way and cram it down *their* stinking throat instead!"

Lone grinned in spite of himself. Smith's sentiment was sure as hell one he could relate to. "Ride to the bullet," he echoed musingly. "Got a familiar ring to it. Knew an Army officer once who followed a like-minded tactic. 'Ride to the sound of the guns' was his belief. Served him pretty good, too, durin' the late war. Won him some battles, a heap of glory. Kinda worked against him a little later on, though. You might've heard of the fella I'm talkin' about...name was Custer."

Smith looked up from his coffee. After a beat, he grinned, too. "Well, there you go. If Custer had stuck to riding to the sound of the guns, he might have been okay. His mistake was riding to the sound of whizzing arrows. I'll make sure to avoid that."

Lone wagged his head. "It's plain enough there ain't no changin' your mind. What ain't so plain is why you came 'round to tell me your intentions. You askin' me to ride on this trackdown with you?"

"No. Not that you and your experience wouldn't be welcome," he answered. "But, like you said a while ago, you've already got plenty of scoundrels scattered in your own wake. Plus, since I don't know what I'm apt to discover about my past, you might find yourself riding beside an even worse scoundrel.

"What I came to ask of you probably isn't even necessary, given your reputation. But I'd feel better hearing you confirm it...should trouble come calling after I'm gone—trouble looking for me, I'm saying—will you keep an eye out so it don't cost the Hallams any more for having befriended me?"

Lone eyed him. "I could almost take offense at you feelin' the need to ask that. But I'll let it slide and give you your confirmation. Yeah, you can count on me lookin' out for 'em."

"Good. I've already arranged for Les Varble from the Circle L—he's the old wrangler who was with me and Harold at Gottlieb's that day—to swing over and give Asa a hand on his spread once I'm gone." Smith's gaze returned to the black pool in his coffee cup, as if hoping to find some epiphany there. When none was forthcoming, he lifted his eyes again and said, "Guess all that leaves is to say my goodbyes and head out first thing in the morning. I appreciate the coffee and letting me bend your ear."

The two men drained their cups and left the table. Outside, after Smith had swung up into his saddle, Lone told him, "Here's a couple of things to keep in mind. That first day, after the shootin', I rode out in a sweep behind Gottlieb's until I picked up the incomin' sign of those three. They came in from due north, not so much out of the northwest as would more indicate Montana." He shrugged. "For what it's worth. Like I said, something to keep in mind. And then there's this: You commence your backtrackin' and come to askin' questions of folks you run across, don't focus so much on Weems. The one to ask about is Milt Bossner, the half-assed albino runt who was ridin' with him. He'll be the one anybody willin' to open up to you is more likely to remember."

CHAPTER FOUR

LONE STOOD FOR A WHILE, WATCHING THE SILVERY DUST haze kicked up by Smith's gelding fade away into the moonlit night. Damn. The man's visit and his torment left things churning in Lone's head that he didn't want to think about or have to try and sort out. Yet some of it had already been present. Now, it was worked up closer to the surface and writhing more restlessly, more demanding of consideration.

Why *had* Granger Weems reacted so instantly and viciously at the mere sight of Red Smith? And what did it say about who or what Smith might have been in his forgotten past? Those questions, the very ones haunting the man himself and now driving him in search of answers, were not new to Lone. They had been nagging at him ever since the shooting—not just due to the way Weems had acted but also due to the side of Red that had emerged when he seized Les Varble's gun and went to work so skillfully with it.

Still, being good with a cutter wasn't automatically a black stain against a man. There were plenty of decent men who developed gun skills for the sake of protecting themselves and what was theirs *against* those on the wrong side. Trouble was, truly decent men didn't tend to have an apparent past association, or *bond*, with the likes of a Granger Weems. And that's what went to the heart of what was so troubling to both Lone and Red— the fact that Weems' reaction had seemed like something so deep and fiercely personal at its core.

Damn.

Lone continued to grind on this as he led Ironsides over to the corral and began stripping off his saddle and bridle. The hell of it was that, as a counterpoint to the troubling thoughts, he'd grown to like Red Smith. He tended to believe he was pretty good at reading people, and these past few days, in the aftermath of the shooting and leading up to Harold's burial, had only solidified his favorable feeling toward the redhead. No small part of it, admirably noted by Lone as well as others, was the strong shoulder Smith had provided the Hallams in their time of grief. And there was that, too— the genuine warmth the whole family had developed toward him. Could so many good people be so wrong if there was some kind of dark villainy hidden by the fog of amnesia?

Once Ironsides was stripped down and turned loose inside the corral, he trotted to the watering trough and began drinking noisily. While he was doing that, Lone added a generous scoop of grain to his feed bunk. As Lone was turning back to close the cover on the grain bin, the big gray suddenly raised his head and issued a slobbery warning snort. Lone instantly dropped into a half-crouch and spun around one end of the bin, reaching for the Colt on his hip as he did so.

"Whoa! Whoa! Hold off grabbin' iron—I mean no harm," came a voice out of the shadows thrown by the lean-to shelter thrusting up on one side of the corral. "It's me, McGantry. Sim O'Greary. You remember me, don't you?"

Keeping his hand on his Colt, Lone said, "I remember the name, yeah. Ease out of those shadows. Slow. Let's have a look at you."

A man leading a bay horse reverse-melted out into the moonlight. He was of average height and build, showing some years, wearing a fringed buckskin jacket and faded "yellow leg" cavalry britches tucked into dusty high-topped boots. Atop a headful of scraggly hair, the same rust color as his drooping mustache, sat a battered Boss of the Plains hat with an eagle feather poking out from its band on one side.

"That horse of yours makes a pretty handy watch-dog," said the man.

Though it had been several years, Lone recognized him well enough as Sim O'Greary. He'd first known the Irishman when he was a trooper guarding Army supply wagons rolling in and out of Colorado's Fort Morgan; and then later when he was a civilian teamster working for a freight company operating out of Sydney, Nebraska. He'd always been a little too brash and a little too fond of his liquor, but competent in the performance of his tasks and somebody who neither shied away from nor went out of his way to engage in bouts of trouble. Lone never considered him exactly a friend yet found him tolerable to be around for brief periods.

In response now to O'Greary's comment about Iron-sides, Lone said, "Yeah, the big gray is mighty handy in a lot of ways. Me and him have been lookin' out for each other for quite a spell."

"Yeah, you always did favor horses and other critters over people," O'Greary recalled. "Time, I didn't much understand that, but over the years I've come around some on such feelin's. Had me a team of mules for near five years, and they was more dependable than most men—and damned sure any woman—I ever met. Lost 'em both in the fierce blue hell of a blizzard one winter when I went on a high lonesome drunk and shamefully didn't see to their proper shelter. They never let me down, but I sure failed them, and it's been a black, heavy anchor hangin' on my soul ever since."

"That's a real sad tale," Lone said dryly. "But there's got to be more reason for you to come skulkin' around in the dark than just to tell it to me. How in blazes did you even know where to find me?"

"My, my," O'Greary responded. "Appears you don't know how much your name is on the tongues of folks hereabouts—leastways that's the case in the saloons over Ogallala way where I've spent the past couple of days. I got the notion you been involved in a handful of doin's in your time, but the shootin' from just a few days ago where you was part of snuffin' out the wicks of three pretty tough hombres, is really gettin' yammered about currently."

"Let me guess. I bet you wasn't shy about joinin' in on the yammerin', was you?"

O'Greary grinned. "You mean happenin' to mention how you saved my hide by clubbin' that knife-wieldin' Dutchman off me that time at the sutler's in Fort Morgan when he was fixin' to split my gizzard with his foot-long Arkansas toothpick?"

"He was out of his head on green rotgut and swingin' that knife—which had more like a six-inch blade—at everybody in the place, not just you," Lone reminded him. "Lucky timin' I walked in when his back was turned to the front door, and I was able to bounce the butt of my Yellowboy off his skull hard enough to finally lay him out."

"You sayin' if I was the only one there he was swingin' at, you wouldn't've did what you done?"

Lone tipped his head as if considering for a moment. "Could be I might've not been so quick to wade in. After all, it took three or four raps with that rifle to flatten the crazy bastard, and he damn near managed to get turned around and lay open my gizzard before I got the job done."

"Ah, but you *did* get the job done. That's what counts," O'Greary declared. "And whether I was on my own or only one of half a dozen others, I benefited from what you did and am grateful. What's more, as somebody who had that blade flashin' in my face, I still say the doggone thing *looked* a foot long!" He paused, and his grin turned sly under the drooping mustache. "Besides, when I tell the story, the longer I make the blade and the closer I say it came to openin' me up, the more drinks I get bought for me."

"Like you need help pourin' who-hit-John down your gullet," Lone said sarcastically. "But once again, I doubt you rode all the way out here to brag how you're usin' something that happened all those years ago to weasel free drinks. Let's cut to the real reason."

"Fair enough," O'Greary allowed. "So happens the reason is sorta payback for savin' my hide back then. It kinda ties in, too, to your red-headed visitor from a few minutes ago. That's why I was hangin' back in the shadows, not wantin' to interrupt 'til your business with him was done."

"Talkin' in riddles ain't hardly cuttin' to it, Sim. And this runaround is startin' to get annoying."

"Maybe it would go better in the house," O'Greary suggested. "I been standin' out here smellin' the coffee you brewed up for the other fella. Might come as a surprise, but I've been known to take a drink now and then of something besides just who-hit-John."

Lone sighed. "Come on in, then. Let's hear what kind of tale you got to spin for me."

A handful of minutes later the two men were seated at the table in the kitchen area of Lone's soddy with fresh-poured mugs of coffee in front of them. After a couple of sips, O'Greary got right to it. "Past three years or so I been workin' down in the Indian Nations, haulin' supplies to the agencies for redistributin' out to the different tribes," he explained. "Not a bad deal. The weather can take some mean turns, but the pay is decent, and you can generally find a plump, willin' squaw to help block the wind on chilly nights.

"'Bout a month back, a fella I work with by the name of Ed Curtis talked me into goin' in with him on a good-payin' side job deliverin' a package up this way to Ogallala. That's what brung me to your neck of the woods. We rolled in three days ago, right on schedule, but the hombres we was to meet to hand the package over to was runnin' late. So we hung around, waitin'. Then, lo-and-behold, we got word these hombres wasn't gonna be showin' up at all. They got delayed real permanent-like...the names of the fellas, you see, was Granger Weems, Milt Bossner, and Yucca Fats."

Lone froze with his coffee cup lifted halfway to his mouth. "I'll be damned," he muttered.

O'Greary chuffed. "Don't know about that, but you sure enough look surprised as hell."

"The biggest surprise," Lone replied, "is hearin' you've lowered yourself to havin' any dealin's with the likes of Weems and Bossner. None of us knew who the Mexican even was...Yucca Fats, you called him?"

"So I was told. And as far as not knowin' anything about him, impression I got was that he didn't rate much worth knowin' about. Now as to me havin' dealin's with the other two," here the Irishman scowled earnestly, "you best believe I never heard their names as bein' part of it until it was too late for me to back out. But, still and all, my part was just a job of work. Deliverin' a package. What those varmints done in the past and whatever might've been ahead for 'em, I meant to have no part of."

Lone regarded him tight and decided he was telling the truth. "Okay, that's good to hear," he said. "What's the nature of this package you was in on deliverin'?"

O'Greary grimaced. "Aye, thinkin' back on it, I guess there's where I maybe should've smelled something fishy right off. But, like I said, it was a tidy-payin' haul and a kinda pleasant one to boot...the whole deal, see, amounted to gettin' this Cheyenne Injun gal transferred from her village down in the Nations up to the Flat Falls Cheyenne rez in North Dakota. Way it was explained to me, she'd been promised to a certain buck, the son of a kinda hotshot sub-chief by the name of Iron Wolf, when the buck and the girl was both real young. But then, a while back as they was both near comin' of age, the Indian Ring gov'ment idjits took a notion to thin out the population on the Flat Falls rez and send fifty or so redskins from there down to the Cheyenne plot in the Nations. This busted up the two young lovers. Eagle Soaring is the buck's name, Bright Moon is the girl. Well, Iron Wolf was fit to be tied over this. I ain't exactly sure how—not all on the up-and-up, I don't expect. I ain't that soft-headed—but he twisted some arms here and there and set up this deal to quietly slip Bright Moon away from the Nations and get her brought back up to his son."

"If I recall correctly," Lone said, "the Flat Falls rez is off the edge of Dakota gold country. Leastways, it was figured to be, or you can bet the government would never have plopped any Injuns on it. I'm bettin' Iron Wolf found some gold still on Cheyenne land—or close by—and that's what he used to grease the deal he made. And Granger Weems, with his history of, among other things, runnin' moonshine to Indians would have made a convenient go-between."

"Sounds like it could've gone that way." O'Greary took a drink and then made a sour face, though not because of the coffee. "But I'm afraid there's also a few more fingers in the pie."

Lone made no reply and waited for him to continue.

It came in the form of a question. "Ever hear the name Pike Grogan?"

CHAPTER FIVE

THE NAME PIKE GROGAN CAUSED LONE'S EXPRESSION TO nearly match O'Greary's. "Unfortunately, yeah, I *have* heard of him. Runs an outlaw gang up in Montana, right? Come to think of it, I heard some recent reports of Weems ridin' with him. Bossner and the Mexican part of his outfit too, you tellin' me?"

"That's the size of it. But Grogan ain't been raisin' hell in *just* Montana," O'Greary said. "Over the past year or so, he's spilled his outlawin' across the boundary into parts of North Dakota as well. Shakes out Grogan is the one who's got some kind of tie-in to Iron Wolf and did all the arrangin' for gettin' the girl out of the Nations and brought for Granger Weems and them to pick her up at the halfway point."

"So me and Red Smith killed three of Pike Grogan's key men and queered whatever deal he's tryin' to cook up with Iron Wolf," Lone recapped. "You got any more good news to share? Like maybe the fat Mexican was the brother to some high-fallutin', vengeance crazy general from south of the border or some such?"

"No, I think you're clear in that regard," the Irishman said wryly. "Hell, as far as just you, you may not have quite so much loomin' over you at all on account of the shootin'. Critters like Weems and Bossner was born to get gunned down sooner or later; just a matter of time. And Curtis has traded some telegrams with Grogan, agreein' to go ahead and take Bright Moon on the rest of the way. He hired a couple of saloon toughs to ride with him—I took my pay cut and bowed out. If I would've shied away knowin' Weems and Bossner was part of it, I sure as hell didn't want to get sucked in no deeper after learnin' that bloodthirsty Pike Grogan was ramroddin' things on the other end."

"Has this Curtis and the toughs he hired headed out yet?" Lone asked.

"No. They plan on leavin' first thing in the mornin'."

"In that case," Lone said, "I'd advise you wastin' no time kickin' up dust and gettin' clear of them pronto. Just in case Grogan don't like hearin' the news about you cuttin' out in the middle of things."

O'Greary frowned. "I don't think Curtis would turn on me like that."

"I warned you, but go ahead and have it your way. I'll try one more time and point out that if Curtis—who I don't know from a buffalo's ass—was willin' to deal with the likes of Grogan right from the get-go and is ready to deal himself in even deeper, then he don't strike me as somebody who sets a particularly high bar for what he *won't* do."

O'Greary rubbed his jaw. "Maybe you're right. Hell, I got my gear all packed. I could just as well make camp somewhere tonight and start back for the Nations come daybreak, without ever returnin' to Ogallala."

"No reason you can't bunk here tonight," Lone told him. "After all, you went out of your way to come warn me."

"Yeah. About that...there's more I ain't got to yet," O'Greary said, somewhat reluctantly.

Lone cocked a brow. "Just a minute ago you said gunnin' those skunks might not rate as too big a deal, especially since Curtis is goin' ahead with deliverin' the girl."

"I said that about *you*," O'Greary reminded him. "But the same ain't hardly true for the red-haired hombre who was in on the gunnin' with you. Red Smith, you call him? Me and Curtis heard the story of him and his memory loss when we first learned about the shootin' of Weems and Bossner. Then we started hearin' plenty more, or leastways more speculatin' once Curtis commenced tradin' those fresh telegrams with Grogan.

"This Smith...sounds like a bunch of things point to him actually bein' somebody named Wade Avril. 'Wild Red' Avril. Up until the middle of last summer, Avril rode with Grogan. Was practically second in command, the way Curtis was able to piece it together. But then something went bad sour. Avril had a big fallin' out with Grogan and broke away from the whole gang. Whatever it was that happened, they all wanted in the worst way to spill his blood. They hunted him relentlessly for weeks, months. But had no luck runnin' him to ground...not until, accordin' to how things seem to be stackin' up based on descriptions of that shootin' you and him did, this mysterious Smith character once again poked up his headful of familiar red hair."

Despite a bellyful of hot coffee, Lone went cold inside.

Christ Almighty. Was this all of a sudden the way it was going to play out? That Red Smith's lightning-erased past actually belonged to somebody named Wade Avril, an outlaw who once rode with Pike Grogan's notorious gang of robbers and killers? There was no denying that the timing of what O'Greary related fit with formerly known circumstances. Avril made his break with the gang in midsummer, and then a little later, the man who came to be called Smith got caught in that storm on the Slash H range. What better place and manner for Avril to disappear from his pursuers than in a new identity as a minor cow hand on a remote ranch in the Nebraska Sandhills? And then what else glaringly fit was the fierce reaction by Granger Weems upon unexpectedly spotting the hunted man that day in Gottlieb's saloon.

All of this raced through Lone's mind like the rushing torrent of a river. Damn! Damn it to hell and gone.

It took Lone a minute to realize O'Greary was still talking. "Bad as Grogan would like to personally deal with Avril—or Smith, whichever way you want to call him," the Irishman explained, "he can't get away right now from the dealin's he's got goin' with Iron Wolf. But he damn sure ain't about to let the redhead give him the slip again. Grogan didn't waste no time puttin' out a bounty on him and spreadin' the word fast and wide. Five thousand for bringin' Avril to him alive—on account of his cravin' to kill the poor bastard personal-like—or twenty-five hunnerd for his head in a sack as proof the job got done, even if by somebody else."

Lone grimaced. "Whatever Avril did when he made his break, he sure chafed the hell out of the gang boss."

"Uh-huh. But it sounds like his days of gettin' chafed back are about due," O'Greary said. "Word of Grogan's bounty is bound to draw every hardcase and gun tough from hell to breakfast. Some of 'em might even spill each other's blood, tryin' to get to Avril before it's over. But I can't see him comin' out of it with his head still on his shoulders, one way or 'nother."

"It's a callin' for damned bloody business, that's for sure," Lone growled.

O'Greary eyed him intently. "That's why I came to warn yuh. You got a chance to steer clear of it—but only if you steer clear of Avril. He might've survived that lightnin' storm a few months back, but he ain't gonna survive the lead storm Grogan is sendin' his way. And neither will you or anybody else who's fool enough to side with him. Best way to be sure is to find someplace else to be for a while. Won't be long before it's all over for Mr. Avril-Smith and then I'm bettin' Grogan will be too busy with other matters up in the Dakotas and Montana to care much anymore about what goes on down hereabouts."

Lone met his gaze and it only took a beat for O'Greary to avert his eyes. "That almost sounded like a hint for me to run out on a friend in trouble," Lone said. "Ain't something I particularly like the sound of."

"Never meant it as no offense," O'Greary responded. "Like you said to me a little bit ago—I warned you, so you go ahead and do what you think best. If Smith is, in fact, a friend, then I guess I understand where that leaves you."

Lone expelled a ragged breath and said again, "It's a bloody damned business."

The Irishman drained his coffee and stood up. "I appreciate the offer of a bunk, but I reckon I'll go ahead and be on my way. You need some alone time to sort out all I laid on you."

Lone didn't try to change his mind. He stood up also and saw O'Greary to the door. "I appreciate you comin' by, Sim," he said. "It was damn decent of you to go out of your way to fill me in like you did."

O'Greary paused in the open doorway and looked back over his shoulder. "I owed you for clubbin' that Dutchman off my back, remember?" Grinning, he then added, "And I still say that blade of his looked to me like it was a doggone *foot* in length."

He no sooner got turned back around before the first rifle shot cracked from somewhere out in the darkness. The impact of the slug jolted O'Greary, driving a sharp, surprised grunt out of him and knocking him half a step backward. A second shot and a second slug came an instant later, spinning him in a half-turn and slamming him against the edge of the doorframe.

Spitting a curse as he dropped into a half-crouch behind the stricken man, Lone reached up and grabbed him roughly, desperately pulling him out and down from the open doorway. O'Greary fell on top of him, and Lone rolled both of them off to one side of the opening as two more tight-spaced bullets came screaming into the soddy.

Lone scrambled out from under O'Greary. He pistoned his legs, kicking the door shut and letting its thick wooden slabs absorb the next wallop of lead. Staying low, he crabbed quickly over and blew out the lamp he had lighted earlier. Then, spinning back around on one knee and drawing his Colt as he did so, Lone returned to crouch beside the fallen O'Greary. The shooting seemed to have stopped, at least for a moment.

The Irishman was dead. Blood streaked the front of him, leaking from two holes in the center of his chest. Lone swore under his breath.

Shifting past the motionless form, staying below the cabin's single window, Lone reached out with his free hand and felt for a moment in the murkiness until his fingers closed around a thick wooden peg attached to a twelve-inch square block of wood. Tugging slowly but steadily, Lone pulled loose the block and the chunk of sod wall that came with it, drawing the combination inward until a clear opening to the outside was created. When Lone and Peg O'Malley had first built the soddy a number of years back, their backgrounds—as a former Army scout/Indian fighter and an ex-mountain man, respectively—made them decide to include several strategically placed and semi-concealed shooting ports in case of trouble. Lone had just opened one of these.

As he did, more shots came pouring in, hammering against the closed door and shattering the window glass above Lone's head. This provided a pair of muzzle flashes—one over behind the well housing and another from a grassy hump off to the right of that—for Lone to shoot back at. He fired first at the grassy hump, snapping two quick rounds that yielded a responsive yelp of surprise or maybe pain. Swinging the Colt's muzzle within the confines of the shooting port, he next triggered two rounds into the sandstone blocks of the well housing. Not waiting to gauge exact results, he twisted away from the port and went in motion toward the other side of the room.

Crossing before the door, Lone reached up and snagged the Winchester suspended on hooks above it. The rifle was another Yellowboy model, brother to the one he carried in his saddle scabbard. Five feet past the door, he stopped and unplugged another shooting port, this one located higher, at chest level. Outside, the two shooters had opened fire again, signaling that the yelp from the one in the high grass had not meant—unfortunately—he'd taken a significant hit.

Hoping to correct that miss, Lone pushed the Yellowboy into the shooting port and sent another .44 slug slicing through the grass. Next, levering home a fresh round and adjusting quickly, given he had a slightly better angle now on the back side of the well housing, Lone pumped more lead at that target, too.

Then, pulling away and turning, he broke into a short sprint back to the other side of the room. Using the busted-out window this time because it afforded him more room to work with the Yellowboy, he cranked out a sweeping volley of shots just as fast as he could reload and squeeze the trigger.

That did it. The incoming fire stopped, and two shadowy shapes could be seen ducking and dodging away deeper into the darkness. Lone chased them with a couple more shots, just for good measure, before he let up.

Returning to the higher port across the way, where he could look out while minimizing himself as a target, Lone stood for a time, just watching. He had a fairly wide view out across the front of the cabin and beyond. He could see nothing moving, hear nothing but his own still-elevated breathing. The hitch rail where O'Greary had left his gelding stood empty, the animal having apparently bolted when the shooting started. Over in the corral, out of range of Lone's vision, Ironsides was now quiet. Lone had heard him carrying on some during the gunfire but his being settled down now was a good sign, conveying that no one else was skulking off in that direction; had it been otherwise, the big gray would have been still making a commotion.

With the Yellowboy held at the ready against his chest, Lone continued to sweep his gaze in a wide, slow arc. Looking for new movement or anything out of place, simultaneously straining to hear any noise that didn't belong. Vaguely, in the distance, there was the hint of what might have been retreating hoofbeats. But it was so thin and so short-lived that the former scout couldn't be certain if it had been there or if he'd only *hoped* it was. At any rate, he remained motionless— except for his sweeping gaze—for several more minutes before finally moving away from the shooting port.

He went to the door, opened it, and stood looking out at a wider expanse of the moonlit stillness. Something much closer caught his eye, a shiny smear of wetness on the door frame. O'Greary's blood. Lone touched a fingertip to the stickiness, and the muscles at the hinges of his jaw bulged visibly. Once before, the blood of another Irishman, another friend—an even closer one—had stained the ground where this soddy stood. Those responsible for that had paid and paid hard...*And the sonsabitches who'd struck here again tonight were by God due nothing less.*

CHAPTER SIX

A CONVERTED TACK ROOM AT ONE END OF THE SLASH H horse barn served as personal quarters for Red Smith, apart from the main house where he took his meals with the Hallam family. He sat there on the edge of the cot now—rousted an hour and a half ahead of the sun —barefoot and still in his long handles, tousle-haired and bleary-eyed as he listened to Lone relate to him the information provided by Sim O'Greary and then the subsequent shooting that had taken the Irishman's life. The expressions that gripped Smith's face as he tried to absorb all that was being told to him ranged from shock to confusion, but lingered mostly on a look of anguish.

"I don't quite understand why," he said when Lone paused in his telling, "if the ambushers meant to stop your friend from warning you about Grogan and the bounty and all, they didn't make a try for me when I was right there?"

"The only thing I can figure," Lone answered, "is that they were followin' Simy but got there a little late. Maybe after you'd already gone, or maybe they simply didn't recognize you in the dark. Besides, I don't think the bounty was necessarily even on their minds. If they were the two saloon toughs that Curtis hired to replace O'Greary—and that's who I'm bettin' 'em to be—then I don't count 'em as ambitious enough or gutsy enough to make a play for the bounty. They'd already signed on for the simpler and safer job of helpin' escort the Indian gal the rest of the way north. But what I *do* count 'em as bein' is a couple of lazy-ass, bottom feeders who saw O'Greary and the payoff they knew he'd recently got from Curtis as easy pickins for a little side bonus. And they would've figured they needed to kill O'Greary to keep him from squealin' back to Curtis."

"So they killed O'Greary for nothing, since you ran them off before they got the money he'd been paid."

Lone made a sour face. "Unfortunately, the bastards *did* get the money. When O'Greary's horse came back around after the shootin' was over, it was stripped of saddlebags, bedroll, possibles pack—everything but its saddle and bridle. There was nothing but a few dollars in O'Greary's pockets. I figure he must have had his pay-off money stuffed somewhere in his gear. I'm guessin' the sneaky bastards must've slipped around while me and him was talkin' inside the cabin, stripped the gear, and found the money, then waited until O'Greary came back out so that, like I said, they could shut him up permanent-like."

"Cold-blooded curs," Smith muttered.

Lone gave him a look. "You ain't seen nuthin' yet. Like I told you, I rate that pair as not much more than a couple of bottom feeders. The kind of hard cases Grogan's bounty offer is bound to sic on us, are the real cold bloods we're gonna have to worry about."

Smith eyed him in return. "'Us'? 'We'? I thought you said O'Greary had a hunch you could slide on this mess as long as you steered clear of me?"

"Yeah, but a hunch on his part is all it was," Lone snapped. "And, just in case you ain't been payin' attention, even at that, it was before he got gunned down in my doorway. You think I'm gonna let something like that just *slide*?"

"But if his killers were only a couple lowlifes out for a sneaky side bonus and no part of the bounty hunting," Smith insisted, "then you can go ahead and deal with them but still stay clear of getting involved with me and putting yourself directly in the way of Grogan's interests."

"Ain't gettin' that squaw up to Iron Wolf part of Grogan's interest? Meanin' if I settle the hash of those two skunks now part of takin' her there, which I full intend to do, then I'll already be puttin' myself in his damn way." Lone's voice was becoming an irritated growl. "All of this traces back to Grogan somehow or other. And if he sees any of it bein' even a hint of an inconvenience or threat, then everything I ever heard about him says he'll react by smashin' it flat to make sure it *don't* cause him any trouble. You, you're a certainty he's out to flatten—by his own hand, if possible. Me, I might be just flickerin' around on the edge of things for now, but if my name pops up too often, then he damn sure won't hesitate to call for me gettin' swatted too...only I don't happen to be in no goddamn mood to wait around for him to make up his mind."

Smith grinned crookedly. "Ride to the sound of the guns, eh?"

"No. Ride to the bullet is how you called it. Remember?" Lone's expression stayed grim. "You said if there was a bullet out there with your name on it, then you meant to ride to whoever marked it that way and turn it back on him. I like that way of thinkin'. In just a little while—probably already started, as a matter of fact—there's gonna be a whole lot of bullets out there with your name on 'em. Mine, too, sooner or later. But, again, they'll all trace back to Pike Grogan. He's the one who put the mark on 'em, so he's the one who, in the end, they need to be turned back against. We cut the head off the snake, his rattle don't mean shit no more. You clear on that?"

Smith's grin was long gone. "Yeah. But you're forgetting one thing."

"What's that?"

"If everything O'Greary said was true, and it's hard denying how it all seems to fit, then at one time, I crawled in the same nest with that snake. I was Wade Avril, reportedly Grogan's second in command. No matter what else, that has to mean I was part of robbing and killing before I slithered away...is that somebody you're willing to ride to the bullet alongside?"

"If I hadn't already decided about that," a narrow-eyed Lone replied, "then we wouldn't be havin' this talk. Far as I'm concerned, you're the fella I've come to know as Red Smith. Unless or until you show me something that says you *want* to go back to bein' the other hombre, then Smith is who I came here figurin' to ride alongside with a shared goal in mind. You made the break from Grogan and his bunch for a reason—since you don't know otherwise, why not choose to believe it might've been as simple as wantin' to be done with the outlaw life? Well, you are. You made it. Now the only question is how hard are you willin' to fight to keep it that way?"

Smith's mouth pulled into a straight, tight line. He stood up from the cot. "If you want me to show you the answer to that, then I'd better get dressed and pull on my boots...we got some snake stomping to go do."

CHAPTER SEVEN

DAYBREAK FOUND LONE AND RED SMITH AT GOTTLIEB'S store in Sarben. The final pre-dawn hours had seen Lone interrupt the slumber of several people. First, there'd been his rousting of Smith; then, together, they'd awakened the Hallam family; and now they had dragged Gottlieb out of bed. In all cases, the main purpose and message had been the same: To relate what had been learned about Smith's past and then warn of potential danger from the bounty hunters almost certain to be showing up as a result of Pike Grogan's response to the reappearance of his hated former comrade. Until word spread that Smith/Avril had gotten his own warning and was freshly on the run, the earliest of the hunters would logically descend on the Slash H and the general Sarben area where their quarry had first shown himself again.

It was these men who prompted Lone to convey the message he wanted driven home the deepest. For anyone who'd gotten to know and like "Red Smith" over recent months, Lone certainly felt no satisfaction in altering their perception of him by revealing his previously blurred past—but *knowing* his past was important to understanding the kind of men who would soon be coming around to try and cash in on it. They would be harsh, uncompromising, menacing individuals. Anyone attempting to stand up to them, to try and speak in defense of Smith, or worst of all, refuse to answer questions or be misleading, would only risk harmful backlash.

That was the last thing either Lone or Smith wanted. For this reason, they revealed nothing about their plans, except that they'd be riding out together and needed to leave with all haste. The less anyone knew, the less they could tell and the less reason they'd have to be evasive or uncooperative if asked.

Needless to say, all of this hit the Hallam family hard. It was only a matter of days since they'd lost their son. As an extension of that, they'd managed to brace themselves for how Smith was already planning to leave and go in search of why Granger Weems reacted the way he did, a result of that reaction including the bullet that caused Harold's death. And now this. All of it still connected to the shooting that claimed Harold's life and jarred Smith's new existence—but on top of that, the sudden, shocking disclosure of the redhead's *past* existence!

Yet, even after the news was laid bare, not one—Asa, Livvy, or Judith—hesitated in the slightest to profess and stand by their belief in the man they'd taken into their home and gotten to know as Red Smith. Gotten to love, in Judith's case. "I believe this," Asa had announced solemnly. "I believe that lightning bolt, the way a red-hot iron cauterizes a festered wound, burned out the poison of Wade Avril and left the cleansed, healed man we took into our midst as Red Smith. I accept him as no other!"

To which Judith added, as Smith took her in his arms in a farewell embrace, "And I will accept him as my future husband just as soon as he returns safe and sound!"

Watching and listening to this, damned if Lone didn't get a big ol' lump in his throat. But he couldn't let it deter him from prodding Smith along and getting them hastened on their way.

Now, in Gottlieb's store, he was continuing to prod along the process of selecting and packing provisions for the long trail stretch ahead of them. By the time he'd buried Sim O'Greary on a gentle slope not far from his soddy, Lone had already made up his mind he would be going after the Irishman's killers and then, ultimately, setting out to deal with Pike Grogan as well. Given that, he'd commandeered O'Greary's sturdy, broad-backed mustang gelding, reckoning it would make a suitable pack horse. As such, the mustang was out back of Gottlieb's now, hitched beside Ironsides and Smith's bay, getting loaded up with the supplies being bought on the inside.

Lone figured he'd pounded home his message to the Hallams and Herman Gottlieb the best he could on how to deal with the bounty hunters he expected to soon be coming around. He counted on them to spread the word among others as necessary. Another message he prepared for delivery was the one he wrote down to have Gottlieb's nephew Rudy send when he showed up for work. Among his other duties, Rudy operated the settlement's telegraph hook-up located in a back room of the store. The message Lone left for him to send was for Keith Overstreet in North Platte, briefly informing the marshal of these latest developments and advising him to be on the lookout for the expected influx of manhunters to the territory.

With that arranged and the last of the supplies secured on the packhorse, Lone announced, "Now, one final bit of business to take care of. Hans, I need a black bandanna, a black hat that will fit Red here, and a couple tins of boot blacking."

Hearing this caused Smith's eyebrows to lift. "Why the sudden concern for my wardrobe?" he wanted to know. "I've got a proper broke-in hat, thanks, and my boots happen to be brown."

"Ain't your boots I give a hang about. It's that headful of flamin' red hair," Lone explained. "Barrin' no other distinction to look for, right about now, every gun tough from Omaha to Cheyenne is gonna start keepin' their eyes peeled for your kind of cherry-colored locks. I'm suggestin' we hide yours with a layer of the boot black, and the hat and bandanna are to help keep it from bein' visibly smeared on your neck or your lighter-shaded hat."

Smith didn't look quite ready to buy the idea. "I sure as hell ain't the only red-haired fella around, you know."

"No, and I expect plenty of those other fellas are gonna get a good chousin' in the days to come," Lone replied. "But that's for them to worry about. Our worry is to keep you from drawin' unwanted attention—not to mention maybe some unwanted flyin' lead—before we get to where we're ready to make our play."

"What *is* our play exactly?"

"Don't all the way know yet. I'm countin' on it sorta takin' shape as we go along."

Smith scowled. "And in the meantime, I'm supposed to keep my hair caked with that shit? What if I get hot and start dripping beads of black sweat?"

Lone grinned. "That's easy. Just don't lose your cool."

Smith rolled his eyes before reluctantly thrusting out a hand. "Okay, Hans. Give me a tin of that goop and then go pick me out a hat and bandanna."

A minute later, Smith had pried open the tin and was digging in with two fingers, scooping out a glob of the waxy black contents and raising it to smear into his hair. Lone looked away, pretending to be busy examining a display of fancy belt buckles in order to hide the smile tugging at his mouth. The logic for Smith altering his hair color was sound, but seeing his sour-faced discomfort at having to comply was nevertheless somewhat comical.

Lone's hidden smile was quickly erased, however, by Gottlieb's tone when he spoke quietly from where he stood, sorting through a selection of hats up near the store's front window. "Lone...there are three strangers coming down the street out here. They appear in no hurry, but they also appear none too friendly."

Lone and Smith exchanged quick looks.

Shit. Was it starting already?

Lone eased up behind Gottlieb and leaned over his shoulder in order to get a full view of the street. Sure enough, three hard-looking hombres on three hard-ridden horses were plodding right down its middle. They rode in a fanned-out pattern, narrowed eyes sweeping from side to side as they took in the layout of the mostly still-sleeping settlement. The just-risen sun at their backs cast their long shadows out ahead onto the dusty street, somehow making the approach of the riders appear even more ominous.

When Lone and Smith had first rousted Gottlieb, the interior of the store had still been dim enough to warrant the lighting of a couple lanterns for the sake of adequate illumination. The glow of these lanterns showing through the windows now, in contrast to the darkened windows of other surrounding buildings where no one was up yet, was like a beacon to the three riders. As Lone and Gottlieb watched, they steered their mounts accordingly.

Without looking around, Lone said over his shoulder, "Go out the back, Red. Grab a rifle and circle around to the front corner on the saloon end of the building. Hang loose until we find out what kind of noise these polecats are gonna make."

"Got it." Smith glided away silently.

Snagging a clerk's apron off a nearby nail, Lone said, "You stay back out of the way, Herman. Let me and Red handle this, okay?"

"As you wish." Looking anxious, the store owner edged off to one side.

Outside, the three riders drew rein at the hitch rail in front of the store. One of them, a whip-thin specimen wearing a short-waisted corduroy jacket, wide-brimmed sombrero, and sporting a faceful of unshaven whiskers, dismounted. The other two remained in their saddles. The one who'd dismounted, strode up to the front door. He walked with a banty rooster strut, with elbows hitched slightly back to make sure the hem of the jacket rode well above the ivory grips of the twin pistols holstered prominently on his lean hips.

After trying the knob and finding the door locked, Banty Rooster rapped a fist impatiently and hollered, "Hey! Open up in there! You got payin' customers out here who've rid hard and long and are in need of fresh provisions!"

Lone stepped up to where Banty could see him through the door's glass. He had removed his hat and slipped the bibbed apron around his neck. He left it untied at the small of his back, however, so that the front hung loose and flared out somewhat to conceal his gun belt and holstered Colt while still allowing him quick access to it if need be. Responding to Banty, he called back calmly, "We ain't open for business yet. Another hour or so. I'm in here takin' inventory 'til then."

"Inventory my ass!" Banty snapped. "You sayin' you'd rather *count* your damn product than *sell* some of it? I'm telling you we're paying customers in need of supplies. We ain't in no mood to wait—and there ain't no café or any such like in this pissant excuse for a town even if we was so inclined."

"I ain't supposed to open up before openin' time," Lone explained simply, stubbornly. "That's the owner's policy, and he'll chew me out if I don't follow instructions."

Banty's expression turned ugly. "You know what me and my pards will do to your sorry ass if you don't listen to reason and open this door? Make your boss's chewin' out look like a smooch from a pretty girl, that's what— not that you'd likely ever know about such. Now unlock this goddamn thing before I signal my pards to bust it down and ride their horses on through!"

Lone donned an anxious, fearful expression. "Okay,

okay! Lordy, no need for anything like that," he wailed, stepping closer and fumbling clumsily to undo the door lock.

"Thought that might jar you to your senses," Banty smirked. "But don't think it was no idle threat. You drag your feet and annoy me and my pards any more, we'll turn your lousy store and this whole goddamn eyesore of a town upside down!"

"No need for that," Lone repeated, pulling open the door. "You and your friends come on in and pick out the supplies you need." Playing up his meek, conciliatory act, he added, "You don't see what you want, just ask, and I'll do what I can to provide it."

The other two men swung down out of their saddles and followed Banty inside. The air of all three was insolent, boots clumping purposely loud on the slice of boardwalk out front and then on the store's hardwood floor. Each made it a point to give Lone a shoulder bump as they passed by where he stood, holding open the door. The first one trailing behind Banty was a stoop-shouldered number in a bowler hat. He looked to be a couple of years on the back side of forty, dark-complected, with shifty eyes and a smoldering cigarette hanging from one corner of his mouth. Bringing up the rear was a tall, heavy-gutted slob with a whiskey-veined nose, wearing a two-sizes-too-small frayed vest over a sweat and food-stained shirt once red in color but now faded—except for the most recent stains—to a dull pink. All were packing six-shooters in low-slung holsters—though only Banty adopted the showy, two-gun style—worn with the swagger of men wanting to send the message they wouldn't hesitate to use them.

Bowler Hat and Whiskey Nose spread out and

began picking and plucking at items with purposeful carelessness, knocking some over and even spilling a few things to the floor. Banty stopped partway down the center aisle and swept his gaze, looking around. Surprisingly, none of them spotted Gottlieb—at least for the moment—where he stood motionless off in a shadowy corner.

Lone called attention back to himself by repeating, "If you need help findin' something, just ask."

Banty's eyes swung around and locked on him. "Well now, that's real accommodatin' of you, friend," he stated. Then, addressing his pals: "You hear that, boys? Anything we want, all we gotta do is ask, and Mr. Inventory here will fetch it for us."

"Then commence asking him," grumbled Bowler Hat, "so we can get after what we came for ahead of somebody else showing up. No purpose hanging around here any longer'n we have to—ain't nothing in this musty ol' shithole even worth stealing."

"Except for some grub," disagreed Whiskey Nose from where he stood over by the checkout register with his filthy paw stuffed wrist deep in an oversized jar of pickles standing on the countertop. "We need to stock up on food stuff before we pull foot outta here."

"Yeah, like you'd waste away if you went five minutes without shoving something into that tub already threatening to rip open the last notch on your belt," scoffed Bowler Hat.

"You don't like the look of my gut, how about closin' your eyes and not lookin' at it? And while you got your eyes shut, maybe you could take a stroll along the edge of a high cliff somewhere," came Whiskey Nose's response.

"For the luva Christ, you two. Give it a rest already, will ya?" Banty growled. Then, his eyes boring once again into Lone, he said, "Okay, Mr. Inventory, here's your chance to help us like you say you will. We can find and take our own damn supplies. What you can do is give us some information...like where can we locate the empty-headed hombre goin' around callin' hisself Red Smith?"

CHAPTER EIGHT

LONE BLINKED INNOCENTLY AT BANTY'S QUERY. "SMITH?" he echoed. "Jeez, there are lots of Smiths around."

"Don't try to be cute," Banty warned. "You know damn well who I mean—the Smith who shot up the saloon attached to the other end of this dump. It's the talk all over Ogallala, where we just came from, and runnin' all through the territory. Don't tell me you're the one person in the dark about it. We know he's been passin' hisself off as a ranch hand somewhere close around here. We want to know which ranch and how to get to it."

"And we want to know pretty damn quick," Bowler Hat added menacingly.

Lone made a show of gulping down a big swallow. "Okay. Sure. I can tell you that."

"Well? Get to it then," demanded Banty.

Lone gestured to the front door that he'd left standing ajar. "If we step outside, I can show you better. I can point the way and give you real clear directions."

After exchanging glances with Bowler Hat, Banty

said, "Okay. Get on out there, then. Commence givin' us those real clear directions. And if they *ain't* real clear or if you're tryin' to be cagey in some way, we'll come back here and burn this whole prairie eye sore to the ground. You understand?"

"Yessir. I mean, nossir," Lone stammered. "Nossir, I ain't about to try nothing cagey."

He led the way outside. Out across the slice of boardwalk in front of the store, past the trio's hitched horses, and out into the street. Lone moved in a kind of anxious, awkward sideways shuffle, making sure he kept the front of the clerk's apron hanging in such a way as to conceal the Colt on his hip.

Banty and Bowler Hat followed him out, and Whiskey Nose lagged behind. Lone could hear him clumping and clattering on the inside, apparently scrounging for some food items to scoop up and bring out when he came. Lone cursed mentally; his plan was to get all three of the hardcases out into the street. But at least he had the satisfaction—upon tossing a quick glance past Banty's shoulder—of seeing Red Smith in position at the front corner of the saloon.

Lone stopped out near the middle of the street and turned to face Banty and Bowler Hat. Whiskey Nose hadn't come out yet but could still be heard noisily continuing his "shopping".

"Alright, let's have it," Banty demanded. "How do we get to where we can find Smith?"

Lone extended his left arm and pointed west out of town, the direction the three had been headed when they came in. "If you was to stay on the wagon road and continue straight on thataway for about three miles," he said, "you'd come to a fork in the road."

A squinting Banty turned his head and followed the line of Lone's finger. "Uh-huh. Then what?" he said.

"Well, don't take the left fork. You wouldn't find Smith that way."

"Okay."

"And if you was to take the right fork...well, Smith wouldn't be off that way neither."

Banty's face snapped around, and his eyes blazed at Lone. "What the hell! What are you tryin' to pull?"

Lone grinned. "Aw, I was just havin' a little fun."

"Fun!" Banty's face started to take on a shade of purple. "You think this is some kind of goddamn joke, you big oaf?"

"Matter of fact, I sorta do," Lone drawled, a harder edge biting into his tone. "And it's a joke on you, tough talker. 'Cause if you really want to find Red Smith, all you gotta do is turn and look over yonder at the end of the saloon."

Banty's eyes widened slightly and an expression of anger mixed with uncertainty gripped his face. At the same time, the purple flush began to drain away. Very slowly, holding their bodies rigid, both Banty and Bowler Hat turned their heads and cut their gazes over at the corner of the saloon. Smith stood there, partially exposed, holding a Winchester leveled from his waist.

Everything seemed to freeze for a tight, tense moment. Whatever might have otherwise played out next was altered by Whiskey Nose choosing right then to exit the store. He stepped out somewhat clumsily with a lumpy, clanking sack of what sounded like mostly canned goods slung over his right shoulder and a cloth-wrapped side of bacon hooked under his left arm.

His abrupt appearance drew Lone's attention for a single quick eye flick. But that was enough of a distraction for the desperate Banty. Screeching, "Burn the bastards down!" he hopped a half step back from Lone, and his hands streaked down for the iron on his hips.

He was fast; real fast. But not faster than an already drawn gun like the one Lone had waiting for him. While Banty and Bowler Hat's heads were turned to look at Smith, Lone had silently freed his Colt behind the screen of the apron he wore and was now holding it down at his side. When Banty made his desperation move, all Lone had to do was tip the Colt at an upward angle and fire without even sweeping the apron aside. Once, then twice, the .44 spoke. Two ragged burn holes appeared in the apron and a pair of ragged, bloody holes appeared in Banty—one at the base of his throat, a second one four inches lower. The rooster was slammed back and knocked to the dirt without either of his guns clearing leather.

As Banty was going down, Smith's rifle cracked. It caught Bowler Hat in mid-draw—the slug smashing into his shoulder, spinning him a hundred-eighty degrees in a spray of blood and shattered bone fragments before he pitched face down onto the dusty street.

What this left was a situation eerily reminiscent of one presented to Lone and Smith just a few days earlier. Two hard cases down, a single remaining one left with a choice: Give up to the inevitable, or try to make a fight he had no chance of winning. Unfortunately for him, Whiskey Nose made the same foolish decision as the Mexican pistolero had previously. His expression at seeing his comrades fall turned suddenly from agonized shock to a look of blind rage. Bellowing "No!" as he hurled away the lumpy sack and dropped the side of bacon, he made a hopeless grab for his gun. Lone's Colt and Smith's Winchester blasted in unison. The double impact of the bullets hammered into Whiskey Nose and drove the big man back through the doorway where he hit the floor inside with a shuddering thump, skidding briefly until coming to a stop. A dead stop.

———

Not surprisingly, the rap of early morning gunfire within the settlement drew the attention of many residents already on the verge of rising to face the new day. Now, the dozen or so who came forth to gather on the edge of the street out front of Gottlieb's were facing it with looks of shock and concern. They watched, silently for the most part, as Lone and Smith hoisted the two dead manhunters belly down across the saddles of their horses. Far from silent was an excited Herman Gottlieb, who was striding back and forth while providing an eyewitness account of the shooting. This included much praise for the cunning and bravery shown by Lone and Smith against superior odds. Unfortunately, it, by necessity, also included a revelation of what had recently been learned about Smith's past.

Someone else being far from silent was the wounded Bowler Hat—now minus his defining headgear, it having fallen off and been stomped flat by his own horse. But that was the least of his laments. "I'm hurt bad! I need a doctor," he wailed as Lone and Smith pushed him up into his own saddle with the reins of the other two horses knotted to the tie-down straps of his bedroll. "I'll bleed to death if you just send me off without proper care!"

"The only care you'll get here is being left alive," Smith told him through gritted teeth. "That was more than you had in mind for me! Consider yourself lucky the rifle I shot you with was one I used for the first time, so I didn't know it pulled low—else I'd've blown your head off."

"What difference does it make—if I bleed out and die on the trail anyway?" Bowler Hat moaned.

Smith shook his head. "Not a damn bit of one to me."

"If you're so worried about losin' blood—which the good folks of Sarben would appreciate you doin' some-where else, by the way, 'stead of leakin' it all over the middle of their town," Lone said—"then best get a move on while you still got some juice to keep you goin'. And if you *do* keel over, especially since you're already leadin' those other two carcasses, try to make it far enough away so's the crows and buzzards and other scavengers don't come flockin' around to bother these same good folks."

Bowler Hat looked aghast. "That ain't funny, you sick bastard! That ain't funny at all!"

Lone grinned. "Kinda depends where you're lookin' at it from."

A very grave and sad-looking Pastor Isaac stepped out of the crowd. "I am sorry, but I must protest," he said, addressing Lone and Smith. "I recognize the unholy history and ongoing intent of men such as these and find it thoroughly detestable. Nevertheless, inas-much as they are still children of God, to treat them in kind even as they—"

"Save your breath, Pastor," Smith cut him off. "In the first place, scum like these aren't children of God. They were spawned by the other deity. Maybe I came from the same place—I don't yet know for sure. At any rate, let Ol' Scratch worry about this bunch. I ask you respectfully, stand aside."

"That's the way of it, Pastor," Lone said bluntly. "Pray, light candles, do whatever you need to do to fulfill your job and sooth your soul. Just back off and let us do ours."

A moment later, Bowler Hat was sent on his way with a sharp slap to the rump of his horse. Grim faces and eyes under pinched brows were turned to the departing sight he made, the other two corpse-laden horses plodding behind his.

Abruptly breaking the quiet that had descended on the scene, Lone wheeled around and addressed all on hand. Among the faces looking back at him was Ma's. It troubled him that she had to see this harsh side of him firsthand. Not that she wasn't aware he'd dished out plenty of rough medicine in times past, but such an unfiltered display as this was bound to strike differently. He'd have to take a quick moment to explain in more detail, and he knew she'd understand, but he still wished to hell she was no part of this. Nonetheless, he had to forge on with what he had to do and with what he wanted to impress on the rest of the crowd at the moment. "I'm sorry you folks had to see and hear all of that. It was harsh business, I know." He gave it a beat and then continued, "But on the other hand, I'm kinda glad you got a taste of it. Because, as Herman explained, due to what has been claimed about Red Smith's past, you can expect more varmints like those three to likely be showin' up—leastways until word spreads that Red is gone from the area. Which he soon will be. In the meantime, if you're 'fronted by any more skunks like these, *don't* trifle with 'em! They're mean and dangerous and hurtin' and killin' comes to their kind 'bout easy as breathin'. So, do nothing but cooperate. Don't try anything like what me and Red just did. We were cornered and had no choice. Plus, we happen to have the kind of skills to measure up to 'em. That won't be the case for any of the rest of you."

"Lone's right," Smith said. "I'm sorry I brought any of this on you folks. Everybody in and around Sarben has been nothing but kind to me. I sure never intended to repay you like this. So the best thing I can do for now is to leave. Not run, but leave for the sake of your safety and for the sake of trying to pin down the truth about my past. And then my future...if I even deserve one."

CHAPTER NINE

ED CURTIS REALIZED HE HAD MADE SOME BAD DECISIONS. What was worse, he couldn't see any way but to accept being stuck with them. Not if he knew what was good for him. He was in too deep—up to his ears with the kind of hombres who wouldn't take kindly to any craw-fishing.

Damn.

It was all Sim O'Greary's fault. Well, part of it, anyway...

True, it was Curtis who had agreed via an exchange of telegrams to take the Indian girl the rest of the way up to Pike Grogan in North Dakota rather than only as far as the intermediate hand-off point in Ogallala as originally planned. But what other choice was there? It was kind of hard to do a hand-off to three men who were all of a sudden dead. And yeah, it went without saying that getting even more directly involved with a notorious outlaw like Grogan came with risk; but getting on the wrong side of him by declining his request to finish bringing him something he badly wanted seemed a hell of a lot riskier.

Even at that, it would have worked out okay—hell, maybe *more* than okay, depending on how appreciative Grogan might be for the added cooperation—if that doggone O'Greary had been willing to go along with it. He'd never been comfortable about doing a job connected to Grogan, though, not from the moment he belatedly discovered that was part of it. Still, he went ahead and honored the commitment he'd made to side Curtis as far as making the hand-off. But nothing more. Once his initial obligation was fulfilled, he stubbornly refused any more involvement. He took his pay-out and took his leave, heading back to the Nations.

That's where Curtis made his next bad decision—an even worse one, he was beginning to recognize—than opting to go ahead and get in deeper with Pike Grogan. Feeling angry at O'Greary and desperate to proceed with making his delivery, Curtis had hit several of Ogallala's rougher saloons on the lookout for someone suitable to hire as O'Greary's replacement; somebody with sufficient bark on him and not so high-minded about who he might be rubbing shoulders with in order to earn some quick, easy pay. Well, Curtis found his man. Two of them as a matter of fact. The Tate brothers, both well-fitted to the requirement of having some bark and not giving much of a damn about the kind of work they hired out for.

Trouble was, in the course of his saloon "shopping," Curtis had not only bought quite a few drinks to keep conversations flowing freely, but he had also tossed back quite a few rounds himself. To the point of being a little too loose with the details, he gave out concerning the job. Recollection of this didn't really hit him until the wee hours of the morning, after he started to sober up and after he'd already hired the Tates. He felt immediate pangs of remorse and concern over such carelessness, but inasmuch as it was too late to change it, all he could do was grab a few hours sleep before daybreak—the time settled upon for heading out once again with the girl and their new traveling companions—and hope for the best.

He took some further hope in finding the Tates right where they were supposed to be at first light, waiting with horses saddled and packed, everything ready as Curtis spirited Bright Moon down the back stairs of the hotel where he had been discreetly keeping her. A discordant note got struck soon enough, however, once Early Tate got a good look at the lovely Indian girl and remarked, "My oh my, now here's the kind of job I been waitin' all my life for...real convenient, too, how long we're gonna get to *handle* the merchandise before reachin' its delivery destination."

"Best keep in mind," Curtis advised sternly, "this is mighty important merchandise in the eyes of some key people—namely, Pike Grogan and Iron Wolf. Any *mis*-handling of it would be frowned on real serious-like. Understood?"

Early swept his hand in a brisk, exaggerated salute. "Yes *sir*, Cap'n. Understood loud and clear."

Curtis knew he was being mocked, and it made his ears burn. But he set his teeth and gave no response. Once he'd assisted Bright Moon up onto her mount, he swung into his own saddle and got them on their way, threading through the shadow-cut streets of the just-waking town and them aiming north toward the Dakotas.

Jesus. In the morning sunlight, and filtered through the lingering effects of his hangover, the Tate brothers looked even rougher and coarser than Curtis remembered. He'd gone in search of somebody with some bark on 'em, well, to whatever degree appearance counted, he'd gotten a double dose. At just past forty, an even six feet in height and still pretty solidly built, Curtis packed his own layer of tough hide. But, though he'd never admit it out loud, he knew instinctively he didn't possess the kind of hardness or menace to be found at the core of men like the Tates. Nor Pike Grogan, either. Hence, Curtis's feeling of sinking in too deep—possibly over his head—with their ilk.

The Tates were on the minus side of thirty, only a year apart in age. Early was the oldest, then Late. Early and Late Tate, names bestowed by a loud, boisterous father inclined toward the kind of humor appreciated by saloon rowdies like himself. His first son was born more than three weeks sooner than expected by his mother and the attending midwife; so Early he got dubbed. When his brother then came along and arrived an almost equal amount of time *past* his expected due date, his fate was sealed to be named Late. An added touch of irony to all of this came in the form of Early, in his premature birth state, being considered possibly too frail to survive, eventually growing to brutishly muscular proportions, towering six-six in height, with hands as big as grain shovels. Late, a plump twelve-pounder coming out of the womb, would mature to only average size, not quite six feet tall, lean and wiry of build. But the size of their quick tempers and rattlesnake mean dispositions were equal.

Increasing realization of this only worsened the hangover throb in Curtis's head and the sour lump of regret in his gut as they put Ogallala farther and farther behind them. His frequent sidelong glances over at Bright Moon revealed nothing as far as her reaction to this change in those now accompanying them. Her face remained the same smooth, coppery, flawless mask of impassivity it had been along. In all the days of riding with her, Curtis had never been able to get any sense of what was going on behind that mask and her dark, liquid eyes which simply stared ahead without emotion. Although she was capable of understanding and speaking English, she said even less than she outwardly displayed. Curtis had no idea how she truly felt about leaving the village in the Nations and returning to the North Dakota reservation where waited a young buck she'd been promised to for most of her life.

Before this, the half-assed romantic in Curtis had been hoping she liked the idea okay and that her and the boy would find happiness together. Now, overriding that simple wish was a more frantic hope that his ill-conceived hiring of the Tates hadn't introduced something that would dreadfully and forever tarnish any future happiness Bright Moon would be able to carry in her memory. Whether or not she had noticed the lewd, lustful gleam in Early's eyes when he poked about "*handling* the merchandise," Curtis hadn't missed it... and it worried the hell out of him.

But the real knife in the guts came a few hours later

when they made a mid-morning stop to give the horses a breather and take on some water. That was when Curtis noticed for the first time the saddlebags slung behind Late's bedroll. There was no mistaking the colorful Indian-bead trim they were decorated with. Curtis knew that trim well. He'd been riding alongside it for the past dozen days, right up until only about forty-eight hours ago—those saddlebags belonged to none other than Sim O'Greary!

Whatever showed on Curtis's face caused Late to pin him with a hard glare and demand in a snarl, "What're you lookin' at?"

Curtis pointed with a thrusting gesture. "Those saddlebags—where did you get them?"

"That's my business. What's it to *you*?" Late challenged.

"Because they look mighty familiar. Last I saw 'em, just a couple of days ago, they belonged to my former partner."

"You mean the partner you told us about who bailed out on you?" Late sneered. "What was his name— O'Mally or some such?"

"O'Greary," Curtis corrected tersely. "And he didn't bail out. He fulfilled the job he signed on to do then wasn't interested in stretching it out any farther." It felt a little odd to now be defending O'Greary for taking the very stance that Curtis, in his disappointment over it, had previously cursed. But his eyes were being suddenly jerked open to a lot of things he hadn't been willing to see before. And he could only divert them so much. Which brought him back to his inquiry of Late. "So, knowing O'Greary well enough to know what a

high store he set in those saddlebags, I'll ask again—
How is it you come to have 'em?"

Late's eyes narrowed. "You're developin' a kinda
snotty tone there, Cap'n. You got something stuck in
your craw you want to hack out a little plainer?"

Sensing how heated the exchange was getting and
aiming to cool it back down, brother Early spoke up.
"Late *bought* those saddlebags from your ex-partner.
How else would he get 'em? This O'Toole—"

"O'Greary."

"Whatever. The sorry-ass Irishman was broke,
needed a grubstake and was willin' to deal to get it,"
Early explained. "Brother Late liked the look of those
beaded bags. Made an offer, it got accepted, and the
transfer was done. Just that simple."

Curtis frowned. "Sim was broke? How could that be?
I'd just got done paying him off for..."

When his words trailed off, Early finished for him.
"Yeah, you told us how you paid him a tidy sum for
sidin' you on the trip up from the Nations. So it ain't
your fault—nor nobody else's—how the blamed fool
took his pay-off to the Crystal Palace gamin' tables and
went on one of the worstest and fastest losin' streaks
anybody had ever saw. Me and Brother Late came in in
time to see the sad, sorry end to it."

"That's when," said Late, picking up the narrative
with an abrupt and wholly unconvincing show of
sympathy, "the unlucky, wrung-out poor rascal started
scroungin' for a grubstake so's he could hit the trail for
home. Like he shoulda done a whole lot sooner."

Curtis felt sick to his stomach. He wanted to rage
against the lies he knew he was being fed. But for a

swarm of reasons, he held himself in check. Fear for himself was undeniably among them, but also concern for Bright Moon if he acted too recklessly. And, of course, there was no ignoring the weight of crushing guilt he felt for having run his mouth about the "tidy sum" he'd paid the "ungrateful" O'Greary, who then left him in a lurch. Yeah, Sim had left him in a lurch, and his careless tongue had gotten even by setting his old friend up—Curtis was growing nauseatingly certain—to be robbed and killed.

To drive one more nail into the confirmation of this, Curtis said with a feigned bitterness, "Blackjack. I bet the blackjack table was where that fool Sim took his beating, wasn't it? He never was worth beans at playing that damn game yet was too much of a sucker to ever give up trying."

"Yup," crowed Early. "That's where he was right to the end...drainin' his pride and his wallet on one final bust from the flip card!"

Curtis ground his teeth together. There was the clincher. In truth, Sim seldom gambled at all. But above all, he avoided blackjack. Hated the game and was often heard to claim he'd never be caught dead playing it.

Well, ironically, now he *was* dead. Of that, Curtis felt convinced. And blackjack was being blamed as an accomplice.

But *he* was the real accomplice. And those who carried out the deed were the killers presently taking Sim's place, riding stirrup to stirrup with Curtis and Bright Moon as they continued north. What a hell of a situation. *But I know the truth, and they don't know I know*, Curtis told himself. He'd have to play it smart and squeeze everything he could out of that advantage. He glanced again at Bright Moon. He had failed Sim...he'd be damned if he would let down this innocent beauty, too. He didn't yet know how, but for both of their sakes, he had to find some way to break them free from the grip of these ruthless, murderous Tate brothers that his half-drunken over-eagerness had placed them in.

CHAPTER TEN

It was crowding noon when Lone returned from Ogallala to where Red waited for him half a dozen miles northeast of the town. After leaving Sarben and the bloody day's start they had found there, it was decided that riding into Ogallala together might not be a good idea. Though Red wasn't known there, Lone was. And since word had spread about how Lone had been in on the Weems-Bossner shooting with the mysterious red-headed stranger since revealed to be "Wade Avril," anyone riding at his side was sure to draw unwanted scrutiny—in spite of the hair-blackening disguise.

Still, Lone felt a stop in Ogallala was warranted. According to what O'Greary had reported last night, and seconded by remarks from the three manhunters who'd shown up this morning, the rowdy old cowtown sounded like a hotbed of activity and talk swirling around the resurfacing of the man alleged to be Avril and the revenge bounty placed on him by Pike Grogan as a result. Lone wanted to catch up on the latest in all of this. He also sought to get a better line on O'Greary's former partner Ed Curtis, and the two toughs he'd hired to replace the Irishman; the bushwhacking snakes responsible for his murder, Lone was convinced.

Inasmuch as his recurring trips to the area during his roaming years had been centered mainly on visiting Ma in North Platte, Lone had naturally developed more acquaintances there than in Ogallala. Nevertheless, he'd spent enough time in the neighboring "Gomorrah of the Plains," as it had been called back in its heyday, though considerably tamed down in the present, to get to know a few old reliables there too. They were who he'd called upon as he made a quick pass through that morning, and then rode off, having gained sufficient updates to call it time worth spending.

Not knowing how long Lone would be, Red had gone ahead and made a meager camp for the duration. A spot on the north bank of the North Platte River suited his needs. Plenty of graze and water for the horses, a nice splotch of shade under a cluster of cottonwoods and birch for him. He stripped down and picketed the animals, built a small, smokeless fire over which he cooked some coffee, then leaned back against a tree trunk and waited.

This was how Lone found him when he came riding up. Drawing rein and planting a forearm across the top of his saddle horn, Lone gazed down and said dryly, "Gee. I hope you haven't caught a chill stuck there in all your nice, cool riverside shade while me and Ironsides been hoggin' up all this blazin' hot sun out here in the wide open."

Smith held up his tin coffee cup. "Managed to ward off any serious frostbite by relying on plenty of hot brew to keep my insides warm."

"Glad you were able to tough it out." Lone swung down from the saddle, bringing with him a lumpy, grease-spotted paper bag. "How about vittles? You scrounge yourself anything to eat?"

"Was thinking on working up some kind of lunch before too long. Hadn't yet decided on what."

Lone held out the bag. "Well, I decided for you. For us. Got ham sandwiches on cornbread in here, also a couple chunks of cherry pie. Gonna cost you some of that coffee, though. Fresh."

Smith pushed away from his tree and stood up. "Done deal. While you're cooling and watering your horse, I'll cook up a new pot. Then we can wash down the sandwiches and pie with it while you're telling me what you found out in Ogallala."

So that's how they spent the next half hour. The pie and sandwiches Lone had purchased at a café in Ogallala were delicious, and Smith proved capable of turning out some pretty fair coffee. Not quite as good as his, Lone judged, but passable. For what they were setting out to do, the former redhead's already proven gun skills were the most important thing. But considering the long trail miles that lay ahead, also having some skills around a campfire sure didn't hurt none.

As far as what Lone had learned in town, there really wasn't anything new about the situation surrounding Pike Grogan's bounty offer. Just that the intensity of it hadn't lessened any; in fact, it had only increased as word spread wider and more and more manhunters with blood and dollar signs in their eyes were reported to be flocking from every direction. None other than the marshal of Ogallala had confirmed this to Lone, commenting how he was seeing many such men pass through daily and was getting reports of the same from elsewhere. A curious aspect commented on by more than a few was how neither Grogan himself nor any direct members of his gang—except for the initial venture of the ill-fated trio headed by Weems—seemed to be on the way to join the chase firsthand. Whatever they had cooking up in North Dakota—it was speculated—must've been something mighty big to hold them there while letting others take up the pursuit of the now-flushed quarry they hated so badly and had previously chased so hard to bring down by their own hands.

Nor did Lone learn much he didn't already know about Ed Curtis—or Sim O'Greary either, for that matter. Neither of them had drawn much attention from anyone for the brief amount of time they'd been in Ogallala, not until O'Greary faded from the picture and Curtis hired the Tate brothers to replace him. There's where Lone picked up some worthwhile insight. The curiously named Early and Late Tate, he learned, were a bit more than the saloon dredge bottom feeders he'd calculated them to be. According to the marshal, while they didn't rate as top-line gun toughs, they were nevertheless well-known hard cases who made do as bouncers and heavy freight handlers when they had to, but jumped at any chance to hire out for thug work or strongarm intimidation if the opportunity for such came along. Then, too, there'd been some hints of rustling involvement that claimed not only the loss of cattle for a few scattered ranches but also the lives of a handful of wranglers trying to hang on to them. Nothing could be proven, however, not against the Tates or anybody who might have been working with them. Nor did anyone seem to know the nature of the work Curtis hired them for in this latest instance. But when the Tates pulled out at first light this morning, having mentioned a couple of places the night before how they figured to be gone for a spell, more than one voice was heard to mutter at the news how little they'd be missed if they failed to ever find their way back.

Lone, of course, did know the nature of the work the Tates were hired for—to assist Curtis in getting the Indian girl, Bright Moon, the rest of the way back to the Flat Falls reservation. Somewhat to his puzzlement, at no point in talking with anybody had there been mention of an Indian girl. Yet Curtis and O'Greary were known to have each booked a hotel room for the nights they were in town. So where/how had they managed to keep Bright Moon so invisible during that time? Likewise, when riding out this morning...though doing so at daybreak would likely have accounted for that part.

"Only a couple possibilities it could boil down to," Smith concluded. "Either they kept her hidden away in one of the rooms—or stashed somewhere close on the outskirts of town. No matter which, it doesn't sound like very respectful treatment for what's supposed to be such a valuable package."

"Like white men treatin' an Indian disrespectfully is something new," Lone said dryly.

Smith frowned. "That aside, if those curly wolves hadn't delayed us first thing back in Sarben, you damn near would've reached Ogallala about the time Curtis and his bunch were leaving out. Might've even been there to intercept them. We could right now be on their tails tight as ticks."

"Might've worked out that way," Lone allowed. "But

the way things stand, we still ain't necessarily left in too bad a shape."

"How so?"

Lone took a drink of coffee. "If I'd've caught up with the Tates last night or even first thing this mornin', my inclination would've been to waste no time cuttin' 'em down. Payback for O'Greary...and I ain't sayin' they don't still have that due...but now that I've had time to cool down some and reflect a little wider on things, I'm thinkin' maybe there might be worth in not hurryin' that so much."

Smith eyed him silently and waited for him to continue.

"Last night, after I got done buryin' ol' Sim and before headin' out to fetch you," Lone said, "I took a scout around my property and found where the ambushers had stashed their horses ahead of workin' up closer on foot. There was enough moon for me to make things out pretty clear. It showed me that the left hind foot of one of their horses had a nick out of its shoe.

"After leavin' Ogallala a little bit ago, before anglin' toward here, I rode a sweep back and forth outside of town until I picked up fresh sign of five horses headed due north. Not more'n half a dozen hours old. One of 'em showed a nick in the shoe of its left hind foot."

"Five horses?" Smith questioned.

"Curtis and the Tates account for three. The girl on a fourth, and then a pack animal. It fits."

"Yeah. Yeah, it does."

Lone said, "With no more of a jump on us than that and a clear trail to follow, an afternoon of steady ridin' could damn near put us tick-tight on their tails by nightfall."

"But a minute ago you said there was no worth in hurrying," Smith pointed out.

"What I said was not hurryin' to cut down the Tates," Lone reminded him. "But that don't mean not closin' the gap on 'em, then stickin' close, and puttin' 'em to work for us."

Smith looked ready to say something but Lone held up a hand, palm out, stopping him. "I know what you're thinkin'—just 'cause I ain't in no rush to take care of the Tates don't mean you're ready to commence your dealin' with Grogan at the same slowed-down pace. Especially knowin' how the hounds he's called out to hunt you are gatherin' faster and thicker by the minute."

"You could say that weighs on my mind just a tad," Smith responded tersely.

"But don't lose sight of how it's all linked together," Lone insisted. "The Tates are part of it on account of sidin' Curtis in gettin' the girl delivered safe to Grogan and Iron Wolf. Right? Well, if you hear me out, I think you'll see how we can use that link as an advantage for both of us achievin' what we're after in a surer, safer— though, yeah, maybe a bit slower—way."

Smith scowled. "I'm willing to listen. You haven't steered me wrong so far, and I don't want to seem ungrateful. But, I've got to tell you, too much time spent on this business with the Indian girl—especially since you're now saying you're in no hurry to take vengeance on her escorts who killed your friend—seems to me like time lost going straight for Grogan. And how is it you figure tailing them amounts to 'putting them to work for us'?"

"Because, when the time comes, the delivery of the girl could be the key that opens Grogan's front door. Damn it, stop and think," Lone grated. "As far as gettin' to Grogan, all we know is that he's holed up somewhere in the vicinity of the Flat Falls Cheyenne rez in North Dakota. That's a mighty big chunk of wild, wide-open country. We go chargin' up on our own and...what? Start turnin' over rocks and callin' for ol' Pike to come out and play? How do you think that's apt to work out for us? Or...do you think we might have a better chance if we fall in tight behind Curtis's bunch and fog 'em unseen until they lead us to where Grogan is waitin' for the girl to be handed over?"

Smith drained the last of his coffee, upended the cup and tapped the remaining grounds out of the bottom. Regarding Lone, he said, "A minute ago, I told you I was grateful for you not steering me wrong. And I meant it. But, by the same token, having you be right *all* the goddamned time could get annoying after a while." He paused to heave a sigh. Then: "Go ahead and finish your coffee while I saddle my horse. We've got a lot of ground to make up before night camp."

CHAPTER ELEVEN

EARLY TATE SANK HIS TEETH INTO A CUT OF BEEF JERKY and tore off a big bite. As he began chewing the mouthful of salty, stringy meat, his face remained set in a brooding expression. "I tell ya, brother," he said as he chewed, "this whole thing is startin' to get old. Comin' up on four days now we been on the trail. Bakin' under the damnable hot sun with nary ever even a wisp of a cloud to throw shade, eatin' dust every mile, chilled every night in the middle of nothing but these treeless, endless grassy hills. Gettin' to be a miserable slog, and don't tell me you ain't feelin' it too."

His brother Late sat on the ground beside him. It was the middle of the day, and the sun was high and hot straight overhead in a cloudless, bleached-out blue sky. Their group was halted for a noon break, the chance for people and horses to rest, drink, and eat. Graze for the animals was plentiful in the form of sun-baked high grass, though some of it still with spring greenness down nearer the base of the stems. A sparse meal of jerky and biscuits leftover from last night's supper, washed down with tepid canteen water, sufficed for the riders. It was too damn hot to cook coffee.

The brothers were settled at the base of a high, sharp slope clogged with tall yucca growth, their backs pressed against said growth, trying to find a thin slice of shade thrown by its irregular outward swell. Curtis and Bright Moon sat several yards apart from them. He also hitched back against a ragged, grassy cutbank, trying to find a sliver of shade, and the girl sat cross-legged out in the open, seemingly oblivious to the sunlight pouring down, burnishing her smooth skin to an even richer copper color.

In response to his brother's lament, Late said, "A-course I'm feelin' the miseries of bein' out on the trail in this heat and dust. How could I not? And if there *was* any chance I didn't notice, your near-constant belly-achin' about it would sure keep me reminded."

"Well, excuse me all to hell," Early huffed.

Late scowled. "What did you expect when we signed on for this ride-out up through the Sandhills? Ain't like you never got a gander before how barren and empty they are."

"Yeah, a gander maybe. Even that was too much. Never had a hankerin' to spend so blasted much time plumb in the thick of 'em."

"So you oughtn't be disappointed then at the prospect of bein' near out of 'em. Wipe the sweat outta your eyes and take a good look yonder." Late stretched an arm and pointed off to the north and a bit east. "See that dirty-lookin' smudge along the horizon there? Them's the Black Hills of South Dakota, so named by the Sioux Injuns on account of how the pine trees grow so thick along the rocky ridges up that way they look almost black from a distance."

Early squinted to make out what his brother was indicating. His wide mouth spread in a grin. "Hey. Trees growin' that thick would sure be a welcome thing. How far away are they?"

"A day or so, I'd say. Way we're headed, though, what I'd also say is that we ain't gonna ride right into 'em, but more like we'll pass a ways off the western end. Sorta squirt between them and the Nebraska Pine Ridge area farther west, I calculate."

"Well, shit." Early's grin curved down into a frown. "You had me hankerin' to get in among some trees and now you—"

"Relax," Late cut him off. "You'll still get your fill of trees. And soon. Maybe even an early taste of 'em by night camp. Look ahead and you'll see how all this empty is fixin' to break up and turn ruggeder in a kinda long, rocky spine that reaches for a long way across the top of Nebraska and the bottom of South Dakota. We get in the middle of that, you might even find yourself missin' these bare, gently rollin' hills."

Early grunted. "Fat chance of that." He swallowed his lump of chewed jerky, and his frown deepened. "How come you to be so familiar with all this? We ain't ever been up this far before, have we?"

"*We* ain't, no," Late answered. "But I was once. Remember that time we threw in with that pack of ex-Johnny Rebs still fightin' the war by sticky-loopin' cattle from ranches over Big Springs way? And you got horned bad the night we struck, so had to stay behind while the rest of us took the beeves north to the sellers that had been lined up? Well, this neck of the woods is where we brung our catch."

"Yeah, I remember the job," said Early. "Guess I never realized how far you had to come to unload the take."

"It was early spring, a lot cooler. Still, it was no picnic pushin' fifty cow critters and all the while lookin' over our shoulders for pursuit. But the herd was so scattered on the sprawled-out ranch we took 'em from, I don't think the rancher knew we grabbed any of his stock until it was too late to try and give chase. In fact, it went so slick those Rebs reckoned to do it all over again." Now Late pasted on a frown. "In fact, I was ready to throw in again, too, except you talked me out of it. I never could quite figure out why."

"No matter why, you oughta be damned glad I did." Early looked grim. "That sprawled-out rancher was plenty ready the second time, wasn't he? Ready to the tune of every last one of them Rebs gettin' either shot to pieces or hung from a propped-up wagon tongue before the next mornin's sun. Had you been with 'em, no reason to think you'd've fared any better."

"No argument there. Shivers me to think about comin' so close," Late allowed. "But I still don't know why you held me back."

"Okay. Reckon it's time to fess up about that." Early bit off another chunk of jerky and then went on talking as he began to work it inside his mouth. "Remember the Reb leader—that wild-haired, hate-the-world cuss with just one eye and more craziness whirlin' in it than a whole passel of whiskey-fueled Injuns? What was his name—Tilbertson or some such?"

"Tillotsen," Late said. "Yeah, you bet I remember

him. I spent near a month ridin' with that spooky bastard, and practically every minute of that time, I was primed for him to snap his last wire. Ain't proud to admit it, but mostly why I said I'd be willin' to ride with him again was worry over settin' him off by sayin' no. Luckily, you pleaded me away by claimin' that horn wound of yours wasn't healin' right and I needed to get you to a proper doctor."

Early cocked a brow. "That wasn't an altogether false claim. It was true enough my wound still needed some more healin', though it had got to passable shape. The reason it didn't get healed more was on account of Tillotsen's sister, who he left me in the care of. Remember her?"

"That mousy little thing who stayed behind with you in that cave while the rest of us herded off the stole cattle? Yeah, I remember."

"That 'mousy little thing'—her name was MarJean, for what it's worth," declared Early, "turned out to be more wildcat than mouse! The dust haze of you fellas and those cow critters had barely thinned outta the air before she was on me like a starvin' she-griz comin' outta hibernation. You know what a strong ruttin' crave I got myself, right? Well, I'm here to tell you that even two hundred percent healthy I couldn't've kept up with her. She's the reason that wound never completely healed. Soon as my eyes fluttered even the tiniest and I showed any sign of wakin' up—boom!—she was under the covers, crawlin' all over me and makin' demands. I swear, if you fellas had been gone another handful of days, I think she mighta drained me plumb to death!"

Late eyed him tighter. "Why, you dog. Here I have been believin' all this time it was my interests you was lookin' out for by pullin' us away from that bunch. Now I find out it was your own hide you was out to save!"

"*Both* of our hides," Early said stubbornly. "What's more, I was at double risk. First from MarJean near ridin' me to death. And then, for all I knew, from her spooky ol' one-eyed brother. I had no way of knowin' how he'd react if he found out what the two of us—no matter it was mostly on account of her—had been up to while he was away. Or, if he didn't care about that, what if she threw some kind of jealous fit? Was I to claim I was worn out and wanted to be done bedroll bouncin' with her? In case I didn't mention it, she was startin' to sound mighty possessive there toward the end."

Late wagged his head. "You dog," he said again. "Ever think you was gettin' payback for all the gals you bedroll bounced and then turned your back on?"

"Aw, nuts to that," Early protested. "I didn't lead none of 'em to expect any different. Hell, most of 'em were *paid* not to expect any different. Besides, like I said before and like you damn well know, I got me a powerful ruttin' crave that no one woman could likely handle anyway."

Late grinned. "Except for MarJean. Sounds like she was up to handlin' it...and then some."

"Now don't start rubbin' that in, I'm warnin' you. I opened up to you, but I don't want to hear no more about it," Early grumbled. "I was sick and hurt, and MarJean was a spooky little bitch who woulda wore down any man—hell, any *three* men!"

"Okay, okay," said Late placatingly, knowing better than to prod his brother too hard, especially about certain things. "We both know you're ruttin' crave, as you call it, didn't suffer no lastin' damage."

"You damn betcha it didn't." Early chewed his mouthful of jerky furiously, and his gaze cut over to Bright Moon. "And that damn squaw over there has got me near bustin' to prove it. Damn, brother, ain't she one prime piece of womanhood?"

"Yeah, but don't torment yourself by startin' in on that again," Late warned. "You know she's off limits, has to stay untouched."

"Says who? Why? And who's even gonna know?" Early demanded. "She's been livin' on a rez, first up north and then down in the Nations before headin' back again now...you think the heathen bucks in those places have kept their hands off her?"

"We can't help whether they did or didn't. We just got to make sure she gets left alone for the time we got say over her. And don't forget Curtis is watchin' like a hawk to make sure of that."

"Bah! That groveler don't worry me none." Early scoffed. "He probably already had his turns with her on the way from the Nations to Ogallala. He knows damn well how you came by those beaded saddlebags he spotted that you took off his Irish pal. Yet he didn't have the stones to brace us hard about that, did he? What makes you think he'd make a hard stand to try stoppin' us from havin' some fun with the girl?"

"He don't have to stop us. All he has to do," Late pointed out, "is tell Pike Grogan about it. Listen, we're lookin' at a mighty healthy payday for this job, right? Plus we already tucked away a tidy little bonus off that Irishman who Curtis stupidly clued us in about. And, long term, like we talked about before, if we make a favorable impression on Grogan that might mean an openin' to ride full time with his gang. The big time. No more scrapin' by on whatever nickel and dime shit comes our way...is your damn ruttin' crave strong enough to make you want to jeopardize all of that?"

Early turned his head to one side and spat a gob of jerky too stringy to swallow down. Bringing his eyes back to Late, he said, "Okay, little brother. For now. But accordin' to Curtis, we got another seven or eight days yet to go. Never can tell what might happen in that long a time."

FOUR HUNDRED YARDS to the south, Lone pushed back from the crest of a low, grassy hill and let the field glasses he'd been peering through dangle loose on the leather thong around his neck. He turned and made his way in a controlled slide down to the base of the slope where Red Smith sat on his haunches, hat pushed back, mopping sweat from his face with a black-streaked hanky.

"Looky there," said Smith, holding up the hanky. "Just like I warned you, my hair keeps dripping down over my face."

Lone grinned. "Don't worry. When it cools down come evenin', you can rinse out the hanky and slap a fresh layer of paint on your head."

"That might be okay for a while," Smith allowed. "But if this heat keeps up, I'm gonna run out of boot blacking before the week is through. We'll either have to find a place to buy some more or have me end up with a striped head of hair like one of those African tigers or some such."

"That might work even better as a disguise from

those bounty hunters lookin' for some plain ol' red-headed hombre."

"Yeah. Very funny."

In accordance with Lone's plan, they had closed the gap on Curtis's bunch that first night out of Ogallala and had been fogging them unseen ever since. This was the middle of the third day, each one a long, monotonous haul over the rolling, treeless, seemingly endless expanse of the Sandhills that made it seem like they were making hardly any progress at all, yet Lone could tell the steady pace being set by Curtis was in fact eating away the miles. About the only thing that broke the monotony were fringe sightings of cattle herds here and there, though Curtis steered their route clear of any ranch headquarters. Whatever his other shortcomings might be, Lone had to give the man a nod for knowing how to cover distance.

Settling himself on the slope base next to Smith now, Lone set aside his field glasses and then took the canteen held out to him. He tucked his chin down onto his chest and raised the canteen, pouring water from it over the back if his neck. That done, he rocked his head back and put the canteen to his lips for a long drink.

Watching him, Smith said, "I watered the horses after they'd cooled while you were up having your gander at our fellow travelers. Just so you know, the main water bag on the pack animal is down below half full."

"That's okay," Lone replied, lowering the canteen. "We'll be reachin' plenty of fresh water soon. By night-fall, matter of fact. Land's about to change, grow more rugged pretty sudden. It'll be broken and rockier, tougher goin' in spots, but there'll be green grass and trees and, like I said, no shortage of fresh, cool water."

Smith nodded. "Man, that sounds good."

"By the look of it," Lone told him, "I'm bettin' our friends up ahead will feel the same. They're startin' to appear a mite frazzled around the edges."

"I know the feeling," Smith said ruefully.

"Aw, you're doin' okay. Ain't none of us holdin' up near as cool as the Indian gal, though. She don't appear to be showin' hardly no sign of wear."

Smith frowned. "I'm still surprised they're not keeping her bound or restrained in any way. I mean, I'm glad for her sake they're not. But I somehow expected she might be making this trek against her will."

"Don't look to be the case." Lone seemed to consider something and then a hint of a frown also tugged at his face before he added, "There's some kind of tension cracklin' among that bunch, though. Ain't sure what or why, but how they hold their bodies most of the time kinda rigid, poised; and the way they eyeball one another, sorta sly and suspicious-like...makes me think of a bunch of greenhorns who crawled barefoot out of their bedrolls only to come late to considerin' how there might be a scorpion or two on the ground between them and where they left their boots."

"There's a colorful image. What do you think it means?" asked Smith.

"Blamed if I know." Lone's frown stayed in place. "But we need to hope it don't add up to 'em gettin' their fool asses stung some way or other before they lead us to Pike Grogan."

CHAPTER TWELVE

Almost as if Lone's words were prophetic, scorpions of the human variety showed up that very evening.

Late in the afternoon, as anticipated by Lone as well as Late Tate, the land underwent a significant change. The empty, blunted rise and fall of the Sandhills gave way to an increasing number of rock outcrops and sharper-crested hills—some peaked by their own low, jagged rocks thrusting up like rows of broken teeth—that then dropped down into bowl-like depressions carpeted by shorter, greener grass studded with spruce and cottonwood trees. Where the vast underground aquifer stretching below the Sandhills mass often left stagnate surface pools and even small, still lakes in some of the pockets between hills, in this broken land could contrastingly be seen quick, twisting, shade-dappled streams.

The welcome change in terrain quickened the pace set by Curtis until he brought his group to an elongated oval-shaped meadow rimmed on one side by a brush-choked low ridge and a tree-lined creek meandering along the opposite side. Here, he signaled an early halt for night camp with the last sliver of sun still glowing in the heart of a pinkish-gold smudge just above the western horizon. In short order the horses were stripped, watered, picketed, and the campsite was laid out. As the three men then took some time to douse themselves and splash about like adolescents in the cool water of the creek, Bright Moon quietly went about building a fire and setting a pot of coffee to brew. After the others had wrung themselves out and came straggling to the fire, the Indian girl left the rest of the evening meal preparation to them while she withdrew to a remote spot further upstream behind a screen of willows and dense brush to attend her own cleansing.

A quarter mile away, from the lip of a wide, shallow gully angling across the front edge of the meadow, Lone and Smith observed these activities by taking turns looking through Lone's field glasses.

"Looks like our neighbors have planted their picket pins a mite early and are making themselves plenty comfortable for the night," Smith remarked.

"Appears so," agreed Lone. "Nor is it a bad example to follow, says I. Don't know about you, but neither would I mind a splash of that cool, fresh water and an extra hour or so of rest and shuteye come dark."

Smith said, "I vote the same, though I think I'll wait a bit before enjoying any of that water. Seeing how we're downstream from where those three hombres just did their wallowing, I reckon the flow could use a little more time to run clear first."

A thin offshoot tributary of the meadow-side creek trickled into and down through the middle of the gully floor behind and below them. Since this and the thick grasses bracketing it would meet the needs of their animals, and the overall sunken feature of the gully appealed to the shadow riders as an aid to keeping themselves out of sight, they had marked it as a good spot for their own night camp once they finished reconnoitering Curtis's group.

"Reasonable point about those wallowin' hombres," Lone responded to what Smith had said. "But in case you didn't notice, the Injun gal has now gone off to do her own ablutions. We gonna wait out her run-off too?"

Smith gave it a beat and then eyed him from under a cocked brow. "As a matter of fact, I did notice the Indian girl. I noticed her real good. Having said that, and at the risk of sounding somewhat crude, it strikes me that a trace of run-off from any 'wallowing' she might do wouldn't be such a distasteful thing."

Lone grinned. "You might've fancied up the words some, but you still came across soundin' crude. Which ain't meanin' to say I disagree. Come on. Let's drop back, wash up and get some coffee cookin'. There's enough dry kindling for a smokeless fire and what little breeze there is is in our favor for carryin' off any telltale wisp or cookin' aroma..."

———

Unfortunately, notice of Bright Moon and what was meant to be some private attention paid to herself did not end there. Not with Lone and Smith turning away to begin laying out their camp; nor even with the slack-jawed gawking of Late Tate—all the while being glared at disapprovingly by Ed Curtis—trying his damnedest to gain a peek through the distant screen of creekside foliage.

No, far more intrusive notice came in the form of four riders who appeared suddenly, topping the crest of a low rise less than a hundred yards away on the opposite side of the creek. From that vantage point, no trees or brush of any significance lined the bank to interrupt a full view of the copper-skinned beauty bared for the purpose of bathing herself. The hoofbeats of the riders' horses, muffled by the thick grass on the back side of the rise, soon rumbled louder as the animals were brought only to a brief pause before being spurred on eagerly down this near side by the vision now in sight. One of the riders displayed particular eagerness by letting out a whoop and hollering, "Yeehaw, boys! Looks like we found ourselves the prize stray anybody ever turned up on Twin V range!"

Bright Moon's nature was not to panic or cry out at the first sign of trouble. She'd endured too much, even at her young age, to overreact at what was so far only a relatively minor disturbance. What she did do was cross her arms to cover her bare breasts and, at the same time, bend at the knees to ensure from the waist down, she was below the surface of the water. Her clothing, folded neatly on the bank, was too far away to attempt a quick retrieval. Making a dash for them at this point would have revealed far more to the hungry eyes of the rapidly approaching horsemen than if she just stayed put.

The riders spurring toward her were cut from a similar bolt that marked them as cowboys, wranglers from some nearby cattle spread. The one who called out had mentioned the "Twin V range," seemingly identifying the brand they rode for. He and the others were all clad in the standard garb of chaps, colorful bandannas, and wide-brimmed hats. Bright Moon took all of this in with a quick sweep of her dark eyes, the expression on her face showing nothing. Without looking around, she was confident that Curtis and the Tate brothers would soon be coming up behind her, responding to the appearance of these newcomers. Strangely, the thought of that—of the two brothers, especially the openly lecherous one called Late, seeing her so exposed—made her skin crawl almost as bad as the looks she was getting from the closing riders.

Back in the camp, exactly as Bright Moon expected, Curtis and the Tates were indeed alerted by the sight and sound of the intruders. Rising up from the task of slicing strips of bacon into an oversized frying pan, Curtis tossed aside the carving knife he'd been using and instead snatched up the gun belt he'd taken off earlier for his dip in the creek. Hurriedly buckling the rig once more around his waist, he barked, "Grab your rifles!" as he broke into a run toward where Bright Moon was suddenly receiving unwanted visitors. The Tate brothers were instantly in motion at his heels. They raced across the stretch of open meadow and came pushing through the underbrush and willows on the near side of the creek just as the four wranglers were drawing rein on the other bank.

Still partially immersed in the water, Bright Moon crouched a bit lower. Her eyes snapped anxiously back and forth between the converging groups of men.

The horseman who had hollered from higher up the slope now leaned a forearm casually across his pommel as a wide, cocky grin split his face. On closer appraisal, he appeared a shade younger than the others; barely halfway into his twenties, and clearly prone to putting more care into his appearance. His face had been cleanly shaved that morning, its thin blond mustache neatly trimmed. Attire-wise, his clothes, though dusty and showing some wear, were a cut or two higher in quality. Less faded, with no patches or frayed cuffs. And the tooled leather of his saddle and the holster riding high on his hip—not to mention the six-gun with engraved grips nestled in it—displayed workmanship that didn't come cheap. All of these features, along with his cocky grin and the way his horse was reined up slightly ahead of the rest, added up to this smug character holding some kind of leadership role over the rest of the pack.

"Well, well, well. What have we got ourselves here?" he drawled, his gaze lingering on Bright Moon in a prolonged leer. There was a certain added glassiness in his eyes that, mixed with the smell of exhaled whiskey fumes drifting through the still air, told a tale of him and his pals having combined a good deal of bottle-tipping with their afternoon of alleged stray hunting.

When he finally raised the level of his glassy gaze to make a slow scan over the men on the opposite bank, he was met by a hard scowl from Curtis, standing poised, rigid. The Tates bracketed him, their own menacing frowns reinforced by the rifles held at ready angles up across their chests. None of this seemed to phase Mr. Smug, though the three riders backing him sat their saddles also with a certain rigidity, eyes flinty and free hands hovering close to the guns holstered at their sides.

"Appears pretty clear to me," Curtis spoke in

response, "that what we got is four rude brushpoppers, stickin' their noses in where they got no business and then failing to turn away and show decent respect."

The cocky smile never faltered. "My, my. I fear that amounts to us having a serious difference of opinion, stranger."

"Whatever your opinion is, I don't give a damn, and I don't want to hear it," Curtis declared. "If you know what's good for you, you and those other gawking morons had better ride away and leave this poor girl alone!"

Now, the smile turned ice cold. "If *we* know what's good for *us*? You better re-think that business about listening, mister, and get this damned straight! The only ones who ain't got no business being here is you three saddle tramps and your bare-assed squaw whore. Everything in any direction you look is Twin V range—that means everything on it belongs to our boss, Vance Veldon, and your sorry bunch ain't nothing but unwelcome trespassers!"

"This is open range and all we're doing is passing through," said Curtis. "We have every right to do that."

"Veldon, don't make a habit of seeing it that way. And on his land, what he says is how it goes!"

"You tell him, Wyatt," urged one of the other wranglers, a scrawny number with a lumpy, pock-marked nose. "Seein' their campfire over yonder is what got our attention. Weouldn't surprise me if, on top of trespassin', they're cookin' a stole Twin V beef over there."

"That's a damn lie," Curtis responded through gritted teeth.

The wrangler who'd spoken out, stiffened even more in his saddle, and his hand dropped to the grips of the gun at his waist. "Nobody calls me a liar! Especially not no—"

Early Tate's rifle swung level in a blur, bringing the muzzle directly in line with the wrangler's chest. "That hogleg lifts half an inch out of its leather," he grated, "I'll blow you clear off the ass end of your horse."

"Hold it! Hold it, for Chrissakes!" Wyatt suddenly straightened up out of his slouch, face still flushed with anger, but his cock sureness had now given way to uncertainty edged by alarm. "Damn! This ain't worth throwing lead and somebody maybe getting killed over."

"Now you're making some sense," Curtis said, even as his own hand hung claw-fingered and close to the Colt on his hip. "For crying out loud, man, we ain't here meaning to arouse any trouble. We're just looking for a little grass to graze our horses and some water to cook coffee and wash up with, that's all. Like I told you, we'll be moving on first thing in the morning."

Wyatt's anger, quick-triggered by nature and made even less stable under whiskey influence, flared anew. "If you ain't looking to arouse," he snapped, "then why in hell are you letting your squaw parade around jaybird nekkid like she is? What do you expect when a ranch crew comes along and sees something like that?"

"If it was a crew of mine," Curtis countered, "I'd expect 'em to pretty quick figure out they'd barged unexpected-like on what was meant to be a private moment and then have the decency to turn and ride away."

"There's a laugh," Wyatt jeered. "You called me and my men 'gawking morons' a minute ago? Look at those two slobs of yours—they're practically drooling into the creek. And if you want to talk acting decent, while we're doing all this jawing, I don't see that squaw acting like she's in any kind of hurry to cover herself up!"

"Jesus! You think that *might* be because she don't want to come out of the water with an audience gathered round?" Curtis's tone rang with equal parts sarcasm and exasperation. "Tell you what...if getting the girl covered up and out of the way will help cool everybody down and get back to talking sense, I can damn well take care of that."

So saying, he began shrugging out of the light jacket he'd donned after his own dunk in the creek and, at the same time, took a step forward. His intent was clearly to wade out and wrap Bright Moon in his jacket so she could discreetly exit the stream and then retreat somewhere away from all the prying eyes to dry off and get dressed.

Curtis only got as far as planting one foot in the water, however, before another of Wyatt's crew—a grim-faced gent who'd taken his eyes off Bright Moon for scarcely a second since riding up—sang out sharply. "Just a goddamned minute! Who's sayin' everybody has had their fill of seein' the squaw uncovered? That sure as hell didn't get my vote. Matter of fact, I say she ain't yet uncovered *enough*!"

"I vote with Lenny. Now he's talkin' *real* sense," cackled Lumpy Nose, the cowpoke who'd piped up before.

Curtis waded forward another defiant step before pausing to glare at Wyatt. "That the way it works in your pack? You let the mongrels do the howling and decision-making for you?"

"Goddamn it, *I'm* the ramrod of this crew!" Wyatt insisted angrily.

"And sure as hell don't need no help from outsiders like you," Lumpy snarled. To emphasize his words, the fool jerked up his hand—the one that had been resting on the grips of his hogleg—and swung it to thrust a warning finger at Curtis.

But Early Tate, who'd been continuing to hold his Winchester leveled on the outspoken wrangler, misread the sudden motion of his gun hand and Early's trigger finger closed in response.

From there, everything turned to hot lead and holy hell...

CHAPTER THIRTEEN

Ironically, the same jerky motion by Lumpy Nose that caused Early Tate to shoot him created a last-second shift to the way the wrangler was positioned. Enough of a shift so that Early's bullet hit differently than intended. Instead of punching into the middle of Lumpy's chest, the slug went high and ripped through meat and muscle above his right collarbone, just off the side of his neck. The impact was nevertheless powerful, twisting him violently in his saddle and sending him toppling from his mount as he emitted a screech of pain.

Before Lumpy ever hit the ground, other gunfire began erupting, and in a matter of seconds, the air over the formerly peaceful stretch of creek was filled with streaking bullets and roiling clouds of powder smoke.

Cursing at the failure to hit his target squarely, Early Tate immediately jacked a fresh round into his Winchester and planted another slug into the thrashing, wailing Lumpy. It knocked him into a flailing roll through the grass, but he refused to remain still and wailed even louder.

Off to Early's right, his brother also stood braced with his Winchester now held at waist level, repeatedly racking fresh rounds and pouring lead into the horsemen on the opposite bank. The Twin V men were responding with drawn pistols—none brought into play any faster nor blasting any steadier than the fancy cutter wielded by the ramrod himself.

In the middle of the stream, Ed Curtis's instant reaction to Early's first shot had been to whirl his jacket matador-like and throw it around Bright Moon. He immediately followed it, wrapping her and the jacket in his arms and then pulling both of them lower into the water as he churned frantically to work around so he made himself a shield between the girl and the Twin V shooters. Engulfed in his arms, Bright Moon could feel his body shudder and hear him hiss through his teeth as bullets began slamming into his back.

Up on the bank, Late Tate, limping from a leg wound, was shouting to his brother, "Fall back into the trees!" But the warning command came too late. Early suddenly stiffened and staggered backward as a bullet found him. He fought to steady himself and swing his rifle in response, but another bullet hammered into him before he could get off another shot. He dropped to his knees. He seemed barely able to grasp his Winchester, and his powerful arms hung limp, unable to lift the weapon.

"No!" Late bellowed, twisting back from where he had started for cover.

He watched helplessly as Wyatt fired a third and fatal shot into Early. An instant later, though, Late had his rifle lined up and was pulling the trigger. The roar of the Winchester and the curse spat from Late's twisted lips came simultaneously. The curse added no harm; but the bullet leaving the rifle muzzle in a red lick of flame did. It blew Wyatt backward out of his saddle and dropped him to the ground in a lifeless heap.

Only two men remained capable of throwing more lead.

Early Tate, Wyatt, and the unnamed Twin V rider who'd never spoken a word were all dead. A still moaning and whimpering Lumpy Nose lay immobile in the grass. Ed Curtis, with a backful of bullet holes, was still shielding Bright Moon and stubbornly pushing his feet against the creek bottom, trying to nudge the two of them closer to the bank.

On the other side of the water, the Twin V man who'd earlier been addressed as Lenny, was sprawled behind the carcass of his horse that had been cut down by a wild shot. A bullet crease across Lenny's hairline was pouring a curtain of blood down over his eyes faster than he could keep it sleeved away. His clouded view barely caught the sight of Wyatt getting blown out of his saddle. Yet the sight was clear enough to send an enraged reaction coursing through Lenny, one that only thickened the blood flow, impairing his vision. But this didn't stop him from making a wild sweep at the scarlet screen with his free hand while thrusting up behind the horse carcass and extending the blood-smeared Colt gripped in the other. Screaming, "You murderin' sons-abitches!" He began triggering round after round at the blurry shape he could make out, standing on the other bank.

Seeing the bloodied man rise up like a screeching,

crimson-masked demon sent a momentary immobilizing shock through Late Tate. But when the bullets started sizzling in closer and closer, he quickly snapped out of it and his Winchester—along with his own roar of rage—began talking back.

Still in the creek, almost being smothered now by the weight of the steadily weakening Curtis, Bright Moon heard but could not see this desperate exchange of gunfire. Yet something about it told her it marked a crucial moment in the battle.

Then, it suddenly stopped.

In the otherwise eerie silence that fell over the scene, all Bright Moon could hear was the ragged breathing of Curtis pressed against her, the soft lap of the water they were immersed in, and somebody whimpering and sobbing over on the other side...

————

DRAWN by the shouting and shooting from the direction of the Curtis camp, Lone and Smith threw caution to the wind as far as revealing their presence. Leaping onto their horses without taking time to saddle them, they went tearing from their own camp as fast and hard as they could.

Though visibility was sufficient due to the glow of lingering yet fading twilight, once they were clear of the gully and out onto the fringe of the meadow, the crackling fire in the center of the Curtis camp made a beacon marking their course even more distinctly. They closed the distance rapidly, only slowing their mounts as they drew within about twenty yards. Even at that, they held back very little due to no sign of anything that looked alarming or seemed to fit with all the commotion they had heard. The camp was laid out in an orderly fashion, with no appearance of disarray; all five horses belonging to the group were picketed nearby, calmly munching grass. The only thing unusual was some cooking utensils and a partially sliced slab of bacon left unattended—and the absence of any people belonging to the camp.

"What the hell?" muttered Smith, looking puzzled as his gaze raked back and forth over the scene.

Lone was having a similar reaction until he swept his eyes in a wider scan and spotted something. Pointing, he said, "Smith. There's movement over yonder by the creek."

Both men slipped from the bare backs of their horses and broke toward where Lone had pointed. They drew their guns and proceeded at a measured trot, allowing their eyes to re-adjust away from the flickering brightness of the campfire. Fanning out, Lone angled toward the near end of the tree cluster while Smith swung in a slight curve and came in more to the middle of the foliage.

As he got closer, Lone saw more of the movement that had initially caught his eye. He could make out now that it came from a bulky, shapeless mass right on the edge of the creek bank. The mass had some size to it, and for a moment, he thought it must be an animal—a horse or a deer maybe—struggling weakly from an injury. But then part of the mass lifted briefly apart from the rest, and Lone saw the profile of a human face with long, thick dark hair spilling back away from the facial outline.

Good God, it was the Indian girl!

Lone moved closer in a rush and then was able to discern the rest of what made up the bulky mass. It was a man, turned face down, his legs and feet still trailing out into the water; and the girl was tugging awkwardly but determinedly in an attempt to pull him all the way up onto the bank. So intent was she in the task that she had no awareness of Lone's presence.

Stepping still closer and crouching slightly, speaking soft in hopes of not giving the girl too much of a start, Lone said, "How bad is he hurt?"

Not surprisingly, this startled her regardless. Her face whipped around, eyes huge, and she likely would have tried to bolt if not for the fact that her legs were partly pinned under the man as a result of her desperate grappling to try and pull him along with her.

For good measure, Lone reached out with his free hand and closed it firmly but with reasonable gentleness on one of her wrists. "Please. I mean you no harm. I'm here to help," he assured her, without knowing if she even understood English.

Lone felt heightened tension run through the arm he had hold of. The girl's eyes flared, and her lips started to peel back. Lone braced, ready for her to come at him with her teeth.

"Who you talking to over there?" Smith called.

Staying on guard, Lone called back, "The Indian girl —Bright Moon."

Suddenly, some of the fire went out of Bright Moon's eyes. Not all of it, but some. Cooling it were traces of surprise and curiosity. The tenseness in her wrist also eased a bit.

Then, those eyes boring hard and direct into Lone's,

she said in a soft, somewhat husky voice, "How is it you know my name?"

"It was told to me by a man named O'Greary," Lone answered.

Hearing that appeared to sit well, cause her to relax some more. But before she had a chance to say anything in response, the wounded man groaned and lifted his head slightly. "O'Greary? Is he here?" he said in a thick voice.

"No. He's not."

"Wh-who are you?"

"Make it McGantry. Lone McGantry."

The man struggled to lift his head higher. Lone got a good enough look at him to recognize him—after viewing him numerous times through field glasses over the past three days—as Ed Curtis. "I know that name. Heard it back in Ogallala...yeah, Sim mentioned how he knew you. Said he might even pay a visit before he...did he? Did he make it out to see you?"

"He did." Lone bit out the words.

Curtis expelled a ragged sigh. "Good, good...so he's okay then?"

Anger welled up in Lone, making his voice tight. "You ought to know. You sicced your two new partners on him—what did they tell you?"

Curtis jerked as if stricken. His next words came out in a pained hiss. "No! It wasn't like that! I never meant for those bastards...oh, god." His head dropped back down.

"He is badly wounded," Bright Moon said sharply. "He took bullets protecting me. He needs care, not harsh words!"

"Matter of opinion," Lone grunted.

When Bright Moon reached down to place a comforting palm on the side of Curtis's face, Lone realized for the first time that, except for a soaked, oversized jacket wrapped loosely about her, she was quite naked. In spite of himself, he gawked at the display of ripe bronze femaleness. When she lifted her face suddenly and caught him looking, he quickly averted his eyes and felt an instant rush of embarrassment burning his ears.

The awkward moment was quickly pushed aside by Smith calling again from where he'd emerged all the way out of the trees and brush. "Lone. Jesus! There's dead bodies sprawled all over hell—here, and on the other side of the creek too!"

"What in blazes happened?" Lone demanded of the girl.

"Some horsemen showed up," Bright Moon answered, haltingly at first but then increasingly steadier. "They said we did not belong on their land. Some arguing broke out...and then it turned to shooting. A great deal of shooting. Ed Curtis threw himself on me to protect me, like I said, so I could not see very much of it. I could only hear...until, as suddenly as it began, it was over."

CHAPTER FOURTEEN

ONLY IT WASN'T OVER. NOT THE AFTERMATH THAT LONE and Smith suddenly found themselves stuck in, trying to figure out how best to deal with.

Their whole plan for evading bounty hunters and shadowing Curtis's bunch to Pike Grogan's front door had been knocked sideways to hell and gone. What was left in its place were five dead men, two badly wounded ones, and a stranded Indian girl.

The second wounded man—a lumpy-nosed runt who said his name was Hank Meechum, a wrangler for the Twin V spread—was discovered on the other side of the creek. He was suffering from painful, bone-smashing bullet hits to his right clavicle and left hip. Curtis's wounds consisted of three bullets to the meaty parts of his back; luckily, none close to his spine, though one shoulder blade was shattered. All of these injuries were serious, the only good news about any of them being that they hadn't hit any major arteries, so the bleeding was able to be brought under control. Unfortunately, this came only after both victims had already lost considerable blood.

Meechum was carried over and laid out on the near bank next to Curtis. Then, working frantically in diminishing light, primarily as directed by Lone, successful stanching of further blood loss was achieved by packing the wounds with leaves and creek mud bound in place by strips of cloth torn from the clothing of fallen men.

In the course of this, told in fits and spurts by the patients between groans and spasms of pain, Lone and Smith got a more detailed account of how the shootout had come about. Naturally, each man had his own bias where the blame and any subsequent accounting should be directed. The one thing they agreed on was the part Bright Moon's bath had played, reminding her in a spurt of embarrassment and modesty to withdraw and trade Curtis's too-revealing jacket for her own clothes.

Once they'd gained an understanding of what had taken place and had done what they could as far as providing emergency care, Lone and Smith were still left needing to decide on a course-correction to the wreckage of their original plans. Not only what to do next, but how much more did they owe these wounded men now dumped in their laps? From a coldly practical standpoint, they didn't owe the pair a damn thing. In fact—especially considering the life-threatening circumstances Lone and Smith were skimming on the edges of—you could even say they couldn't afford *the risk* of owing them anything more. Especially Curtis, Lone reminded himself bitterly, who had, even if inadvertently, set up his old friend O'Greary to be gunned down. In that same vein, Lone had already been forced to swallow a dose of bitter regret by missing out on his vengeance against the Tate brothers due to them falling instead to the guns of the Twin V riders.

On the other hand, when it came to Curtis, it was hard to look past how the sonofabitch had gained himself a big chunk of redemption by the way he'd protected Bright Moon at the cost of blocking those bullets with his own body.

And then, last but not least, there was Bright Moon herself to consider.

Lone had at first half expected her to try and take flight after what happened. When she didn't, he realized she really had no hope of bettering her situation, considering how she would be on her own in a rugged and totally strange country, far from any place familiar to her. A case of better to stick with the devil one knew. Especially for a lone, attractive young woman—an Indian girl to boot, which made her an even more vulnerable target should she run into additional rowdies like the Twin V men she'd already encountered. Also, Lone could see she had reached a certain comfort level with Curtis. Understandable, he supposed, after all the miles they had traveled together—and now she no doubt felt an extra indebtedness to him because of the sacrifice he'd made for her.

If there was any doubt about her feelings in that regard, she made them clear as soon as the creekside wound patching was complete. Looking up from where she kneeled beside Curtis, covering him with a blanket she had fetched from the campsite, she said to Lone, "You have done everything you could and done it well. But care from a real doctor is still badly needed, is it not?"

Lone winced slightly at the bluntness of the question coming from right there where the wounded men could hear. But he didn't sugarcoat his response. "Yeah, that's about the size of it."

As feared, the exchange got a panicked reaction out of Meechum, who'd been regularly wailing and carrying on in sharp contrast to the more stoic Curtis. "I knew it! I could tell...I'm shot to shit and ain't gonna make it, am I? What the hell was packin' me in river mud supposed to accomplish anyway?"

"It was meant to stop the bleedin', and it did that," Lone told him. "Now take it easy, damn it, or you'll get it started again."

"So get me to a doctor then—before it does start up again." Meechum pushed up on one elbow, his expression pained and pleading. "There's Doc Risen in Coraville, less than ten miles away...oh, god, don't let me just lay here and die, mister." Then he dropped back once more, emitting a half groan, half sob.

Catching Smith's eye, Lone jerked his chin in a faint "follow me" signal and then stepped off a ways over toward the stand of trees. Smith drifted after him. Bright Moon remained beside Curtis, who continued to lie quiet.

In a low voice, Lone said, "Ain't neither one of those hombres gonna last long if they *don't* get attention from a proper doc."

Smith frowned in the deepening shadows. "So what does that leave? They're not in any shape to sit a horse, and we got no way to haul them to that town. Even if we did, that wouldn't be something we'd want to stick our necks out for, would it? I mean, explaining how they got shot would naturally lead to telling about these five who got more than just wounded. If the town is big enough to have a doctor, then it likely has a lawman of some kind, too. We're sure not looking to draw that much attention to ourselves, are we?"

"No, not hardly," Lone allowed. He rubbed his knuckles back and forth along his jawline. "But, damn, ridin' off and leavin' 'em here to almost certainly turn to buzzard bait don't exactly sit easy neither."

Lone said, "Other wranglers from that cattle spread those jaspers on the other side of the creek rode for— the Twin V or some such, Meechum called it—are bound to notice pretty quick they've got four missing men, right? Hell, some horses with empty saddles might have already shown up back at the ranch by now. That will bring searchers. For sure, by morning, maybe tonight. They'll have as much chance to hold off the buzzards as we do. What we need to worry most about is not getting caught in a fix that ends up with buzzards circling above *our* heads."

"Yeah, that sounds like a reasonable goal," Lone agreed with a wry twist to his mouth. "But what about the girl?"

"What about her?" Smith echoed.

"Strikes me," said Lone, "she could still turn out useful were we to take her on to Iron Wolf's rez, where she originally came from and the place we reckon has our pal Grogan for a neighbor. Bein' the ones to bring her home ought to at least get us that close, maybe even welcomed for a little while—until we decide it's time to trespass on over into Grogan's yard."

"Okay. So we take her with us then," Smith agreed somewhat offhandedly.

Lone smiled thinly. "Guess you ain't noticed how

Bright Moon appears a mite attached to Curtis. And now, understandably, all the more beholden. I don't figure convincin' her to ride off and leave him in the shape he's in would come as an easy chore. Might get less of a fight tryin' to hogtie a bobcat with a ball of yarn."

Lone eyed him. "Okay. I can see that, as usual, you got something in mind. Go ahead and cut to it."

"Alright. For all the reasons you outlined," Lone said, "takin' the wounded men *to* the doctor in town ain't appealin', even if we had a way to do it. But what if one of us was to go fetch the doc and bring him here? We could say we had a man out on the trail too hurt to move, and it wouldn't even be too much of a stretch. Oughta be enough to convince him to come without stirrin' any undue attention from anybody else in town. Once we got the sawbones here, we could turn the situation over to him while we went ahead and kicked up some dust before the law or any others had cause to stick their noses in."

"Back to the girl, if we worked it that way. What about her?" Smith wanted to know.

Lone looked over to where Bright Moon remained beside Curtis. He ran his knuckles along his jaw again before saying, "I'm countin' that, once she sees we've done what we can to see proper care is at hand, she'll be agreeable to goin' with us if she understands we'll take her on to North Dakota. It's clear that Curtis, if he makes it at all, won't be goin' nowhere any time soon. There'd be nothing for her here, and it don't seem she's been dragged this far against her will. From what we've seen in the time we've been shadowing, it appears she wants to get back to the Flat Falls rez and the young buck waitin' for her there. We'd be offerin' her the chance to continue makin' it there."

"And, just incidentally, hopefully doing us some good at the same time," added Smith.

"Nothing wrong with sharin' the benefits of a thing," Lone told him.

Smith heaved a sigh. "Very well, you win. That annoying damn habit of once again laying out a plan that sounds reasonable. I'm not so sure the girl is going to be as easy to convince as you think, but we'll have to find out." He paused, made a face. "I may have tried to sound like a cold bastard before, but I wasn't really all that keen about just riding off and leaving those two jackasses to die."

"I know. I also know it was still damn temptin'." Lone's mouth pulled tight. "But this way is better, makes for a decent chance all the way around."

"So you up for being the one to go for the doc?" Smith asked.

"Like I said before, I'm willin' to share."

"And like I said before, you win. That means you get the ride-taking honors. Even with this black goop in my hair to disguise me, I think it's understandable I want to avoid showing my mug anywhere there might be bounty hunters with itchy trigger fingers hanging around. Besides, you're a better horseman and a surer bet to find your way to the town and back over this unfamiliar country."

Lone grunted. "Don't lay the flattery on so thick, I smell it for what it really is. Come on, let's go let Bright Moon know what we got in mind."

Twenty minutes later, Lone was once again astride Ironsides and riding away from the spot Curtis's group had laid out for their night camp. In the interim, he and Smith had lifted the two wounded men on spread-out blankets and, one by one, carried them from the creek-side to the campsite where they could be kept warmer and more comfortable. They'd also used the time to relate their plan to Bright Moon and to get directions from Meechum on finding Coraville. Before proceeding to the town, Lone would swing by the abandoned gully camp long enough to retrieve his saddle.

It was fully dark by that point. The moon hadn't risen yet, but the sky was clear, and a wash of bright-ening stars gave this early stage of night a reasonable level of visibility. In the camp, Smith was adding fuel to the already crackling fire that bathed all in its proximity not only with warmth against a creeping chill in the air but also provided a wide, pulsing glow of illumination.

It was within this glow, away from the creekside gloominess and the urgent activity of ministering to the wounded men, that Bright Moon had the opportunity to take her first good look at the man called Smith. Even at that, under these rapidly shifting circumstances and given the somewhat odd, intensely black hair showing below the man's hat brim, around his ears, and on the back of his neck, recognition was slow in coming. But when it hit, it was as certain as it was startling.

Rocking back on her heels where she kneeled beside Curtis, Bright Moon's wide eyes locked on Smith and she proclaimed, "I know you...you are Sad Eyes!"

CHAPTER FIFTEEN

LONE HAD LITTLE TROUBLE FINDING CORAVILLE. Meechum's directions—ride cross country due west until coming to a well-traveled wagon road; follow the wagon road south into town—had been simple and accurate. Before reaching the road, the terrain was somewhat broken in places, but not too bad. The moon finally putting in an appearance had given some welcome brightness to navigating the more rugged stretches. Once on the road, it was smooth, easygoing.

The hour was moderately late when the town came in sight, though a number of windows still glowed with light in the residential pockets located on either side of a main street that the wagon road fed directly into. The welcoming sign posted on the outskirts stated CORAVILLE – A GOOD PLACE TO LIVE AND DO BUSINESS, but gave no population. It was decent-sized, however, larger than Lone had expected. From what he could tell, it was a seemingly quiet, tidily laid out cluster of mostly wood-frame businesses and homes. A far cry, thankfully, from the boisterous, hodge-podge assemblage of structures that made up places like Deadwood, Lead, and others spawned by the gold fields located not much farther to the west.

As he started down Main Street, Lone could see that most of the businesses lining it were closed at this hour. Farther along, though, bright splashes of light poured out in front of two or three of the establishments. Saloons, most likely, enjoying their prime business hours. Lone smiled wryly; Coraville wasn't quite *that* tranquil.

He'd only proceeded a short way before he spotted another business showing signs of still being open. It was a livery stable with one of the large double doors at the front of its barn standing ajar and light showing from within. Lone steered Ironsides over to the building, dismounted, and left the big gray ground reined.

As he approached the open door, he could hear voices talking on the other side. Entering, he saw two figures—a stocky man and a boy of eleven or twelve—walking toward him down the wide center aisle. A lighted lantern was hanging on a post off to one side of the doorway and the boy was swinging another one as he walked. At the sight of Lone, the pair slowed their stride but didn't quite come to a halt. In the glow of the boy's lantern, Lone could see that both were flushed and sweaty as if from recent physical strain.

The man thumbed back the battered, wide-brimmed straw hat perched above his beefy face and said, "My name's Gunther. Something I can do for you, mister?"

Gunther's Livery was the faded lettering Lone had been able to make out on the face of the barn outside. He responded to the proprietor, saying, "I just got into town, saw your lantern light through the open door. Was hopin' I could trouble you for some directions."

The man and boy were now stopped a few feet in front of Lone. "We'll sure help you if we can," Gunther told him. He spread his big hands and showed an amiable grin. "We might look a little wrung out and not smell so hot right at the moment, but I reckon we know the lay of things around here as good as any. This is my boy Josh. We just got finished helping one of our best mares get through a very difficult delivery, by the way, which is why you find us in our present condition."

Josh's eyes went wide. "The new colt is a boy. A stallion he'll be someday! I helped pull him out, and Pa says if I keep pitchin' in and helpin' regular, I might get to claim him as my very own."

Lone grinned. "That sounds like a pretty good incentive, and it sounds like you already got a pretty good start."

"What's in-incembative?" Josh asked, frowning.

"It's what makes you do something for the sake of getting something in return," his father explained.

"Okay. I get it...I think."

"Like, for instance, the bottle of sarsaparilla I promised you if you helped me with the messy job we just successfully completed." Gunther lifted his shaggy brows. "Does *that* get the idea across a little plainer?"

"You bet! So, do I get the sarsaparilla now?" Josh wanted to know.

"*After* we get cleaned up. And after," Gunther added, "we get back to helping this stranger we've so rudely kept waiting when all he asked for are some simple directions...what—or who—is it you're looking to find, friend?"

Lone replied, "A doctor. I'm in hopes you have one in this town. We've got an injured man back on the trail, you see—too badly hurt to sit a horse and make it the rest of the way in. I'm countin' on findin' a doc who'll ride out to tend him and bring along some kind of rig we can then load the patient on and fetch him back for the longer care I expect he'll need."

"Doggone," said Gunther. "I wish you would've explained that right away, me and Josh wouldn't have prattled so much. But anyway, yeah, we got a sawbones. Dr. Risen. Pretty darn good one too...well, leastways..."

"How's that?" Lone prodded when the livery man's words trailed off.

Gunther shook his head. "Never mind. Step outside, I'll point you plain."

A moment later, they were standing out in front of the barn, and Gunther was extending a thick arm and a blunt, calloused finger. "Continue straight on down the main drag here," he was saying. "First cross street you'll come to, not all that far, is Clinton. Swing right, the doc's place will be the second house on your left. Blue trim, little fence in front, post with a sign saying James Risen, M.D. Can't hardly miss it."

"Sounds like it'd be hard to," Lone agreed. He swung up into the saddle and touched a finger to his hat brim. "Obliged." As he wheeled Ironsides in a half turn and started down the street, Gunther called after him, "Good luck."

That, coupled with the half-finished "Well, leastways" remark, gave Lone a curious feeling about this Dr. Risen. Yet, in practically the same breath, Gunther had also called him "a pretty darn good sawbones." So what the hell was the deal with the medicine man?

It wasn't going to take long to find out, the former scout told himself, as he turned Ironsides down Clinton Street and promptly spotted the blue-trimmed house with the signpost out front.

The heavy, old-fashioned iron ring knocker hanging on the front door clacked loudly when Lone put it to use. The windows of the house were glowing brightly, he'd noted as he rode up, so it didn't take long to get a response. When the door opened, an attractive, auburn-haired woman looked out at him through rich brown eyes above a measured, businesslike smile. "Yes? Can I help you with something?"

"I hope so," Lone answered. "I have need of a doctor. Is Dr. Risen in?"

A troubled, somewhat hesitant look passed briefly over the woman's face. "No. No, I'm afraid he isn't," she said. Then, opening the door wider and assuming a rather bold stance, she added, "But I'm his sister and nurse of half a dozen years' experience, is there perhaps something I can do?"

Middle twenties, Lone guessed she was, well formed and very fetching in merely a simple white blouse and pleated, cranberry-colored skirt flowing from trim hips. A part of his brain—even under present tense circumstances—couldn't help jumping to the thought that there was plenty such a woman could do for a man. But this was instantly followed by a blistering self-chastisement. *Jesus Christ, McGantry, what's wrong with you? Get your mind out of the gutter, especially with everything else that's going on!*

All of that passed in a flash, and then, with a meek flush of embarrassment he hoped wasn't noticeable to the woman, he replied, "I kinda doubt it, ma'am. You see, the person needin' help is a fella who's been hurt back on the trail. Hurt bad, maybe busted up on the inside. His horse threw him when it got spooked by a rattler. He's in no shape to go back in a saddle. I was hopin' maybe the doc could go do some mendin' on the spot and then fetch him back with the aid of a buggy or wagon of some kind."

The woman put a hand to her throat. "My goodness. Of course, we must try to do something." Her eyes darted past Lone and out toward the main street. Again, that troubled, hesitant look passed over her face. Her gaze returning to Lone, she said, "My brother finds relaxation some evenings by engaging in games of chance at one of our local saloons. I believe you'll be able to find him a ways farther down the street at an establishment called the Rancher's Rest. Tell him your situation as you've explained it to me, and I'm sure he'll be willing to help. Tell him I will be preparing his medical bag and bringing round the horse and buggy we keep stalled out back."

With that, she urged Lone on his way and retreated back into the house to presumably make the preparations she had indicated.

CHAPTER SIXTEEN

THE RANCHER'S REST WAS A TYPICAL COWTOWN SALOON, not much different than a couple hundred others Lone had been in over the years. Less tawdry than many, but still presenting the standard layout of a bar running along one side of the room, a scattering of tables and chairs in the middle, billiard table at the back. The hardwood floor was lightly sprinkled with sawdust. A layer of cigarette and cigar smoke hung in the air, wrapped within it a heady hybrid odor made up of the smoke itself, stale sweat, cloyingly sweet yet ineffective bay rum, spilled liquor, and the tangy final touch of horse and cow dung inadequately scraped from boot heels.

There was a modest crowd on hand that night, a fairly even blend of cowhands and townsmen by the look of it, numbering about a dozen and a half in total. Mingling among them were two bored-looking, averagely pretty gals who would never see thirty again. Both wore heavy makeup and spangly, short-skirted dresses that left their shoulders bare. Lone didn't make them for crib girls though; more like just bits of window dressing to help lure in the men and entice them to stay a little longer for one more drink accompanied by another close-up view of some cleavage and maybe even a discreet little squeeze of the goods on display.

The barkeep overseeing all of this was a sawed-off number wearing a bowtie, a shiny silk vest, and a sour expression Lone had a hunch seldom changed. Maybe it had something to do with the soggy, over-chewed, unlit cigar stub that poked disgustingly out one corner of his mouth.

"What'll it be, stranger?" The question came in a voice that was like rusty iron dragging on rusty iron.

"I'll have a beer," Lone told him, experience having taught that things generally went better in such settings if you made a purchase before trotting out any questions.

When the beer came, Lone laid some coins on the bar and then said, "I was told I could find Dr. James Risen here. If that's accurate, can you point him out to me?"

The barkeep's stubby fingers hesitated ever so slightly as he scooped up the proper amount of coins. Once he had his fist closed around them, he lifted his eyes to Lone's face for a beat and then cut them abruptly toward a table near the back of the room. "The card game goin' on back there nearest the billiard table. Blond fella in the white shirt and string tie. There's your Doc Risen."

Lone took an obligatory drink of his beer. "Obliged."

The barkeep jingled the coins in his grip and then gave an odd little grunt. "They claim he's a pretty good sawbones. Never had call to do any doctorin' with him myself. Ever I do...well, all I can say is I'd hope he was a helluva lot better at dealin' out the gadgets from his medical bag than he is at layin' down a decent poker hand." Then he rocked back his head and released a honk of laughter that threatened to spew the tortured cigar remains halfway across the room. Lone didn't waste any time getting out of the line of fire and heading for the table where the man he'd come looking for was seated.

The three other men engaged in the game with Risen consisted of two cowpokes and an elderly shop-keeper type wearing bright red suspenders and a pair of round spectacles perched on the tip of a pointed nose. The doctor, Lone saw as he drew closer, was a trim, somber-faced gent in his midthirties, fair of skin and hair, displaying a permanent faint flush on his otherwise pale cheeks that indicated the early stages of chronic alcohol abuse. The bottle of gin and half-filled glass at his elbow—whereas a pitcher of beer and accompanying foamy mugs seemed to be satis-fying the thirst of the other players—did nothing to dispel this.

Lone stepped up close to the gin drinker's chair, cleared his throat, and said, "Pardon me...Dr. Risen?"

In the act of shuffling the cards, getting ready to deal, Risen gave him a quick eye flick before respond-ing, "Indeed I am, my good man. Risen may be my name, but my luck is certainly not on the rise when it comes to the way these blasted cards are falling this evening." The lack of winnings in front of him compared to the other three, especially a heap of crum-pled bills before one of the cowboys in particular, seemed to silently confirm this. "What can I do for you?"

"There's been an accident out on the trail. One of the fellas I'm ridin' with got hurt. Hurt too bad to put back in a saddle and try to bring in," Lone told him, once again laying out his fabrication. "I'm hopin' you'll come have a look, see if you can't patch him up good enough so's we can get him on a wagon or some such and then fetch him the rest of the way in for whatever else he might need."

Risen frowned as he continued to shuffle the cards. "Good lord. What happened to him?"

"Got pitched from a rattler-spooked horse, landed on some rocks. He's got a busted hip and some ribs for sure, I fear he might be busted up on the inside, too."

The cowpoke with the heap of bills in front of him, a string-bean with carrot-colored hair and an underslung chin, guffawed half-drunkenly. "Man who can't stay on his horse—maybe he ought to have a rockin' chair fetched out to him for ridin' from now on."

The other puncher, narrow-shouldered and thick-gutted, apparently a brand mate to Carrot Top, snorted out a short laugh in support of his pal's attempt at wit.

The shopkeeper scowled at the pair. "The plight of this man's friend sounds serious—hardly something to be made light of," he scolded.

"Aw, stuff it in your boot, Harold, you old sourpuss," Carrot Top snapped in response. "Nobody asked for your two cents' worth, less'n you want to lay it down in a bet. And as far as me and Lou pokin' a little fun, we ain't hurtin' a damn thing."

Risen stopped shuffling and placed the piled deck flat on the table. "Unfortunately," he said, "some hurt *has* been done. And, much as I'd like to stay and try to recoup at least part of my losses from you, Fain, duty calls."

Fain, the carrot-headed hombre, smiled tauntingly. "Then why be in a hurry? Hell, Doc, I'd like for you to stick around and try your luck some more, too. I can't make no money outta the deep pockets and short arms of these other two jaspers."

"Sorry," Risen said, pushing the deck toward him. "There's duty and there's also the matter of a certain oath I took once upon a time."

Fain's hand shot out and stopped the doctor from pushing the cards any closer. His smile suddenly gone cold, he said, "You want an oath? Try this—you don't sit back and keep dealin' 'til I say I'm done winnin' money off you, I swear I'll break your goddamn wrist! How about that?"

Lone had heard enough. He edged up tighter between where Fain and Risen were seated. "I got an answer for you. It ain't worth shit," he grated. "If the doc is ready to leave with me, he's comin'. You try gettin' in the way, you might need some mendin' of your own— *after* he's done takin' care of my friend out on the trail."

Fain's eyes lifted slowly, and when they locked on Lone, they were blazing with anger. He snarled, "I don't know who the hell you think you are, mister, but you're really pushin' your luck. First, you barge in and interrupt our game, and now you think you're gonna tell me—"

He was cut short by the raspy-voiced barkeep calling out. "Fain! You been warned before about startin' trouble in here!"

Without taking his off Lone, Fain hollered back, "To

hell with you, Elmer. It ain't me startin' any trouble, it's this big galoot thinkin' he can—"

Now, it was Harold, the shopkeeper, who interrupted him, saying, "Blast it, man, this fellow is only seeking help for an injured friend. You have no call to interfere with that."

Thick-bellied Lou promptly jumped in, thrusting a finger at the shopkeeper and advising him sharply, "You got told once to stuff a boot in it, Harold. Wasn't that plain enough for you?"

"This is getting ridiculous!" exclaimed Risen, starting to stand up.

Fain lunged in his chair, grabbing the doctor's wrist and slamming it down on the table, pinning it there. "Goddamn you," he seethed, "I told you you ain't goin' nowhere until I say so! Now sit the hell back down and deal those cards."

Lone was a veteran of enough such scenes not to recognize when talking simply wasn't going to cut it, and since punches were bound to start flying, it was only smart to go ahead and get in the first lick. So that's exactly what he did. Twisting at the waist, he brought a right hook hard around and smashed his fist square into Fain's already sloping chin, driving it even more sharply inward. The impact lifted the cowboy up out of his chair, blurting a strange "awwgghk!" sound as he let go of the doctor's wrist and went toppling to the floor, out cold.

Again calling on past experience, Lone had a strong hunch what to expect next. Twisting back around, he saw he was exactly right as he spotted hefty Lou struggling to push to his feet while at the same time clawing for the gun holstered on his hip. Lou's struggles froze abruptly when Lone's Colt seemed to leap into his hand, and Lou found himself staring down the black tunnel of its muzzle.

"Sit back down, Fatty, if you know what's good for you," Lone snarled. "Pouch the iron and slap those hands flat on the table."

Lou plopped obediently back onto his chair seat and pressed his palms tightly down on the tabletop.

Lone thought that was the end of it, thought he'd nipped the disturbance in the bud. He didn't figure any of the other patrons—a few tilted against the bar, the rest at neighboring tables chewing the fat or otherwise engaged in their own business—would try to take a hand.

He figured wrong.

A husky, brooding individual occupying a table only a few feet away—a recently terminated freight hand, it turned out—happened to be just drunk enough and in just a foul enough mood to welcome an excuse to lash out at something or somebody. In spite of the knockout punch Lone had just delivered to Fain, something about him apparently appealed to the freighter as somebody suitable to unload on.

"Watch out!" came a warning shout from Elmer the barkeep.

If not for that, Lone would have been caught full force by a blindside blow that very possibly might have dropped him as cold as he had Fain. As it was, he got his head snapped partway around in time to catch sight of the freighter surging out of his chair and see the blur of his fist hurtling forward, aiming to land on Lone's left ear. The former scout's keen reflexes—triggered by Elmer's shout and then spurred even more by the

glimpse out the corner of his eye of what was coming—
allowed him just a split second to partially tuck his head
and hunch his shoulder. The blow still hit with plenty
of impact, but it slammed into shoulder meat first and
then skimmed only glancingly up across Lone's temple.

Nevertheless, Lone was spun half around on sagging
knees and sent staggering. The Colt fell from his grasp.
He nearly upended Harold, the shopkeeper, out of his
chair. Shoving away from that collision, Lone took
another lurching step, fighting desperately to stay on his
feet. Tripping over the fallen Fain nearly caused him to
go down anyway, but it was the freighter charging after
him and grabbing him by his shoulder and shirt collar
that kept him from pitching onto his face. The save
wasn't done as a kindness, however. It was only meant to
hold him upright long enough to be the target for some
more punches—a left hook to his ribs and a windmilling forearm clubbed down onto the back of his
neck.

The forearm sent Lone staggering again. Until he
slammed against the wall on the far side of the room.
The rib punch had knocked a big gust of breath out of
him, and the blows to the side and back of his head had
his vision swimming. But suddenly, finding himself
pressed to the firm, solid wall gave him a moment of
steadiness and tenuous sense of balance he'd been
lacking ever since receiving that first blindsided wallop.
He understood frantically that he now had to seize the
moment and damn well make use of it before he got
pounded senseless.

The freighter bulled forward and grabbed for him
again. Lone was tensed, ready. The instant those clutch-
ing, calloused fingers touched him, he shoved away

from the wall and whirled to face the man they belonged to. He swept his well-muscled left arm around hard in a swatting away motion and batted down the reaching hands of the freighter. Continuing his pivot, one foot planted firm against the base of the wall, Lone put all his momentum into drilling a low right hook to his attacker's gut. The freighter doubled over, his forward motion halted, and a great woof of air exploded out of him. His lowered face was immediately met by Lone's left fist rising in a smashing uppercut.

The freighter was straightened up and sent staggering backward half a step. But he was a durable bastard, not willing to go down easily. While he stood momentarily teetering, Lone sidestepped and shifted partway around behind him. Moving fast, he hooked the man's belt with his left hand and reached up to clutch a fistful of hair with his right. Now he was the one doing the holding and manhandling. Not wasting any time in taking advantage of this, Lone shoved the freighter as hard as he could toward the wall—applying extra pressure to push his head forward and down so it was sure to make initial contact. It did, resulting in a solid, satisfying thud when it hit. For added measure, Lone pulled back on his fistful of hair and then rammed head and face to the wall one more time.

When Lone let go and stepped back, the freighter slid slowly down and collapsed in a heap, bubbling sounds coming out of his crushed nose. Lone wheeled to face out at the room—battered and breathing hard, but ready this time in case anybody else wanted to try and get in the way of his business.

Elmer, he discovered, proved to be thinking along those same lines and was already taking steps to keep anything like that from happening. He'd come out from behind the bar and was planted in a wide stance before it, brandishing a sawed-off shotgun that, even with its barrels chopped down, still looked almost as long as he was tall. There was nothing lacking about his ability to use the big gun, though, as he demonstrated by aiming it upward and triggering one of its barrels. A reverberating boom shook the room as a cloud of cottony white smoke was released along with a sheet of glittery pellets that rattled like fury-driven hail against the already heavily pock-marked tin-covered ceiling. Tight on the heels of the blast, Elmer's raspy voice did its own room-shaking as he declared, "Now, by God, that's enough! Anybody lookin' to prolong this fracas more, better be ready to get their asses burned with a second barrel of rock salt, and that ain't no bluff!"

Nobody looked the least bit ready to test Elmer's words. All patrons held still and silent, the only sounds were that of the bubbling noises still being made by the fallen freighter and the patter of a few rock salt bits that hadn't embedded deeply enough in the ceiling falling loose and dropping down onto the floor.

Elmer's eyes made a sweep of the room and came to rest on Lone. "You, stranger...you about ready to wrap up your business with the doc?"

"Been ready for that ever since I walked in here," Lone replied flatly.

"How about you, Doc? You willin' to go help this hombre?" Elmer wanted to know, his gaze cutting to Risen, who stood frozen and ashen-faced still in the same spot where Fain had tried to pin his arm to the table.

"Of course he's ready to go help. It's his duty." The

voice answering Elmer's question was not that of Dr. Risen. It was a female voice—his sister's—spoken as she pushed through the batwings and came marching boldly into the room.

All eyes swung to her, including those of the doctor, who abruptly shook himself free from his stunned immobility. "Sue! What in Heaven's name are you doing here?" he blurted.

"I brought around the buggy and your medical bag," she answered smartly. "This man," gesturing toward Lone, "came by the house first and made it clear he has a friend out on the trail in need of your prompt attention."

Before Risen could respond to that, a new presence bulled through the batwings and stepped up behind Sue. He was a burly number, an even six feet in height, face lined by near forty years of hard living, brittle eyes, and a blunt, thrice-broken nose above a walrus mustache flecked with gray. A town marshal's badge was pinned to one lapel of a corduroy jacket.

Obviously, having been drawn by the sound of the shotgun blast, he immediately demanded, "Elmer, what in blazes is going on here?"

"Everything's already taken care of," the barkeep was quick to assure him. "A couple of rowdies decided to try and get over-frisky, but me and the stranger and old Beulah here settled it all down right quick."

The marshal wrinkled his nose at the tang of powder smoke still hanging heavy in the air and then cut a scowl up at the freshly scarred ceiling. "If you and old Beulah keep settling things down the way you make a habit of," he grumbled, "then one of these days you're gonna settle that ceiling smack down on your head."

"That's why I have the owner put up a fresh sheet of tin every two or three years," Elmer countered. "We consider it our contribution toward helping to keep the peace here in Coraville."

"Instead of being so quick-triggered with Beaulah, how about leaving the peace-keeping to me and my deputies for a change?" the marshal barked.

Elmer thrust out his chin defiantly. "Be glad to do that very thing—Just as soon as you or any of your deputies can respond to trouble as quick or quicker than Beulah can clear her throat and have the job done."

The marshal looked ready to reply but then settled for a brief rumble deep in his throat and a dismissive wave of one hand. This was clearly an argument of long standing wasn't going to be resolved here tonight.

Instead, the lawman settled for heaving a resigned sigh and asking, "So what was the nature of the trouble, and are there any charges I oughta throw somebody in the hoosegow for?"

Turning to face him, Sue, the doctor's sister, said, "The biggest trouble, Marshal Kurtz, at least from the standpoint of needing the most immediate attention, is that this man," again a gesture to Lone, "is trying to get some medical aid to an injured friend out on the trail and seems to be running into interference."

Kurtz looked past her and locked his gaze on Lone. "That right, mister?"

Lone nodded. "Like the lady said."

Kurtz extended a finger and flicked it to indicate the two fallen men. "That your doing?"

"I'd call it more like their own doin'," Lone answered. "I was tellin' the doc here about my hurt friend, and those hombres—again, like the lady said—took a notion to interfere."

"Took a notion to *try* and interfere," said Risen, suddenly stepping forward. "It was exactly as this man is telling it, Marshal, and as any honest observer will further attest." The doctor paused for a moment to glare meaningfully at heavyset Lou, who remained seated at the card table looking wholly frazzled and uncertain. When Lou wouldn't meet Risen's eyes and offered no peep of objection, the medic went on, saying, "The stranger did nothing to antagonize either one of these men. In fact, if anyone has a right to bring charges, it's him."

"Which I'm not interested in doin'," Lone was quick to say. "All I want is to get some help to my hurt friend without losin' any more time."

"And I'm ready to give it," Risen declared. "If Sue has my bag and buggy ready, then it sounds like there's a poor injured devil who has been left suffering quite long enough."

"What about those two?" the marshal asked, tipping his head to again indicate the fallen men. "They look like they might need a little patching up themselves."

Risen replied coolly. "No doubt they may. But my prognosis is that it's nothing too serious, so I'm afraid they'll have to wait their turn. They earned no better consideration." He turned his attention to Lone. "Now then. You'll need to lead the way to where we can find your injured friend."

CHAPTER SEVENTEEN

LONE WASN'T HAPPY WITH HOW THINGS HAD GONE IN Coraville. Yeah, he'd been able to fetch a doc as planned. But it had taken longer than expected, and in the process, he'd drawn a hell of a lot more attention to himself than ever intended. And if that wasn't enough, Dr. James Risen wasn't the only person he found himself leading out of town toward the scene of injury and death. The doctor's sister insisted on coming along to assist as his nurse.

Lone was quick to realize she was making this demand due to concern that Risen's gin consumption during his card playing—both being too-common occurrences, the former scout suspected—might affect his ability to administer treatment; so Sue wanted to be on hand to intervene if necessary. Under different circumstances, Lone might have found this admirable, even if a little tragic. On this occasion, though, it was an added complication he could have surely done without. But with so many people listening and looking on when they got out front of the Rancher's Rest and Sue piling into the buggy right alongside the doc...well, there hadn't been anything Lone could think of to say to get her to change her mind.

So up the moonlit trail, north out of town, they went. Lone leading the way astride Ironsides, the sleek black buggy, with Sue at the reins of a high-stepping steel dust in the harness, rolling smoothly close behind. Lone's mention of some rugged terrain to be covered before they reached their destination was met with assurances that the doctor frequently made house calls throughout the countryside, meaning both rig and animal would be up to the challenge.

When they came to the trailside rock outcrop that Lone had memorized as the marker for where they needed to turn off, he signaled for their departure from the wagon road, and they began the stretch over broken country. Luckily, the sky remained clear, and a high, bright moon aided by an array of stars, provided welcome illumination for them to make their way. As promised, the buggy and its puller proceeded steadily along.

Even though he wished she wasn't present, Lone couldn't help but admire the determination and capability of Sue. He glanced back frequently, impressed by her sure-handed skill with the steel dust. Nor could he keep from again noting, no matter how unbidden and ill-suited to the moment, how attractive she was, especially in the splashes of pale, silver-blue lighting that crept in under the buggy awning from time to time.

Her brother, on the other hand, in spite of his willingness to answer the call of his profession, was showing little else to be impressed by. He slouched in the seat beside Sue, looking by turns, barely able to hold his head up or casting about with an anxious look like he might be sick and ready to vomit over the side. He apparently had been drunker than Lone realized and now the jarring and bouncing of the buggy as it passed over this rougher terrain must be bringing all that gin in his gut to a threatening foam. Seeing this stirred a double dose of anger in Lone. Anger at the thought of how ineffective this sot might be when it came time to do the wounded men any good. And anger over the question of how many times his sister likely had to put herself out in an attempt to cover for his sorry, drunken ass.

A pleasant surprise came when the time it took to re-trace Lone's route over the broken land to where the meadow campfire appeared in the near distance seemed shorter than it had on the way out. Not long after that, they reached the camp itself and found Smith and Bright Moon waiting to greet them.

But as soon as he quit Ironsides' saddle, Lone sensed something was wrong. And then he spotted that there was only one form occupying a bedroll over near the fire.

Following his gaze, Smith said in a low voice, "Curtis didn't make it."

From where he stood assisting his sister down from the buggy, Risen overheard this. He looked around sharply and said, "You mean the individual we came to aid is dead?"

"There's still a man here who needs your services," Lone was quick to assure him. He paused, grimacing as he faced the pair now standing beside the buggy. Then: "Time you knew that the details I gave in town about what you'd find out here were a little short of the full story."

"What's that supposed to mean?" Risen demanded.

"For starters, it means that when I left here, there were two injured men I hoped you'd be able to do some good. As you can see, now there's only one." Lone jabbed a thumb toward the form by the fire. "But that don't lessen the fact he still needs doctorin'."

From where he lay, Meechum struggled to lift his head and call out weakly, "Is that you, Doc? Doc Risen? Oh, Lordy, am I glad...these folks have tended me best they could, b-but I'm wounded bad...and hurtin' fierce... and scared, scared of..." His head dropped back and his voice trailed off.

Sue thrust out the medical bag to her brother, saying, "We must see to that man. He's obviously suffering."

Risen took the bag reluctantly, all the while scowling at Lone. "I don't like being deceived," he stated. "And I have a strong suspicion there's going to be a good deal more I won't like about this matter before it's finished."

"I can just about guarantee that'll be the case," Lone told him. "There's a hell of a lot about this I don't like either, pal. But, as you oughta know, sometimes you're flat stuck with havin' to play the cards you get dealt."

"If that's supposed to be some sort of philosophical wisdom, I can do without it, thanks," the doctor snapped.

"Maybe what you *can* do something with," Smith spoke up, "is the knowledge that the hombre you need to start paying attention to has a couple gunshot wounds in him."

Cursing under his breath, Risen took a hurried step toward where Meechum lay.

Sue hesitated long enough to favor Lone with a disappointed scowl that stung like a barb, even before she added words to it. "I spoke up for you. I trusted you. Why the need to lie? Surely, you must have known we would have come as quick or quicker for a bullet wound as for a horse fall injury."

"I had my reasons," is all Lone said in response. Then added, "You'd best go help your brother."

"If there are bullet wounds to be dealt with," Risen called out as he kneeled beside Meechum, "then I'll be needing some boiling hot water." It struck Lone that, at that moment—for the first time since being in the man's presence—Risen's tone and stern expression made him abruptly seem like the MD. He claimed to be.

Replying to his request, Smith said, "Already got it covered. There are two pots bubbling on the edge coals of the fire. Just say when you're ready for 'em."

Huddled close over the wounded man, campfire light pulsing over them, the two medics went to work intently and began carefully cutting away the temporary bandaging Lone had applied. They murmured sparingly and inaudibly during this.

While they were confabbing, Smith edged over to Lone and they did some quick, quiet word trading of their own. Smith told how Curtis had died only an hour or so after Lone left the camp earlier; at Bright Moon's insistence, they had buried him over by the creek, near the spot where he'd sacrificed himself to save her. For Lone's part, he gave a truncated version of what he'd had to go through to bring the doc and how he'd been unable to avoid including the sister as part of it. That exchange complete, Smith's eyes had grown big with excitement as he announced he had some major news to report concerning—

Before he could get into it anymore, Risen suddenly called, "We're ready for that hot water now!"

Smith broke away to help Bright Moon get the first of the steaming pots, snatching up a leather patch in order to grip the hot handle. Lone also walked over to stand, looking down on the treatment of the patient.

"Whose idea was it to pack the wounds in this manner?" Risen asked crisply, taking careful cleansing swipes at the torn flesh around Meechum's wound, using a cloth soaked from a cup filled with hot, disinfectant-laced water.

"Mine. Dry leaves and creek mud under a pressure bandage. Old mountain man's remedy for stanching blood flow," said Lone. "It seemed to have been holdin' pretty good when I left, though he'd already bled quite a bit before I got to it."

"Damnedest thing, eh, Doc?" croaked Meechum, lifting his head groggily. He'd clearly been doped with some kind of painkiller or sedative. "I didn't much like the sound of it at first. But blamed if it didn't keep me from leakin' dry."

"It appears so," Risen said, somewhat grudgingly. "Now we'll just have to keep an eye out for whatever crawly little things might have been in the mud that could show up as infection."

The remark was clearly meant as a dig at the crudity of Lone's method of wound treating. The former scout could have let it float. But the snottiness of this half-hungover jackass made him bristle anew. "Seems to me," he grated, "if you succeed in gettin' those bullet fragments dug out good and clean, then any threat of mud bug infection oughta get tamed easy enough at the same time."

Before Risen could reply, Meechum's head lifted once more. Despite however he'd been medicated, he was suddenly upset. "You *are* gonna be able to get those bullet pieces out, ain't you, Doc?" he wailed. "I ain't at risk for lead poisonin', am I? Oh, god, I've seen poor devils check out that way, and I don't want no part of it! I'd rather've gone with a quick kill-shot like my pards over yonder than that!"

"Just settle down. Take it easy," Risen soothed him, acting like a doctor again. "I intend to treat any and all infections that might be a threat. We're not going to let you get blood poisoning."

"Thank God. Please don't." Meechum's head dropped back down.

Risen shot a blistering look at Lone. "I insist you watch your remarks so as not to aggravate his condition any worse!" He then returned his attention to the patient's wound.

But Sue had her gaze locked on Lone in a more probing way. "What did he mean," she said, "about some 'pards over yonder' being killed quickly?"

So there it was. No way to ease up to it anymore now.

After a quick glance Smith's way, Lone brought his eyes back and met Sue's inquiring stare. He expelled some air out through his nostrils. Then: "What he meant was pretty much exactly what he said. The lead your brother is presently diggin' out of Meechum got put there last evenin', 'long about dusk, as part of a shootout that took place over near that cluster of creekside trees. Meechum and three pals, all punchers from a cattle spread somewhere hereabouts called the Twin V were on one side, three hombres from down Ogallala way was on the other...Meechum is the only one still alive."

Sue put a hand to her throat. "My god! And the others?"

"Still where they fell," Lone answered. "Takin' care of the wounded seemed the most important thing to see to. Without—for reasons my friends and me don't feel obliged to get bogged down tryin' to explain—draggin' in the law or any such right away. The dead ain't in no hurry. Once you and your brother get Meechum fit enough to take back to town, then you can send the marshal out to start handlin' his part."

"But where will you be?"

"Gone. Now that you two medics have got things under control, me and my friends plan to pull foot and get on with our own business."

"That's outrageous!" wailed Risen, still kneeling over Meechum with his hands pressed to the damaged shoulder, his own shoulders and head twisted around to glare at Lone. The campfire light pulsing on his enraged expression made him look almost maniacal. "You can't just ride away from this horror you've described and leave it all in our hands!"

A corner of Lone's mouth quirked up. "Actually, I'm pretty sure we can. And I'm even more sure it's exactly what we're gonna do. Remember before when I said you were right to suspect there wasn't gonna be much about this you'd end up likin'? Well, here's what I had in mind."

"Damn you! You duplicitous cur!" Risen fumed.

"If you're really interested in the truth," Smith advised him, "then the best thing you can do is keep Meechum there alive. He's the only one who can tell the whole story of that shootout. Yeah, we got you out here under false pretenses, so I can see where you'd doubt anything else we claim. But the fact remains we had nothing to do with the shootout, only came along shortly afterward. So there's nothing we could offer to help the marshal's investigation even if we did stick around."

"If you're so innocent, then why the big hurry to run away?" Sue wanted to know.

"We have our reasons," Lone said tersely, growing annoyed with this time-wasting back and forth. "That's all you need to know."

"There's where you're wrong, bucko. I got a lot more I need to know—and I damn well aim to find out the answers!"

CHAPTER EIGHTEEN

THE DEEP VOICE COMING SUDDENLY FROM THE DARKNESS somewhere outside the orb of campfire light froze everybody wrapped in the illumination. At least for one startled moment. As soon as that clock-tick of time passed, however, the hands of both Lone and Smith dropped automatically to the Colts holstered on their hips.

"Don't be damn fools!" the voice barked again. "You got three Winchesters dead-centered on ya. Any iron lifts outta leather, we'll cut you down."

Lone and Smith both stayed their hands.

"That's being smart. If what you say is true, there's already too damn many dead men on this meadow. But me and my deputies won't hesitate to add more if you give us no choice."

Lone's mind raced. The speaker's voice sounded vaguely familiar, but he couldn't quite place it. The marshal from back in Coraville, maybe? His talk of "deputies" would fit that. But what the hell had brought him here, caused him to follow? And whoever he was, did he really have the advantage he said he did—the "three Winchesters dead-centered on ya"? Since the darkness made it impossible to tell for sure, merely making such a claim, for the sake of assuring cooperation, didn't necessarily mean it was so.

As if reading Lone's thoughts, the voice spoke again, saying, "I see a dangerous notion flickering in the eyes of Mr. Saloon Brawler. Like he thinks I might be as big a liar as him, and so leaving him to wonder if I'm on the level with everything I laid down. Johnny, Sam...one at a time, off-cock and then quick re-cock your rifles so's to convince Mr. Saloon Brawler you're real and to keep him from trying something stupid that'll only get somebody hurt."

From two different places out in the darkness came the sounds of rifles being adjusted in accordance with the order. Lone swore under his breath.

"Marshal Kurtz? Fred?" Sue queried. "Is that you out there?"

"For a fact, ma'am," the reply. "Just hold steady and stand clear of those two scoundrels. I'll come forward in a minute...but first, real slow and using your off hands, I think it'd be a good idea for you gents to shuck your gun belts and kick 'em away after they hit the ground. Then hoist your paws up about chest high and keep 'em there, steady and in plain sight."

His mouth twisting grimly, Smith said, "You're one mighty careful hombre, ain't you?"

"Uh-huh. And that's why I'm one *alive* hombre after twenty-odd years of standing behind a badge."

Once the gun belts were on the ground and Lone and Smith were holding docilely in place, the marshal advanced. He reverse-melted out of the dense shadows with a Winchester aimed steadily from his waist. A few yards off to either side of him, his deputies also moved in, their forms becoming gradually discernible. One was tall and lanky, with clean-shaven features, appearing to be in his early to midtwenties. The other was shorter and older, wiry-looking, with the measured movements of somebody whose years were catching up to him. Both were wielding repeater rifles in the same manner as the marshal. Whether by design or happenstance, they had been positioned down wind and holding off far enough so that not even Lone's stallion, Ironsides—normally a sharp-eared watchdog who would signal upon sensing a foreign presence venturing too close—had detected them until Kurtz called out.

As the head lawman stepped into the full light, Lone pinned him with a hard look and said, "What's this all about? That saloon fracas wasn't my doin'. Those two peckerwoods set it in motion, I finished it. I thought we had that settled before I left town."

"Yeah, that part was settled okay," allowed Kurtz. "The thing that didn't settle down so easy, though, was my gut."

"Your gut?" Lone echoed, looking puzzled.

"That's right. Every once in a while, you see," explained the marshal, "I get this kinda knot in my gut when something I can't rightly put my finger on refuses to set proper. A gut hunch, I call it. And learning to pay attention to it is another reason I've stayed on top of the sod all these years."

"All these practices you follow, you looking to live forever?" Smith said sarcastically.

"I'll leave that up to my creator." Kurtz showed a smug smile. "My part, the way I see it, until He reckons it's time, is to not let some no-account dust-kicker pinch out my wick ahead of schedule."

"That's real inspirational," Lone drawled. "But it still don't answer why you and your men have showed up wavin' all that hardware in our faces. What 'gut hunch' gave you cause for that?"

Kurtz's smile grew wider and smugger. "Just a couple simple things. You came across a mite too cool, too slick. You proved you could handle your dukes real well, and you had the look of somebody who wasn't shy about pulling iron if you thought it necessary, neither. Yet for all that air of competence, you were in a mighty big hurry to drag away the doc—and Miss Sue, as it turned out—for a simple horse fall injury...something about that just smelled fishy to me."

"Thank God it did!" Sue exclaimed.

Kurtz tossed a one-shoulder shrug. "So the more it nagged at me, and especially after it sank in that nobody had even gotten a name for a complete stranger who rode out of town in the middle of the night with two of Coraville's most prominent citizens...well, I quickly decided it'd be better to risk getting embarrassed if I was wrong than to not act and be sorry because I should have. So I grabbed Johnny and Sam and we followed after, discreet-like, to make sure things were on the up and up."

"And from what we overheard hanging back in the shadows," spoke up Deputy Johnny Case, "they sure as hell ain't!"

"Nobody ever tell you it's rude to sneak around eavesdropping on people, sonny?" sneered Smith.

The deputy gave him a look. "You keep up that tone with me, mister, you'll see rude quick enough!"

Kurtz heaved a somewhat weary sigh. "Speaking of seeing something, Johnny, how about you pull a burning branch out of that fire you can use as a torch and go check over by those creekside trees? See if there truly are bodies there."

Johnny grimaced at the instruction. But then, after throwing another baleful look in Smith's direction, he headed to find a suitable firebrand.

"How many people you need to tell you there *are* bodies over there?" Lone asked the marshal. "If you were listening, ain't the wounded man right in front of you proof enough? You heard him say what happened to him, then me confirm it."

"Another little caution I take," replied Kurtz, "is that I don't believe everything I hear and not even all of what I see. Which brings me to something I've lamped on but ain't yet heard no mention or explanation of. What's the story on the Injun gal standing all quiet-like off beside the fire?"

"Leave her out of this," Smith was quick to say. "She's of no concern to you. She's been through enough already, she don't need you poking at her too."

"You got a knack—a damned annoying one—of rubbing wrong against my way of doing things, you know that?" The marshal's eyes and tone took on a distinct flintiness. "Another one of 'em happens to be that I'm particular about choosing for myself what to be concerned about."

"Seems like," Lone put in matter-of-factly, "you got a plateful of that already. Without goin' out of your way to worry about the girl."

Kurtz's flinty gaze shifted to him. His mouth pulled into a tight line but he didn't say anything for a beat.

Then: "Alright. I'll hold off on the girl. For now...but that don't mean I ain't keeping some concern over her in reserve."

"I think a concern you might *not* want to push too far aside, Boss," drawled wiry Sam, the other deputy, "is Vance Veldon. Hank Meechum does, for a fact, ride for the Twin V. Has for a long time. And this *is* Twin V range we're on. If the dead over yonder includes three more Twin V punchers, there's gonna be hell to pay. You can bet Veldon is bound to want blood for blood."

"Tell me something I don't already know," muttered Kurtz, the flintiness in his voice suddenly losing some of its edge. His eyes drifted to Johnny, following the young deputy as he trudged off toward the creek, holding a burning branch out ahead of himself like a torch.

For just a moment, Lone thought—or hoped rather?—an opening of some kind might be presented if the marshal was distracted enough by Johnny's progress or by thoughts of how the Twin V's he-bull, apparently somebody who had considerable sway hereabouts, was going to react to news of his men getting shot up. Lone could sense that Smith was poised, just as he was, for a chance to turn the tables back around on this trio that had unexpectedly gotten the drop on them. But, so far, credit was due to the marshal and his men for their rifle muzzles never wavering and for staying far enough out of reach to provide no reasonable opportunity to make a sudden grab. The temporary removal of Johnny's rifle seemed to only make the other two star packers—especially Sam—hold that much steadier. And Kurtz's tantalizing appearance of possibly losing focus was gone in an instant.

That didn't mean Lone was going to let up on prodding him, though. "Blood for blood? In that case, it's already been achieved," he reminded the two lawmen. "The ones who took down the Twin V punchers got cut down themselves. Again, you heard as much from me and Meechum. What he can shed light on that I can't, is what brought on the gunplay in the first place."

"Meechum's not going to tell anybody anything. Not right now, and not for quite a while," said Risen over his shoulder. "I put him under pretty deep so he'd hold still while I finish digging out these bullet fragments before I close up the wound. Then I've still got to have a closer look at his hip. Damn it, Sue, get back over here! I could get on with it faster if I had the help you're supposed to be providing."

Sue quickly went and kneeled once more by her brother's side. Lone held his tongue, but bristled at seeing her spoken to and treated that way. He noted the pinched look that came over Kurtz's face, too, indicating he didn't much like it either. Chalk up at least that much in his favor.

"Meechum is gonna pull through okay, ain't he, Doc?" the lawman inquired.

"I don't see why not. As long as I can get all or most of these fragments out—along with the rest that are likely in his hip—and then be able to keep the infection down."

"He's a mighty important witness to this whole mess, you know," Kurtz declared somberly.

Smith's eyes flashed. "Including setting you straight that *we* are no part of it. Except for the bad luck of happening along in time to hear the gun pops but then not getting here until the shooting was all over. Which begs the question, Marshal, of why we've been stripped of our weapons and are being held at gunpoint? For being *in the vicinity* of some place where some other men shot it out and killed one another? That's no basis for charging us with anything!"

"You hear anybody *say* you been charged with anything?" Kurtz snapped. "If I set my mind to it, though, I could damn well come up with some right quick. How about giving false information to an officer of the law? Or threatening to flee the scene of a crime— multiple killings, no less, by your own admission? I could rattle off more, but I think you get the picture...in the meantime, you're being held in custody—that includes no guns—for further questioning until Meechum comes back around to see what he has to say about your claims."

"You ought to do more than take their guns, you ought to put them in irons," Risen said, once again speaking over their shoulder. "Even if they didn't take direct part in this shooting, they're obviously on the run. Only men who've put themselves on the wrong side of the law have reason to be on the run!"

Lone ground his teeth. "Yeah, that's right, you frog-brained idiot. We're such lowdown desperadoes we hung back and went out of our way to fetch a doctor to save a wounded man we never laid eyes on before. If I committed any crime here tonight, it was bringin' back your sorry, gin-soaked ass and siccin' you on an already sufferin' patient."

Before any of those gathered at the campfire had the chance to say any more, Deputy Johnny let out a whoop from over by the creek. "Jesus God! You can bet there are dead men over here, Marshal. A whole heap of 'em!

Two on this side of the creek...and two, no, make that three more on the other side."

"Shit!" Kurtz spat. Then, glaring at Lone and Smith, he said, "There's something I wish to hell you *would* have been lying about."

"That mean you're ready to start believin' the rest of what we've been tryin' to tell you?"

"Not by a damn sight!"

At that moment, from somewhere off on the other side of the creek, came the mournful, drawn-out wail of a coyote followed quickly by some shorter, fainter yips farther away.

"They're back." Smith's mouth twisted grimly. "There's a pack of coyotes working their way in from the northwest. I went over a little while ago and chased off a couple front runners with some rifle shots. But it sounds like there's more forming up."

At another coyote wail, Johnny turned and began his return, the bobbing of his torch marking his hurried steps. "Hey, I'm coming back," he said somewhat breathily. "Nothing more I can do out here."

"This campfire is close enough to make the coyotes a little nervous about getting close. But that don't mean they'll give up," Deputy Sam said. "If those bodies are still laying out there come light, the crows and vultures will start showing up too. They'll be harder yet to drive off."

"Then we must do something—we can't just leave them there!" Sue insisted.

"Damn it, let the marshal worry about that. You need to pay attention to what we're doing here," her brother bitched at her again, "or we'll have another potential meal for the scavengers."

But this time, Sue didn't take it so meekly. "The only problem we're having here is how badly your hands are shaking. Just let me take over, then. I can finish closing that up."

Kurtz didn't like the sound of that at all. "Jesus, Doc, settle down. You know how important—"

"Goddammit, I heard you the first time—get off my back!" Risen rocked back on his heels and leaned away from the patient, spreading his hands wide. Sue immediately leaned in closer and resumed finishing the closure of Meechum's torn shoulder.

Risen was sweating and looked mournful, desperate. He swept his gaze over everybody. "I-I'm sorry. I can get hold of myself, I really can...I just need a..." He didn't finish, instead twisting at the waist and digging somewhat frantically into his open medical bag.

Without looking up from her task, Sue said, "You won't find it in there, James. Not this time. I made it a point to throw it out before I brought you the bag."

"Damn you!"

"No. Damn what you're doing to yourself, James," his sister fired back, still intent on the wound. "You said a minute ago you could get hold of yourself. Well, it's time to start doing so—and not by repeatedly trying to regain your grip at the bottom of a bottle!"

Risen straightened back up, making an anguished sound in his throat. He swept his gaze over the others again, looking desperate. "For God's sake, I just need a jolt. Just a couple swallows...doesn't anybody have a flask of something?"

There was a long moment of strained, awkward silence.

And then Deputy Sam said, "Reckon I do. Hold on a

second." Lowering his Winchester, allowing the snout to dip momentarily downward, he reached across his chest with his free hand to fumble at an inner pocket of his jacket. Kurtz glanced over to see what he was doing.

There it was. The opening they'd been hoping for, been poised for.

Simultaneously, Lone and Smith lunged forward...

CHAPTER NINETEEN

SMITH BARRELED INTO SAM WITH A FULL HEAD OF STEAM, knocking the smaller man clean off his feet. The deputy hit the ground flat on his back, emitting a loud grunt of surprise and pain carried within great gushes of breath driven out of him first by the impact of Smith's shoulder and then by slamming to the ground. Continuing to go with his momentum, Smith plunged down on top of the wiry veteran, immediately grabbing the Winchester and twisting savagely to wrest it free. His whole body brutally jarred and nearly emptied of air, and Sam was too stunned to put up much resistance. As soon as he had control of the weapon, Smith rolled free, twisted around and scrambled upright. Braced on one knee, he immediately locked the repeater's aim on the man he'd just taken it away from.

For his part, Lone turned out to have a harder time overcoming the marshal. Kurtz was bigger and stronger and hadn't been caught quite so off guard. Nevertheless, Lone's unexpected charge was quick enough to succeed in slipping past the big advantage presented by the lawman's Winchester. Thrusting his left arm out ahead as he propelled himself forward, Lone swept it sharply up and outward, the bone and muscle of his forearm smashing against the wood and iron of the rifle's fore-stock. Pain streaked through Lone's arm all the way to the shoulder, but it was worth it to knock away any immediate threat from the gun. This was demonstrated an instant later when the Winchester discharged and sent a slug screaming impotently off into the darkness.

Even with the closeness of the shot battering his eardrum, Lone never let up on his continuing bull rush against the marshal. They slammed together, chest to chest, and Kurtz staggered back barely a step. "Damn you!" the lawman cursed, their faces so close that the spittle from between his clenched teeth splattered Lone's face. A moment later, Lone brought their faces even closer together by drawing his head back for just an instant and then ramming it forward, hard and fast, to pound his forehead down on the bridge of Kurtz's nose. The latter howled anew, and this time, the wetness splattering Lone's face was blood gushing from the nostrils of the nose he'd just busted.

Kurtz staggered another step back, but he still main-tained his grip on the Winchester, even though Lone's left arm was keeping it shoved off high and to one side. His arms being pulled in such a manner forced the marshal's torso to be partially twisted that way, too, leaving his middle and left rib cage quite exposed. Seeing this as something he couldn't let go to waste, Lone immediately pounded three hard, fast right hooks into those ribs.

That knocked the starch out of Kurtz. His knees sagged, and he folded forward as far as he could with

Lone jammed up against him. Suddenly pivoting ninety degrees, Lone reached and seized the Winchester with both hands, tugging hard, trying to yank it from Kurtz's grasp. But the stubborn damn law dog wouldn't let go. Spitting his own curse, Lone abruptly dropped into a slight crouch and then leaned forward at the waist, still maintaining his grip on the rifle, still tugging. In this manner, he dragged Kurtz over his shoulder and into a flailing somersault that ended with the marshal's own shoulders thudding heavily to the ground—no longer with the Winchester in his grip. When he rolled groggily onto one hip and lifted his head to look up, Kurtz found himself staring into the gaping bore of the repeater's muzzle mere inches from his face. Held there by Lone.

Jacking a fresh round into the chamber, Lone grated, "Who's in whose custody now, you mule-headed bastard?"

"Better make up your mind fast and let Johnny-boy know what you decide," Smith quickly added. "He's out there looking like he don't know whether to shit or shoot—and if he chooses wrong, it's a guarantee somebody more is gonna get hurt."

Sure enough, Deputy Johnny stood frozen part way between the creek and the camp. The attack on his fellow lawmen had come so sudden and unexpected, and he'd been too far away—and remained so still—to do anything about it. Yet the pulsing torchlight playing across his facial features now showed a tortured mix of alarm and indecision—of *wanting* to take some kind of action, regardless.

But Lone could see in Kurtz's eyes that he was savvy enough to know when the tide had turned too strongly to attempt any pushback. At least for the moment.

"Tell him!" Lone urged.

His voice, thick due to the blood running back inside his throat from his smashed nose, the marshal called, "Don't do anything foolish, Johnny! They got us cold. Any lead starts flying, there's too much risk to innocents. Lower your rifle, stand down."

"Better yet," Lone advised, "put the rifle on the ground and shuck your gun belt. Leave 'em there, then you come on the rest of the way. Slow and easy."

"And remember—you try anything cute, the first ones to pay will be your two friends," amended Smith, making a short thrust with the commandeered Winchester he held aimed at Sam.

Johnny shed his weapons and came forward, meekly, as ordered.

Dr. Risen leaned back on his elbows and let out a groan. "For the love of God...this only keeps getting worse."

His sister, who—except for displaying a brief start when Kurtz's rifle discharged—had remained intently focused on Meechum's shoulder wound throughout the surrounding flurry of events, now looked up and gave Risen a disdainful glare. "For the love of God indeed, James! Get hold of yourself and straighten up. This shoulder is taken care of for now. But the hip still needs attention—*your* attention—while this man remains medicated. Take a damn drink if you must, but then snap out of it and get back to your job. The job you're sworn to do!"

The dressing-down by his sister succeeded in jarring Risen out of his dual attack of booze craving and self-pity. Waving off Smith's offer to finish digging the flask out of Sam's pocket, he wiped the sweat from his face, re-rolled the rumpled shirt sleeves that had fallen loose earlier, and once again leaned determinedly into the task of ministering to Meechum.

While the two medics were thus occupied, Kurtz and Sam were stripped of their sidearms, as Johnny had already been, and Lone and Smith strapped their own back on. This done, Lone asked Bright Moon to gather up all of the lawmen's weapons, including the outlying ones left by Johnny, and pile them on a blanket.

Lone and Smith then herded the three lawmen into a bunch off a ways from the fire. Kurtz and Sam were a little the worse for wear but able to stand and face what Lone proceeded to lay out for them.

"You brought this on yourselves," he said. "I understand you were just doin' what you saw as your jobs, and I generally don't fault no man for that. But in this case, you complicated the hell out of things for no good reason—none worth the trouble you've pushed it to. No matter what you believe, me and my pal ain't on the run from the law. But we do have some bad hombres out to do us serious harm, that's why we have to stay on the move and can't afford to get hung up here for any length of time over this shootin' business.

"I'll say one more time, we were no part of that. We *were* on the tails of those Ogallala fellas who did get caught in it, though. They were leads to helpin' settle this other business houndin' us. It gets complicated, I don't aim tryin' to explain more."

"Then why explain anything at all?" sneered Johnny. "You're just gonna shoot us and leave us for the coyotes and buzzards, anyway—like those other poor devils."

"That's what we'd do if we were what you're so hell-bent on believing we are," said Smith.

Lone focused his attention fully on the marshal. "We won't hesitate to kill if we have to. But it ain't what we want. We're ready to ride out of here before first light and be out of your hair with no more hurt done...all you have to do is agree to give us twenty-four hours before you send out a posse or start wirin' around to other law dogs in the territory to try and intercept us."

"You know I can't agree to something like that," Kurtz was quick to respond. Then he paused, his eyes narrowing suspiciously. "Besides, even if I said I would, how could you be sure I'd keep my word?"

Lone's eyes narrowed, too. A cold intensity stabbed out from them like dagger points. "Ain't something I'm hankerin' to do, Marshal. But there are ways."

CHAPTER TWENTY

VANCE VELDON'S BROAD, FLESHY FACE WAS PURPLE WITH rage. "You're out of your goddamn mind if you think I'm going to draw rein on something like this! Four Twin V riders have been gunned down—one of them my own nephew, Wyatt, the only son of my widowed sister." The rancher's grief and anger-filled eyes bored hard into Marshal Kurtz. "And you want everybody to just sit on their thumbs and let those murdering sonsabitches ride clear for a whole day and night before giving chase or spreading word to be on the lookout for 'em?"

"Damn it, Vance, that ain't what I *want*!" Kurtz growled back in a thick, nasally tone due to the bloody cotton stuffing pushed up into each nostril. His eyes, too, were etched with pain and anguish and half moons of reddish-purple discoloration were already forming under each one. "Yeah, those are the conditions I agreed to. But did you miss the part where I explained why? They took Sue Leonard hostage with the promise to release her safely only if those conditions are met."

"And you believe them?" Veldon said tauntingly.

"I had no choice!"

"Hogwash. That would only mean anything if you were dealing with men of honor, men you could count on to keep their word. Does this," Veldon swept one of his thick, powerful arms in a slashing arc, indicating the scene and activity taking place about them, "look like the leavings of men who have a shred of honor or can be trusted to hold up their end of any bargain, any worthless 'promise'?"

The two men were standing on the edge of the camp originally pitched by Curtis and the Tates. To the east, the sky all along the irregular horizon line was painted a steadily brightening pale gold, just minutes ahead of the sun poking into sight. Between the camp and the creek, a flatbed wagon was pulled up with a team of restlessly shifting mules hitched to it. The cause for the animals' uneasiness was the death smell coming off the cargo loaded on the wagon—the bodies of the five dead men gathered from the creek area.

Since the Twin V ranch headquarters was closer than town, Deputy Johnny Case had been sent there to report the news of the creek shootout and to seek assistance in the wake of all that had transpired after. Vance Veldon himself had been rousted. Along with four Twin V wranglers, including ranch foreman Tobe Medford, Veldon had ridden out to the scene post haste. The mule team and wagon, to fetch the bodies, followed along soon after.

While the dead men were being recovered, blanket-shrouded and laid out on the wagon bed for transporting to Coraville for eventual burial, Deputy Sam Wiley had gone ahead into town to spread the word and start making preparations there. During all this,

Marshal Kurtz had related everything he knew about what had taken place both before and after he and his men had arrived on the scene...culminating with the departure of the two hard case strangers—no names ever given—the mysterious Indian girl they assumed escorting duties for, and Sue Leonard, the doctor's sister, whom they took as their hostage. Dr. Risen was able to add what verification he could and the wounded Meechum, drifting in and out of consciousness, provided some as well.

So, with that much established, what was at issue now was how to proceed next. For the safety of the hostage, Kurtz was very much inclined to follow the arrangement he had agreed to. Rancher Veldon, fiery-tempered and impatient by nature—and having suffered direct and personal loss—was wanting no part of allowing the fleeing men any more of a lead than they'd already gained.

"Blast it all, Fred," he continued to rail at the marshal, "have you gone soft in recent years? Have you forgotten that the only way to deal with bloodthirsty animals like these is to be just as fierce and relentless as they are, to give them absolutely no quarter? You know damn well that girl is probably already dead by now. The last thing they want is to drag her along any farther than necessary, to slow 'em down during the time they figure she's bought 'em. Only reason to keep her alive at all, maybe for a little while, would be to stop at some point for a quick..."

Veldon let his words trail off, abruptly aware of the haunted eyes of James Risen gazing at him. The doctor, along with Deputy Johnny and the Twin V ramrod Tobe Medford, was standing close by, silently listening to the exchange between Veldon and Kurtz. Meechum, his wounds tended as thoroughly as possible for the time being, was still stretched out on bedroll blankets beside the fire and had once again dozed under the effect of Risen's medication.

Speaking into the sudden emptiness left by Veldon's unfinished rant, Risen said in a low, hollow voice, "Might as well go ahead. Don't let me stop you. There's nothing you can say that would be worse than the horrible possibilities I haven't been able to stop from swirling around in my head ever since those curs rode away with my sister."

Veldon regarded the fair-skinned speaker, looking frail and wrung-out by his dogged determination to finish ministering to Meechum even though emotion-torn by his sister's abduction. The rancher's wide mouth pulled into a grimace while a curious mix of pity and disdain showed briefly in his dark eyes. He could understand pain and remorse, but he had little use for overt displays of the same. He himself was a big, still ruggedly built man, though these days showing—and feeling—the ravages of too many years of tough living; most recently, a busted hip from a bull-ramming incident the previous fall that left him with a limp and chronic dull pain every waking minute. The limp he couldn't hide, but any lamentation about the pain he kept to himself. Though it surely did nothing to soften the gruff, demanding nature behind the way he ran the Twin V and his demands and expectations from those about him.

Responding to Risen's comment, Veldon said, "I'm sorry for your distress, Doc. I truly am. Didn't mean to paint such a black picture. But it can be a mighty tough life, and it's villains like those we're faced with here who add to making it that way. You're a young man, you weren't around for the wildest times hereabout." He paused to cut a sidelong glance over at the marshal. "But old mossy horns like me and Fred were...though he seems to have forgotten some of what it took to tame that wildness down when it rares its ugly head."

"I ain't forgot a blasted thing," Kurtz argued. "It was one of my gut hunches that caused me and my deputies to show up here in the first place, remember? Yeah, I ain't proud to admit we ended up getting caught off guard by an unexpected turn," here he shot a somewhat subdued look of his own in the direction of Risen, "but when you wear a badge and have civilians in the mix, you have to take precautions we didn't necessarily bother with in the old days. And there were times, no matter how wild it was back then, that we stretched the line pretty thin ourselves, Vance."

"Says you. I never did a damn thing any of those times I wouldn't do all over again," Veldon came back stubbornly. "And I damn sure would never have wasted time jaw-jacking back then when there was killers to chase after."

"See? There you go." Kurtz made a frustrated gesture. "Those two strangers may be hardcases, but that don't make them killers—not based on anything we can say for sure. You heard your own man Meechum say they didn't show up until *after* the shooting."

"If they ain't killers, they're skin close to it. If not here, then by God somewhere else, you can bet on that," Veldon insisted. "You're the one who said they admitted to being on the tail of the skunks who *did* cut down Wyatt and my other men. What's the fancy legal lingo—

guilt by association? How about that? Lenny Gleeson rode for my brand longer than anybody save for Tobe here...and I'm supposed to let a couple sonsabitches who had *anything* to do with his killing just ride away clear?"

"Not clear, damn it. Just a lag before giving chase—for the sake of the hostage. After twenty-four hours I'll call out pursuit from Hell to breakfast."

"Not good enough. As for the hostage, can't you get it through your thick skull that when it comes to killers like them—"

Kurtz cut him off. "What if you're wrong, Mr. 'Always-So-Sure-Of-Himself'? What if they haven't killed the girl right away and truly intend to keep their word about releasing her safely if we hold off like I agreed? Are you willing to bet Sue Leonard's life on your damned stubbornness? If those men are crowded too suddenly and made to feel betrayed, then yeah, they might very well react like you seem so hell-bent on seeing them do. Comes to that, Sue's blood won't be on just their hands."

But Val Venton wasn't prepared to give an inch. "Any harm befalls that girl, like it already has my nephew and these others, the blame will belong strictly to those who did the harming. Any blood ends up on my hands, either directly or indirectly, I'll proudly wear knowing it came from going after justice—not biding my time in the name of some 'deal' struck with human vermin!"

"Anything you're planning on doing, I want no part of, Vance," Kurtz declared, his eyes blazing. "You'll do it without sanction of this badge I wear, and I'll do my damnedest to dissuade anybody from my town to join any kind of posse you mean to form. When it's time, I'll form my own—"

Now, it was Veldon who did the cutting off. "*Your* town, *your* posse," he sneered, lips peeled back in an ugly way. "Do you think I give a shit about any posse to come out of there—made up of a bunch of soft-handed clerks and bar flies and daddies worried about getting home in time for supper with the wife and brats? Same for that badge of yours, which is miles outside its legal jurisdiction anyway."

"We can make up all the posse we need right from our own riders, Boss," spoke up a flinty-eyed Tobe Medford.

"You think I don't know that?" Veldon snapped, his ire at the marshal splashing over onto his own man. Then, modulating his tone, he added, "In fact, it's time —and past time—for exactly that. I put it in your hands, Tobe. Go back to the ranch and pick the men you need. Make sure Chico Racone is one of 'em, he's got Yaqui blood in him and is the best tracker in our crew. Put 'em on sturdy mounts, outfit 'em with guns, plenty of ammo, and trail rations for at least three days. Bring 'em back here as a starting point. I want 'em to see our dead piled up before they head out."

Veldon paused, his mouth pulling into a grimace. "I'll be waiting to see you off. God knows that every fiber of my being wants to go with you, but I know damn well this hip of mine couldn't take it. I'd be lucky to last a day and would only slow you down."

"Everybody understands that, boss," Medford assured him.

Johnny stepped forward. "If Tobe will fetch me back a gun, I'd like to be included." The intense expression on his face conveyed two things: His sincerity in wanting to go, and his embarrassment at being weapon-less due to Lone and Smith having ridden off with all the guns they'd confiscated—even including those of the fallen men.

Before either Veldon or Medford could reply, Kurtz said, "You heard me say we'll take no part in this, Johnny. Not until I decide it's time to form a posse of our own."

"With all due respect, sir," Johnny responded, "I think you're wrong. I think Mr. Veldon has the right idea about going after those varmints. The sooner, the better."

Kurtz scowled. "You can think whatever you want. But as long as you wear that deputy's badge and report to me, you'll do as I say."

Johnny's face became a mask of indecision.

Making no attempt to hide a smug smile, Veldon said, "You make the call, son. But if you truly want to go, then Tobe will bring you a gun and you'd be welcome to join."

"Damn you, Vance!" Kurtz spat.

"Don't blame me," Veldon shot back. "He's showing good sense, and you're not. It's as simple as that. And he'd be a good man to have if he wants to go."

"I do," Johnny declared firmly. Then, not without a moment of hesitation, he removed the badge from his shirt and held it out to the marshal. "I'm sorry, Fred, but I feel too strongly about this. I also feel it's in Sue's best interest, if she has any chance at all, to act fast rather than wait."

It took a long beat before Kurtz reached out and accepted the badge. In a quiet voice, he said, "I think you're making a mistake...but, at the same time, I guess I understand." What Kurtz was privy to knowing, as hardly anyone else around town did, was that Johnny harbored a deep love for Sue Leonard that he'd never been able to work up the courage to openly express. Now, he was feeling desperate for a chance not only to save her, but to give himself another opportunity at what he'd been shying away from.

Abruptly, a new voice rang out, stating, "I intend to go too!"

When all eyes swung to the speaker, James Risen, it was Veldon who didn't hesitate to immediately blurt what everybody else was thinking. "You got to be kidding. You—the shape you're in? You wouldn't last twenty miles."

"Damn it, Sue is my sister! I have both an obligation and a right to be part of any attempt to bring her back," Risen insisted. "And, if I set my mind to it, you might be surprised how strongly I can endure."

Johnny spun on him. "You have a 'right'? The hell you do, mister. If she wouldn't have come along out here because she felt the need to babysit your sorry, drunken ass, then she wouldn't be in this fix at all!"

Risen winced, almost as if Johnny had slapped him. But he stood his ground and glared back defiantly. "Regrettably, I can't dispute anything you just said. But don't you see? Those are exactly the reasons I must join in going after her. At least let me try. If I fall behind as expected, then leave me and call it a noble effort...or perhaps my just deserts."

"Who's gonna take care of Meechum if you ride off?" asked Kurtz.

"All that can be done in the near term is to regularly

change his dressings and watch for infection. Any of the midwives in town can handle that," Risen said with casual confidence. "I'll leave my kit and medicine to administer in case infection does flare."

Veldon threw up his arms. "We're losing valuable time! Tobe, you need to get a move on. Bring back a gun and cartridges for Johnny. If the doc thinks he can keep up when you return and are ready to ride, let him try. The results will be on him...now knock on it!"

CHAPTER TWENTY-ONE

LONE DISLIKED HAVING TO TAKE SUE LEONARD HOSTAGE. It went hard against his grain in a general sense and was made even worse by the curiously strong attraction he'd felt toward the woman since first laying eyes on her. Nevertheless, forcing her to accompany them was the best option he'd been able to come up with for extracting him, Smith, and Bright Moon out of becoming too entangled in the creekside shootout back on Twin V range. If Marshal Kurtz stuck to his agreement, taking Sue would buy important time and distance that would translate to keeping them ahead of pursuit as well as staying reasonably on schedule for still reaching Pike Grogan. Getting bogged down in Coraville would not only jeopardize the latter, but— apart from the obvious threat of perhaps facing criminal charges—there was the added risk that holding in one place for too long in the public eye, despite Smith's blackened-hair disguise, could draw unwanted suspicion from some sharp-eyed roaming bounty hunter.

A quick tally of the undesirable possibilities made

the distasteful act of taking a hostage not so hard to bite into.

Much of how successful it was going to be, depended, of course, on whether or not Kurtz kept his part of the deal. Even if he didn't, Lone had no intention of actually harming the doctor's sister. But should pursuit be sighted too early, neither would he go ahead and release her. If she failed to be a deterrent as initially hoped for, that didn't mean she might not still serve as a useful bargaining chip at some later point.

In the meantime, upon first riding away from the camp and the scene of the creekside shootout, there was cause to believe the agreement *would* be kept and so Lone meant to take advantage of every minute and every mile he hoped his group stood to gain. With the moon starting to wane and daybreak more than two hours away, traveling over rugged, unfamiliar terrain was going to be difficult. But progress was progress, even at a slower, more cautious pace. The array of stars still provided decent illumination and Ironsides, ridden by Lone in the lead, had proven many times in the past to be sure-footed over far more broken land than this.

Riding close behind Lone, her mount tethered to his saddle horn, was Sue Leonard. Sullen and stone-faced, she sat her saddle well, clearly no stranger to spending time on horseback even though she was poorly suited, attire-wise, on this occasion. Other than a brief exchange with her brother, she had spoken scarcely a word since hearing Lone's stated intention to take her as a hostage. But the way she looked at him whenever their eyes met spoke volumes—and it was clear that loathing dominated each page.

Bright Moon followed behind Sue in their procession, with Smith leading the pack horse bringing up the rear. Lone had anticipated that Bright Moon could be convinced to come along with him and Smith after Curtis and the Tates had been gunned down, but he was somewhat surprised by the overt willingness she showed when it was time to make their departure after turning the tables on the lawmen. Something had transpired between the Indian girl and Smith while Lone was gone on his trip to Coraville, something that seemed to bond them somehow. Smith had started to tell him about it after he brought the medics to the camp, but had gotten interrupted by Dr. Risen's demand for hot water to assist his treatment of the patient. Then, things had propelled in directions that prevented any chance to take up the discussion again. But Lone fully intended to re-visit the matter and figured to do so at some point in the coming hours when they stopped for a break.

For now, though, the main thing on his mind was covering distance. By his reckoning, the Flat Falls reservation in North Dakota still lay about five days away. Five days of staying steadily on the move, with no more interruptions. No longer drafting in the wake of the solid pace set by Ed Curtis, they had to set and maintain one of their own. And then, once they got there, there would remain the incidental little matter of ferreting out and confronting Pike Grogan.

———

WHEN DAYBREAK CAME, Lone began using his full visibility of the surrounding landscape to set their course in ways that would mask their passage as much as possible. Over rocky, hard-packed stretches that would leave little or no tracks; in and out of twisty, shallow streams that were in abundance throughout the region from an apparent rainy spring; across expanses of high, fresh grass that sprang back quickly, leaving minimal sign of having been tramped through. He chose such areas whenever possible, yes, but never to a degree that zig-zagged their route very far off its aim of due north. Making steady progress toward their destination remained the overriding factor that pushed him on.

All in the party were dog tired, having gone twenty-four hours now without sleep. Each had, one way or another, put in a full previous day and then found themselves caught up in results stemming from the creekside shootout that had subsequently occupied them through the night and to this dawn of a new day. With, if Lone continued to have his say, minimal let-up in sight.

Finally, with the sun about three hours old in the sky, he called a rest stop on the banks of yet another narrow, crooked stream lined by a smattering of trees. Both animals and humans needed a breather. While the others dropped in exhausted heaps onto the soft grass skirting the trees, Lone held the horses back until they'd cooled sufficiently before letting them drink. Then, even though the stop was going to be short, he picketed them to make sure none got a case of wanderlust. He knew he could trust Ironsides, but didn't want to take a chance with the other animals.

While tending the mounts, Lone noted that their hostage seemed to be showing some tolerance toward Bright Moon. While Sue had maintained her silence when it came to Lone—though showing no reluctance

to glare daggers at him whenever she got the chance—
she appeared willing to speak in low tones with Bright
Moon and to show proper appreciation for the beef
jerky and sips from a canteen the Indian girl offered
her.

As they continued to converse sparingly between
bites of the tough jerky, Smith pushed up from his brief
flop onto the grass and came over to help Lone with the
picketing. "This mean we're gonna hold here a spell?"
he asked hopefully as he stomped down one of the
stakes.

"A mighty short spell is all."

Smith's mouth twisted wryly. "I was afraid you were
gonna say that."

"You know as well as I do why we can't let up," Lone
said. "We sure as hell can't afford to get sucked back and
tangled up all over again in that Coraville-Twin V mess.
We got to take full advantage of the time our hostage is
buyin' us."

"You really think that marshal will keep his word?"

Lone held out his hand, palm down, and waggled it.
"Fifty-fifty. Yeah, I think Kurtz would be inclined to do
what he agreed to. But no tellin' how hard he'll be
tugged otherwise by the townsfolk and likely the Twin
V crew too—wantin' him not to hold back puttin'
together a posse soon as possible."

"Even at that," Smith mused, "they couldn't have
drummed up much of a force before daybreak. And if
they started out clear back at the town, that gives us, at
worst, still a pretty fair jump in both time and distance.
And I've noticed how you've been masking our trail
whenever you can."

Now, it was Lone's turn for a wry twist of his

mouth. "If they got a halfway decent tracker with 'em, it won't fool him much. But every little bit helps. Fact remains, no matter how tuckered out we are, our best bet is to keep pluggin' on and try to out-pace any followers no matter how much of a gap they start out with."

"Yeah, once again, I can't argue with you," Smith allowed. "Speaking of the agreement with Kurtz, you figure on letting the woman go like you said?"

"Don't see why not. Long as no posse shows up crowdin' us ahead of schedule. That happens, all bets are off. We'll hang on to her as a bargainin' chip for when it suits us."

"Let's hope it don't come to that. I'm all for getting rid of her. The sooner, the better. Not for any noble reason, mind you," explained Smith, "but mainly because she kinda gives me the willies. The hatred burning in her eyes for us is downright fierce. Comes night camp, no matter how tired I am, I don't know that I'll get much sleep wondering if she won't come in the dark with a rock to bash in my skull or a sharp stick to gouge out my liver."

Lone chuckled dryly. "Hell, what are you worried about? Far as I can tell, most of that burnin' hate is stoked up for yours truly. I don't figure she'd pass up the chance to go for me first—my bloody screams oughta give a fast-draw pistolero like you plenty of time to save yourself."

"Gee, thanks. Now I'll sleep like a baby."

"Besides," Lone went on, "it looks like Bright Moon is havin' a bit of a calming effect on her. Maybe that'll give me a chance to make it through the night, too."

"Could be. It's true she's opening up some to Bright

Moon. Told her she's a widow, that her husband died of pneumonia two winters ago."

"I wondered about her havin' a last name different from her brother."

"Then again, that pneumonia thing could just be an alibi. The truth might be that hubby pissed her off and ended up bumping his head real hard—accidental-like, mind you—on a frying pan." Smith paused, his eyebrows lifting. "On the other hand, Bright Moon seems to be as much at ease with her as the other way around, so I reckon our hostage can't be too awful. I'm learning more and more not to underestimate that little Indian gal."

Lone regarded him. "Yeah, about that...I didn't miss the way you and her seemed to have hit it off pretty good while I was away fetchin' that damn drunken doc. Not complainin', mind you, it was good to see how willin' she was to throw in with us when we pulled foot outta there. But you started to tell me something—some big news, you said—back there before we got interrupted by everything poppin' sideways so unexpected-like. It have to do with something you learned from Bright Moon?"

Smith's eyes widened with excitement, just as they had the first time he'd tried to bring up the matter. "Plenty. I found out some things about her and, believe it or not, some things she knows about me—or, to put it more accurately, who I was as Wade Avril. Maybe you don't want to take the time right now, but I think you'll find 'em worth hearing."

Lone studied the earnestness of his expression. Then he said, "Your tellin' already got put off once. Sounds like something that ought not be left waitin' again. Let's find a spot to get off our feet for a couple minutes, then you can fill me in."

———

ON THE EDGE of the campsite originally pitched by the now deceased Ed Curtis and the Tates, Tobe Medford sat his deep-chested bay gelding at the head of five other riders. Medford was a husky, lantern-jawed six-footer with thirty winters behind him; the last six of those having been spent as the foreman for Vance Veldon's Twin V ranch. Medford was a tough but fair ramrod, respected by his crew, and even guardedly liked. Any reservations felt toward him came from his blind devotion to Veldon—who was *not* always even-tempered and fair in his treatment of others. Meaning that if Veldon made a call at odds with Tobe's more level-headed notion of how to handle a particular situation, the ramrod would nevertheless take care of it as the ranch owner wanted, no questions asked.

The riders backing Medford consisted of Chico Racone, a veteran puncher, near fifty in years yet still wiry and more limber than many half his age, a man of Yaqui Indian blood who had lived with the tribe during his youth and still retained the hunting and tracking skills he learned during that time; Bishop Ikes, another veteran wrangler, tough as rawhide and nearly as good with a hogleg as with a lasso; Jerome "Kid Memphis" Darrold, barely past twenty, every bit the hillbilly his name suggested, but gifted with horses and also handy as hell with a shooting iron. The assemblage was rounded out by Deputy Johnny Case and Dr. James Risen, each with their own bona fides, dubious though his might be, for the task at hand, when it came to the doctor.

Vance Veldon stood beside his tall buckskin, looking up at the group. His eyes were flinty, his strong jaw was set, and the just-risen sun off to the east cast a long shadow out away from him that made him seem an even more imposing figure. He was the only one left at the campsite, Marshal Kurtz having departed some time prior and the wagonload of dead men, once it had been viewed by those just arriving from the ranch, pulling away only minutes previously.

"Men," Veldon said, addressing the riders in a grave voice, "you all should be crystal clear on what's being asked of you. You got a good look at what just left here... the remains of your fellow brand mates, my beloved nephew among them, slaughtered and left laying like dogs. Yeah, those who supposedly shot them down paid too. Our boys gave a damn good account of themselves. But the cowards who left them laying are on the run, on the loose. The fact they ran is proof enough, I say, that they were more deeply involved in some kind of way. What's more, as further proof of what lowlifes they are, they took the doc's sister as a hostage, thinking it will buy them some grace."

Here, Veldon paused, his expression turning even more somber and his voice taking on increased gravity when he continued. "It pains me to think and to say this...and I know it's even worse for the doctor to hear... but I fear the girl is already most likely dead. Believing they've gotten out of her what use she's ever going to be, their kind wouldn't think no more of tossing her aside like an empty tobacco sack. Leave her laying just like they did our men. That's one more thought I want you to burn in your brain, one more reason to run those bastards down and not hesitate to give 'em everything they deserve!" Veldon emphasized those final words by smacking his meaty right fist into the cupped palm of his left hand.

Listening to all of this, Johnny and Risen looked agonized and grim. The doctor's head was hanging mournfully by the time it was over. But the Twin V riders had a different reaction, exactly the one Veldon had been aiming to stir in them. Before he was done, he could see the shine of excitement and bloodlust gleaming bright in their eyes.

Somewhat unexpectedly, though, Bishop Ikes had a question. "What if," he wanted to know, "the woman ain't been killed like you figure? How do we play it then?"

Before Veldon could answer, Johnny shot Ikes a hard look and said, "Why is that even a question? The answer is obvious. If Sue is still alive—which, if there's a just God in Heaven, she *has* to be—then we must proceed with every precaution to keep her that way."

"Whatever the circumstances you find when you catch up with those vermin," Veldon said, his voice now tighter, strained, "I have full trust in Tobe knowing how to deal with it. Look to his leadership without question, and anyone who doesn't will answer to me." His gaze raked the faces before him, then came to rest on Johnny. "And as far as a just God in Heaven...if that was the case, then from my perspective, I would still be in a physical condition that enabled me to lead this undertaking myself. Think about that, mister!"

CHAPTER TWENTY-TWO

THE DAY'S HEAT BUILT RAPIDLY THROUGHOUT THE morning, fueled by a sizzling silver-white ball of sun climbing in a clear sky. To the north and west, however, could be seen a streak of dark clouds smudging the horizon. This potential for a storm moving in only caused Lone to push his group harder and steadier after the brief early respite.

A strong storm would surely affect their progress, and in that regard, be a negative development. On the other hand, in case a posse was in pursuit sooner than agreed upon, then a storm would not only slow their progress as well, but would also help blur the trail of Lone's party. Still, neither was something Lone could count on. For that reason, he kept pressing.

The sun was past its mid-day peak before he finally called a noon halt. He knew he had to, and knew it needed to be a substantial one. Both people and horses required rest and nourishment in order to continue on. A stand of cottonwoods on the edge of the expanse of undulating grassland they were passing over presented a suitable spot. Although there was no nearby stream in this instance, they had plenty of water in their canteens and the large water bag on the packhorse.

While the others wearily and gratefully dismounted, stripped their mounts, and began building a fire to make hot food and coffee, Lone denied himself and Ironsides the luxury of joining them. Not that he didn't feel the weight of his own exhaustion and sense it in the big gray too; but he also knew the limit of their endurance when challenged, and knew they had plenty more to give if required. His decision to call on that reserve now was prompted by a desire that had been building in him to drop back and check their back trail. He hadn't wanted to slow the progress of the group for the sake of doing so before, but now that they were on hold anyway, it was a good opportunity to perform the task. With apologies to Ironsides for having to include him in the added duty, Lone watered him thoroughly out of his hat and treated him to a quick scoop of grain before mounting up again. For himself, the former scout made do with some long gulps from his canteen and a handful of beef jerky stuffed into a shirt pocket he could retrieve and chew on while riding. Telling Smith to expect him to be gone for about an hour and to be ready to start out again as soon as he returned, Lone wheeled Ironsides and started his sweep back the way they had just covered.

The air wrapped around him, steadily hotter and heavier as he rode. The increasing humidity it carried seemed an advance warning that the storm to the north was indeed going to eventually hit. Lone cursed at the thought, the way men have been cursing the weather for eons, but there wasn't a damn thing he could do about it.

Other thoughts churned in his head, too, as he steered Ironsides in what he planned to be a narrow, elongated loop around their previous route. Wide enough to spot sign of any followers paralleling them to either side while also keeping sight of their direct path. Pausing periodically to scan wide from the crests of higher ground, Lone otherwise kept on the move. As did his thoughts—mostly on the things Smith had shared with him at their earlier rest stop.

When Bright Moon belatedly recognized Smith as "Sad Eyes" right after Lone had left for Coraville, it opened the floodgates to a number of revelations. Her knowing him stemmed from the times she had briefly seen him at the Flat Falls reservation, in the company of Pike Grogan and the rest of his gang, just prior to Bright Moon and the other selected tribe members being relocated to the Oklahoma Nations. That short amount of time had been enough, however, for Bright Moon to mentally dub him Sad Eyes because he always appeared so melancholy—particularly in sharp contrast to the loud, raucous carrying-on of the other gang members.

Inasmuch as she'd been just one of many faces looking on whenever Grogan brought his men to the Cheyenne camp, Smith had no particular memory of her. But Bright Moon's almost incidental mention and description of those visits did something that nothing prior had cracked—it stirred in Smith some actual recollections of his own from that time. They were somewhat vague and disjointed, but they were there. Finally. For the first time since regaining consciousness after the lightning strike in Asa Hallam's pasture, "Red Smith" could recall a few pieces of his past before then.

"It's nothing all that earth-shaking," he'd said when he related it to Lone. "It's only a few bits and pieces. But it's a start. And I can't help but see it as bittersweet—confirming now, in my own mind, that I for sure was outlaw Wade Avril."

"I think both of us—not to mention Pike Grogan and the bounty hounds he's sicced after your hide—had already pretty much accepted that," Lone reminded him. "But the key to what you just said is the word 'was.' You ain't Wade Avril no more and you're puttin' your neck on the line to, once and for good, break any link to him and what he was."

"Thanks for saying that," Smith had allowed. "I just wish some of these newly remembered pieces added up to something more helpful toward that goal. I recall the visits to the reservation and I recall why...things had gotten too hot for our gang in Montana and Pike decided that a shift over to North Dakota would not only get us shed of the heat on our tails but a new locale would also offer fresh pickings. The notion for a way to help *keep* the heat off our backs came from Weems, who'd had some past dealings with the Cheyenne. He somehow knew Iron Wolf and suggested we could make a deal with him to set up a hideout on reservation land in return for providing goods and supplies to Iron Wolf's people that the agency weasels were always short-changing 'em on... Iron Wolf went for this in a big way. He was just a sub chief, but an ambitious one who wanted to climb higher in the pecking order. Proving he had sources to make available food and other necessities better than the old chiefs could, he quickly gained popularity and power."

Here, Smith had paused in his telling, struggling to pull together more bits of recollection. "This is where it falters, where the pieces start breaking apart and fading again," he grated in frustration. "I remember something about the arrangement with Iron Wolf started to change something I liked less and less. Something I argued with Pike about. But damned if I can say exactly why. I guess somewhere in there may be what Bright Moon saw as my melancholy, my sad eyes." He paused again, his frown deepening. Then he said, "I only remember one other thing with any amount of clarity. The hideout on reservation land...it was a huge cavern on the side of a mountain. Big enough to fit the whole gang, even all our horses and gear. I guess some would call that mighty convenient. But I recall it as one more thing that chafed on me. Living out of a cave like a goddamn animal! What kind of life was that to be leading?"

The bitter question had hung in the air for a long beat. Until Lone said, "Sounds to me like a long, slow buildup to whatever it finally was that ended in your split from the pack and that life. And there's that word again—a split from what *was*. The trick now is to get all the way finished with that life and come out the other side still in one piece."

This had gotten a rueful smile out of Smith. "Well, hell. Now that you've explained it so clear and simple, the rest ought to be a snap. Right?"

No matter how many times he mentally replayed all or portions of the exchange, Lone kept coming back to that grin and that remark. Damned if he didn't like the man more and more. Whatever his real name, whatever he'd been or done in the past, the person now riding stirrup to stirrup beside him on this venture was somebody Lone felt confident he could count on. And if he— or *they*, when it came right down to it—did come out in one piece, then the better future hopefully ahead would be earned and deserved.

———

LONE HAD COMPLETED NEARLY three-quarters of his back trail check without cutting any sign of pursuit. He'd done the western side of his visualized loop, riding south, then had curled around and up and was returning north off to the east of his group's original passage.

That's when he spotted something. Not pursuit. Something else. Something curious enough to make him draw rein and stop for a closer look.

He was again in the midst of the stretched-out expanse of rolling grassland. To the east was more open country, phasing into choppier hills sprinkled with an increasing number of trees. In the distance to the west and north, where the storm clouds were still building, the terrain appeared to once again turn broken and rocky.

The curiosity that had caught Lone's eye lay in the high grass a bit northeast of where he halted. A horse was moving slowly there, angling inward. It was rigged with a harness for pulling a wagon, but there was no wagon in sight. There was an additional rope looped around the animal's neck, trailing back taut in a way that indicated it was nevertheless pulling some fairly heavy object. But whatever it was, was hidden by the tall grass. Moving behind the horse was the bobbing head of a person—either a child or very short adult—also mostly obscured by the grass.

Once he'd deciphered all of this, Lone was then undecided as to whether it rated any more attention from him or if he should just ride on. Rejoining his group and continuing with them, especially with a storm appearing more imminent, was his overriding priority. Yet something about that bobbing head nagged him. If it *was* a child, which seemed most likely, then what in the world was he or she doing clear out here in the middle of nowhere? And what unseen thing was the horse pulling—and to where?

All of a sudden, as Lone continued to watch and ponder, the barely visible head dropped out of sight and stayed that way. And the horse stopped pulling. That was it. Lone couldn't hold back from going to find out what the hell was going on. He swung Ironsides toward where the head had disappeared and heeled the big gray into a gallop.

CHAPTER TWENTY-THREE

IT WAS A GIRL. A LITTLE GIRL ONLY ABOUT ELEVEN YEARS old. She was clad in a simple flower-print dress and sturdy, high-top laced shoes. Her face—wide-eyed, freckled, pug-nosed—was streaked with dirt and sweat. Her reddish blond hair was also sweat-dampened and somewhat matted. This was the vision that gazed up at Lone as he looked down from his saddle after slowing Ironsides and easing up to the spot where he'd seen her go down.

She was sitting on a log, a twelve-foot section of tree trunk about ten inches in diameter that had been chopped down and trimmed of its limbs. It was the hitherto unseen object roped to and being pulled by the horse. Until the girl, exhausted, had called a halt and sat down to rest. Which was how Lone now found her.

"Hi," she said with amazing calm, peering up at him. "Who are you?"

"My name's McGantry," he told her. "How about you?"

"I'm Mae. Mae Hanes." Her gaze turned shrewd. "Are you one of Cotton Thayer's men?"

"Nope. Never heard of him."

She looked relieved. Then her eyes came to rest on the canteen hanging from Lone's saddle. "Do you have enough water that you could maybe spare me a drink, mister?" she asked. "I'm awful thirsty."

"You bet." Lone swung down and pulled the canteen with him. He squatted in front of her and held it out. "Here. Drink all you like, I've got plenty."

Mae tipped up the canteen and gulped thirstily. When she finally lowered it she breathed a big, satisfied sigh. "Boy, that tasted good! It sure wasn't very smart of me not to bring a canteen of my own when I started out."

Lone let his eyes travel up and down the length of the log, noting for the first time the axe tied to it, then back to the girl. "Where, uh, is it you're started out for... or headed back from?" he said.

"I had to go off yonder east to where those trees are," she jabbed a finger, pointing, "in order to find one big enough to trim down and haul back so's I can help Pa pry up our wagon to get the wheel back on. I been trying to hurry, but I got so tuckered I just had to stop and rest a minute."

Lone's eyebrows lifted. "You mean you cut and trimmed this log all by yourself?"

"Had to." Her reply was matter-of-fact. "Ain't nobody else able after our first pry bar gave out and the wagon dropped and busted Pa's leg. And Ma was already laid up sufferin' in labor."

Lone shook his head, stunned. "Whoa. Whoa. That's one hel—er, I mean one heck of a tale of bad luck, gal.

You sayin' you got a busted-down wagon somewhere hereabouts with two hurt folks and nobody else close by to call on?"

"None but Cotton Thayer. His home spread ain't that close anyway, and Pa said he'd rather crawl to Russet town on his belly than have me go to Thayer for help." For a moment, a look of deep despair gripped Mae's open, innocent little face—a face far too young to have to carry the weight of such an expression. But then she quickly turned it into a look of stubborn determination. "We'll be okay as soon as I get this sturdier pole back, and we can use it to lift the wagon so's the wheel can be stuck back on. Pa can hobble around good enough to help manage that. Then we'll be able to hitch ol' Pete again and then make it to town where Granny Mavis can help Ma get that baby out. It's wanting to come early but something's wrong, it's hung up somehow and causing Ma a powerful lot of pain."

"Well, little gal, I think your run of bad luck may have just reached a turn for the better," declared Lone. "Happens I'm travelin' with a group of people who ain't too far away and includes a lady who's kind of a doctor."

"A lady doctor?" Mae echoed dubiously.

"I said 'kind of a doctor'," Lone corrected. "But I've seen her work and, any way you call it, she's good. I say she's the best bet for your ma—and your pa, too, for that matter. In fact, it sounds to me like fetchin' her and takin' her to them is far more important than messin' around anymore right now with this log. We can come back later for it and the horse. If you'll trust me, climb up behind me in the saddle and show me where we can find your folks' wagon—then I'll pronto-like bring the lady I'm talkin' about."

———

Sue Leonard's expression was grim. "The baby is breeched, partially turned in the birth canal," she announced in a tone matching the look on her face. "That's why your wife is in so much pain and unable to complete the delivery."

Jeffrey Hanes seemed to absorb this information with a kind of wooden numbness. He was a man of average height and build, not much past thirty but looking more like forty. His face, though sun and wind-burned, with deep crow-foot wrinkles at the outer corners of his eyes, still retained a hint of rugged hand-someness. But more than anything, his countenance displayed signs of weariness and anguish that reached back farther than just the hard luck events of this day.

He was seated on a wooden crate beside his tilted, minus-one-wheel wagon with his injured left leg extended straight out before him. Sue had just emerged from inside the canopy-covered wagon that was packed to the gills with household furnishings except for a narrow, blanket-padded space where lay the suffering Sara Hanes. Also gathered close outside the wagon, waiting to hear Sue's report after examining the woman, were Smith, Bright Moon, Lone, and Mae. More than an hour had passed since Lone first came upon the little girl. Luckily, after she accepted his offer to help, they had found her parents' wagon only a short distance away. The camp where Smith and the two women awaited Smith's return was just a mile farther. Since they were packed up and ready when he arrived to fetch Sue, everybody came along. And, despite her disdain for Lone and Smith, when Sue heard there were people suffering and in need, she instantly turned into a care-minded individual totally focused on hurrying to do everything she could to help.

But now, based on what she'd found, the question loomed. What *could* she do? Though none of those who'd just heard her rather terse report likely understood the full details, the term "breech birth" was generally recognized as a serious complication that could have dire consequences for both mother and infant.

Shaking off his initial numb reaction to her words, Hanes now gazed plaintively up at Sue and said, "So what do we need to do? Can you help her? Is there time to still get her to Granny Mavis in town?"

Sue's lips pressed momentarily into a tight line before she replied, "I presume this Granny Mavis is a midwife and likely a very good one. But the fact is, when it comes to a breeched baby, there's only so much anybody can do. Not even the most skilled doctor. You must have heard stories about the risks...and the losses."

Hanes leaned his head back and groaned. "Oh, god."

Mae walked over and silently placed a hand on his shoulder.

"But," Sue said, her voice taking on a firmer tone, "that doesn't mean it's beyond hope. I'm willing to try and do everything I possibly can. But one thing is for certain—if she's to have any chance at all, we must act right away. There's absolutely no time to fix that wheel and get her to town. She's suffered in labor too long already."

"What do you need? What can the rest of us do to help?" Lone asked.

For the first time since back in Coraville, Sue looked

at him without her eyes narrowing in disgust. "It's too crowded and too dim in that wagon. I'll need more room, more light. We'll have to make a bed out here in the warm sunlight and lift her gently, gently down onto it."

Lone nodded. "We're on it. Come on, Smith."

"Somebody needs to get a fire going, too, for hot water."

Hanes pushed up off the crate he'd been sitting on, supporting himself on a pickax. "Me and Mae will take care of that," he said. "We'll get a fire blazin' and start fillin' water pots."

Bright Moon stepped up beside Sue, smiling shyly. "I may not fully understand this 'breech' matter of which you speak," she said. "But my aunt was often called upon by other women in our tribe when they were ready to give birth. Sometimes, I accompanied her and learned to assist in small ways. If you want, I will help you, too, however I can."

"That would be wonderful. A breech birth simply means the baby is turned the wrong way, not coming out head first like it's supposed to. In this case it's only turned part way, but it still makes a problem. What I'm going to have to do is reach in and try to turn it properly." It was almost as if Sue was running through the procedure in her mind and sounding it aloud. "As soon as I get it out, that's when I'll need an extra pair of hands. We have a bit of luck going for us in that the baby is a little premature, so kind of small. And the mother has nice, wide birthing hips. It's not much, but we'll take whatever we can get in our favor."

Bright Moon's smile widened encouragingly. "I think the spirits put you here...in this place, at this time...for a reason. I think it is meant for you to be successful in serving the needs of that woman and child."

Sue's gaze cut meaningfully in the direction of Lone. "I only noticed being drug here by a certain big oaf. But if there *are* any spirits looking on now, I sure wouldn't mind them lending a hand."

CHAPTER TWENTY-FOUR

AND THEN THERE WAS ANOTHER LITTLE GIRL.

Whether the spirits indeed played a hand or Sue's touch alone was delicate enough and skilled enough... in the afternoon sunlight beside a broken-down wagon, a joyfully exhausted Sara Hanes now lay holding a tomato-red newborn girl to her breast; and in the minutes prior to taking the teat in her mouth, the infant's squalls had sounded plenty healthy.

Among the disparate group looking on, there was a shared joy and, for the moment at least, a kind of camaraderie. The miracle of birth, especially one as precarious as the one just witnessed, had a way of brightening all but the most dour spirit. Even Sue Leonard was smiling, basking in the overall moment and rightfully feeling some well-deserved satisfaction for the part she had played.

But the professional in her was never very far removed and would not allow her to relax her concerns for too long. "Much as the warmth and sunlight was welcome before," she said, "I think it's important now to get mother and especially the tender-skinned little baby back out of it. Particularly now, with the wind kicking up a bit and blowing around dust and what not. These are, at best, far from sterile conditions. The risks of keeping Sara's bleeding from starting up again and guarding against infection in either of them now become our greatest challenges."

"I take it," Lone responded, "that would best be served by gettin' this wagon fixed and movin' 'em on into town as soon as possible."

"Yes." Sue paused, frowning. "However, I don't recommend a rough wagon ride right away. I think it would be better to wait until tomorrow morning."

"But in case nobody noticed," spoke up Smith, "the wind that's kicking up is pulling with it those storm clouds moving in from the north. They're coming faster and looking meaner right along, and I'd say they're going to arrive packing more than just a drizzle. Is a wagon ride less preferable than getting caught out here in the open in a hard storm?"

Sue gave him a look. "Is it really the storm you're worried about...or is your true concern being delayed longer in this flight your partner," here a thrusting gesture toward Lone, "has been so relentlessly pushing us on?"

Lone spun on her. "Listen, lady," he grated. "I've given up tryin' to convince you we ain't the lowlife varmints you're so hell-bent on believin' we are. But climb down off your high horse and look around and *think* for a damn minute! Who's the one who came upon these unfortunate folks and halted our progress to help 'em in the first place? You ever hear one word outta me or Smith hintin' we mean to leave 'em in a lurch now—before we get 'em squared away as good as we can?"

Sue tried glaring back at him, but couldn't hold it. Her eyes dropped.

Into the ensuing tense silence, Jeffrey Hanes spoke quietly, a little reluctantly. "We got no chance to beat that storm anyway," he said. "Even if we already had the wheel back on, we'd never make it all the way to town before it hit us. I've got some spare canvas tarps in the wagon. I suggest we get Sara and the baby back into the wagon, batten ourselves down as tight as we can, and ride it out right here."

———

FOR THE NEXT HALF HOUR, another flurry of activity took place in and around the Hanes wagon. As soon as they had Sara and the baby returned to their former nest, Lone and Smith dug out the spare tarps and began enclosing the already canopied rig more tightly to give it added protection against wind and rain. While they were doing that, Sue set and splinted Jeffrey's fractured leg. Mae and Bright Moon took the opportunity to go find Pete the horse where Mae and Lone had left him earlier, then fetch him the rest of the way back to the wagon along with the new pry pole tied to him.

All the while the wind gusts grew sharper. And the approaching cloud bank in the north built up higher and darker. Occasional dim pulses of lightning could be seen within the densest parts of the roiling mass, accompanied by low growls of distant thunder.

But before that threat from Mother Nature moved in all the way, another storm of sorts showed up first.

Little Mae was the first one to notice them as she stood holding a pail of water for Pete to drink from. Her posture stiffened, and she pulled the pail away before Pete was all the way finished drinking. "Pa," she called without turning her head to look at him, "there's Thayer riders headin' our way."

Where Mae's gaze stayed locked was on three horsemen approaching from the east, coming at a purposeful gallop.

Lone looked around. There was that name again. Thayer. Mae had mentioned a "Cotton Thayer" twice back when Lone first encountered her. Neither time had her voice sounded favorable toward the individual. Nor did her tone ring any differently now.

Jefferey Hanes once again pushed up from the wooden crate he'd been resting on. He grimaced briefly at the awkwardness presented by his injured right leg, now splinted with wooden laths pried from the side of the wagon and bound tightly in place by strips of cloth. But he made it upright, once again aided by the pickax serving as a crutch, and stepped around the wagon to look off the same direction as Mae. It took him only a glance before he said to the girl, "Mae, go get my rifle from the under the seat up front of the wagon."

As Mae hurried in response, a frowning Smith, who'd also been watching and listening from where him and Lone were having cups of coffee over by the campfire, edged up closer alongside the former scout. "What's this all about?" he asked in a low voice.

Lone gave a faint shake of his head. "Not sure exactly. But it's pretty clear those riders comin' in ain't looked on as good news by the Hanses."

"Yeah, that much is plain." Smith's gaze tracked the

approaching trio for a beat before adding, "Is there some kind of unwritten law that says trouble-making jackasses always have to show up in threes?"

Lone grinned. "Never gave it much thought before... but, now that you mention it, I guess that's what we been encounterin' of late, ain't it?"

"Uh-huh. But it's odds we've managed to handle okay, so I suppose I shouldn't complain."

"All the same, let's spread out a little and keep an eye on whatever's shapin' up here. Give Hanes a chance to have his say."

A handful of minutes later, the three riders reined up close before where Hanes now stood awaiting them, leaning slightly on the pickax under his left arm and holding the Henry repeater Mae had brought him down along his right hip. After delivering the rifle, the girl had retreated back around the end of the wagon to stand between Sue and Bright Moon who'd been looking in on her mother and new sister.

The middle rider of the newcomers halted his mount a bit ahead of the other two, marking himself as the bunch's leader/spokesman. He was a sturdy-looking specimen, wide through the shoulders though trim-waisted, appearing well into his twenties with a V-shaped face accentuated by a wide-brimmed, cream-colored sombrero cinched tight on his head by the chin strap knotted high on his throat. The sombrero's big brim flapped in the gusting wind, as did the curly strands of dark hair spilling down over his forehead. He, like his companions, wore standard wrangler attire, though all were more heavily armed than most would consider common. The other two men looked a little older, wirier, and more weathered in their whiskery faces, and each sported a battered Stetson rather than the headgear choice of the sombrero wearer.

As expected, it was the latter who initiated the talking. "We saw the smoke from your fire," he said. "What the hell's goin' on here, Hanes?"

"If your eyesight's good enough to have seen smoke blowing in all this wind," Hanes replied evenly, "then surely you ought to be able to make out that we've run up on some trouble here, Fletcher. The busted-down wagon, my hobbled leg...ain't that plain enough?"

A corner of Fletcher's lip lifted in what looked like a well-practiced sneer. "So I see it. So what? Ain't none of it no skin off my nose. Cotton sent me and Lefty and Art here to check and make sure you'd cleared out like you was supposed to. We found your empty cabin and buildings right enough, but here you are, still on Thayer property. That's the only thing we see that we give a hang about...and we ain't likin' the sight of it none at all."

"You think I like being in this fix?" Hanes came back. "Not only that, but I got a wife and newborn baby in the—"

"We not only don't give a damn about *seein'* your troubles," Fletcher cut him off, "but we don't want to hear about 'em neither! The only thing we care about is you and your family clearin' your sorry asses off Thayer property. The property you failed to keep up tax payments on, so you lost your rights to somebody who could. You was given two weeks to vacate. That ended noon today, and it's well past that. Now get a move on before you rile us all the more!"

Lone had heard enough. Cutting a sidelong glance over at Smith, seeing him start to make his way around the other side of the wagon, Lone moved up to stand beside Hanes. Looking up at the man called Fletcher, he drawled calmly, "Just what is it you propose Mr. Hanes should do? Stick a feather up that horse's ass and *fly* his wagon outta here?"

Fletcher's mouth sagged open, and for a minute, he seemed unable to find words to respond. One of the other riders—the "Lefty" Fletcher had referred to, judging by the side the man's hogleg was holstered on— tucked his head down to hide a snicker.

Finally, accompanied by a fierce scowl, Fletcher managed to blurt, "Who the hell are you?"

The calmness in his tone was suddenly gone, replaced by the same flintiness now showing in his narrowed eyes, Lone said, "Who I am is mostly none of your business, buster. All you need to know is that I'm a friend to this family, and the way you and your big mouth are disrespectin' 'em is startin' to annoy the piss outta me."

Fletcher's own eyes took on a menacing gleam. "Is that so? Is annoying you supposed to be something for me to worry about? And I'm includin' that shifty-eyed pal of yours slinkin' around the back side of the wagon. You figure a couple do-gooder saddle tramps is a threat to me and *my* pals?"

"You like the odds, go ahead and play 'em," Lone grated.

Fletcher chuckled nastily. "You simple-minded fool. You're up against a hell of a lot more than just the cards on the table in front of you. You mess with us, you know who you're *really* messin' with?"

"Cotton Thayer, you mean?"

This earned a smug grunt. "You know about him, eh?"

"Heard the name for the first time in my life just a couple hours ago," Lone told him. "But I know him all too well. I've run into Cotton Thayers all over the high plains and from one end of the Rockies to the other. Enough of 'em so's I can paint a picture with only their fat, greedy faces changin'. Land gobblers who can never wrap their arms enough and never get tired of squeezin' out the little operations, no matter how inconsequential. Oh yeah, and they all hire crews of men that include a handful of hard cases who think they're some kind of mini army sworn to protect the almighty brand...got it about right?"

Fletcher trotted out his sneer again. "What you got is a real smart mouth, you know that?"

Lone said nothing. His answer was a hard, flat stare.

Everything but the gusting wind seemed to freeze for a long beat. A growl of thunder, the loudest one yet, rolled in from the north.

The older wrangler who had suppressed a snicker earlier, cleared his throat and said, "Not to horn in, Race. But ain't none of us showin' much in the way of smarts by just sittin' here with that storm breathin' down our necks."

Without taking his eyes off Lone, Fletcher snarled over his shoulder, "You crawfishin' on me, Lefty?"

"You know better than that. Make the call, I'll damn well back you. All I'm sayin' is, whatever we're gonna do, let's get on with it. It's plain this bunch ain't goin' nowhere ahead of the storm. But that don't mean we gotta stick around and end up like drowned rats, too. There's always tomorrow."

Fletcher's scowl seemed to deepen for a moment. But then it gradually eased, and his mouth slanted into a sly smile. "Maybe that ain't a half bad idea, you old bronc stomper. Maybe it'd be fun to let Mother Nature do some of the work for us. Like you said, we can always come back tomorrow to deal with whatever trash she don't blow or wash away."

"If you think it's such a good idea," said Hanes, "don't let us keep you."

Fletcher snorted. "I see some second-hand courage and smart-mouthedness has rubbed off on you, eh? We'll see if it's still there in the morning."

"Count on it."

"If you have any brains at all, you won't be around for me to find out," Fletcher warned. Then he cut his eyes back to Lone. "And that goes double for you, mister. You and your do-gooder partner both. I see either one of you hereabouts after this—on Thayer property or not—we will have some serious business to finish."

"Always hated to leave a thing hangin' fire," Lone told him. "I got some movin' on to do in the near term. But first chance I get, I'll be happy to swing back this way and accommodate you."

"You do that. I can be a patient man when I need to be."

With that, Fletcher wheeled his mount, and him and the other two Thayer riders went pounding off the way they'd come.

CHAPTER TWENTY-FIVE

FROM WHERE HE SQUATTED AT THE SPOT BESIDE THE nameless stream where Lone's party had stopped for their early morning break, Chico Racone swept his eyes over the ground a final time before lifting his face to meet the questioning looks of Tobe Medford and the others. "Six, maybe seven hours ago," Chico reported, "they rested here. But only briefly."

"Well, shit," muttered Kid Memphis. "I figured we woulda closed the gap on 'em more than that by now."

Chico straightened up, saying, "They are the ones picking the course and setting the pace. And they are setting a pretty steady one. What's more, they are starting to disguise their tracks whenever they can."

"So what?" scoffed the Kid. "I can make out their sign most of the time. And even after they fade for a bit, when tracks show again, they're always headed due north. Seems plain that's the way they mean to keep goin'."

"Uh-huh. But what if they take a notion to veer off somewhere?" Bishop Ikes said. "They do that and we just charge north without worrying so much about sign, like you seem to be wanting, what then, knothead? How much of a gap is that gonna close?"

The Kid's eyes flared. "Watch who you're callin' a knothead, mister. I don't like it, understand?"

Ikes smiled thinly. "I'll be sure to keep that in mind."

"Knock it off, you two," Medford growled. "We're gonna continue on with Chico tracking sign. But first, we'll hold here for a little bit. Give the horses a breather, let 'em drink after they've cooled some."

"We needin' a break so soon?" the Kid asked. "I ain't tired, nohow."

"Good for you. I still say the horses need a breather," Medford said.

"Relax, Kid." Chico displayed a tolerant smile. "We will start gaining ground as the day wears on. When the heat comes, those we follow will have to give added consideration to their heavily-loaded pack animal and the two women traveling with them."

This drew sharp attention from Johnny Case. "From the sign here, Chico, both women *were* still with them when they made this stop?"

"That's right. Real plain. Moccasin prints for the Indian girl and Miss Sue's sharp-heeled shoe prints."

Johnny breathed a sigh of relief. "Thank God for that much—for Vance Veldon being so wrong in his certainty they would kill Sue the very first chance they got. As long as she's alive, there's hope."

"Just 'cause she made it this far," Ikes drawled, "don't mean no guarantee they won't still—"

"Damn you, don't say it!" James Risen blurted, cutting him off. "You think the horrible possibilities of what those men might do to my sister aren't already planted deeply enough in our thoughts? They don't need to be repeated anymore—not by Vance Veldon or anyone else!"

"Ooo. Touchy, touchy." Ikes' mouth curved into a taunting smile.

"Damn it, Ikes. Lay off," said Medford.

Ikes shrugged his shoulders dismissively. "Sure. No problem." His smile stayed in place, though, as he let his gaze drift slowly over Risen, taking in the disheveled clothes and rumpled hair, the deathly pale face and red-rimmed eyes. "Ain't like I'll have to bite my tongue for very long. When the day wears on and the heat starts to build, like Chico said...I don't figure Mr. Touchy here will be able to keep up with the rest of us, anyway."

Red-rimmed though they were, there was still a spark of stubborn fire in Risen's eyes. "We'll see about that, mister. We'll just see."

———

WHEN THE FULL force of the storm descended on the Hanes wagon, all gathered in and around it were as ready as possible. The inside had been re-stacked and re-arranged, with some items needing to be put out to the mercy of the weather in order to fit all of the women. This not only provided their best chance to keep dry, but the crowding close together also created a cocoon of warmth around mother and newborn that was an important guard against the sudden temperature drop carried by the wind and rain. The men made do on the ground underneath, each wrapped in a thick, waterproof soogan and covered over additionally with a final piece of tarp. The horses were picketed close along the south side of the wagon, using it as a meager buffer against the driving wind.

Pitchfork lightning filled the roiling sky, and rain slammed down in sheets. The roar of the wind at times seemed almost as loud as the belching, rumbling thunder. The canvas wrapping added by Lone and Smith held fast, but was tested vigorously; flapping and slapping wildly under the gusts hell-bent on trying to tear them loose.

The women in the wagon huddled in grim silence. Brave little Mae took one of her brand new sister's tiny hands in hers and held it firmly but gently while she made comforting cooing sounds to the infant.

Under the wagon, the man teetering on the razor's edge between being Red Smith or Wade Avril was enduring torment from the storm like none of the others. It was as if the brilliantly sizzling lightning flashes were slicing into him and gouging out things that had been deeply buried. Memories. Recollections he had at one time groped desperately for but then had eschewed, never wanting them to resurface. Yet now they were. Bursting forth. Everything. Being caught in a storm out of doors again for the first time since the jolt that had erased everything was now having some kind of reverse effect. It was all flooding back, filling his mind and drenching him in a cold sweat inside his soogan. And there wasn't a damn thing he could do to stop it.

————

SOME MILES AWAY, in the bunkhouse at Cotton Thayer's CT Ranch headquarters, with the storm raging outside, another man was also wrestling with a recollection. But in his case he not only was welcoming it but was probing it even deeper and eagerly trying to share it with others. "It was him, I tell you. I'm positive of it now," insisted Art Tory, the final member—the one who hadn't done any talking—of the three riders who had visited the Hanes wagon just before the storm. "I knew I ought to recognize him from somewhere, but couldn't quite place him. But now I can—it was Lone McGantry, I'm certain sure."

Race Fletcher cocked an eyebrow. "And? That a name supposed to mean something?"

"I've heard of him," said Lefty Sneed. "Made a name for himself as an Injun fighter and Army scout mostly down through Nebraska and some into Colorado, back when the tribes were still actin' up. Was a pal of Bill Cody if I remember right."

"Uh-huh. That's the one," Tory agreed. "Since his scouting days, he's been a drifter and a bit of a hardcase. Never on the wrong side of the law, though, far as I know. I saw him in Deadwood a couple years back where he was working with that Army outfit that ran down the Scorch Bannon gang. That's where I recognized him from."

Fletcher made a show of looking unimpressed. "So now we all know who the big, square-faced galoot who stuck his nose in our business was. What difference does it make?"

Tory's eyes took on an excited gleam and his tone became hushed, conspiratorial. "I'll tell you what difference having McGantry right under our noses makes. Leastways, what a whopping big difference it *might* make!"

The three men had only just entered the bunkhouse

a few minutes prior, having ducked in barely ahead of
the storm. They were clustered around their bunks
toward the far end of the rectangular building, shed-
ding their outerwear and boots, getting comfortable
with plans to hunker in for the night. Other wranglers
from the CT crew, having settled in earlier when they
saw the storm approaching, were mostly gathered in the
common area at the front of the long room, playing
cards or just lounging about, smoking and sipping
coffee, chin wagging until it was time for grub.

The three newer arrivals were segregated by enough
distance so that Tory's lowered voice—especially with
the rain drumming on the roof and the other men not
paying any particular attention to them anyway—fell
only within the earshot of Fletcher and Sneed.
"Remember a couple days ago," he continued, "when all
that talk went rippin' through the saloons and got
carried by all the freight haulers and stagecoach crews...
how Pike Grogan was offering to pay big bounty money
to anybody bringin' him proof they had snuffed out the
wick of Wade Avril, his former right-hand man who'd
double-crossed him?"

Fletcher snorted. "Hell yeah. I remember. Practically
every ranch crew in the territory lost a man or two—not
to mention a few clerks and barflies from some of the
towns—who packed up their guns and took a notion in
their chowder-brained heads to ride out on the hunt.
We even lost a couple men ourselves, didn't we? Those
hillbilly brothers?"

"That's right. The Peecher boys." Sneed wagged his
head. "They wasn't no big loss as wranglers, though.
They might have been hellacious moonshiners or
squirrel hunters back in Kain-tuck or somewhere, but

they sure as hell wasn't cut out to be cowboys. And if they happened to run up against the likes of Wade Avril, I highly doubt their squirrel huntin' experience did 'em much good then, neither."

Fletcher chuckled dryly. "All them gun-totin' fools rode off with dollar signs dancin' in their eyes and the only doggone thing any of 'em accomplished, far as I ever heard, was to make every red-haired man for a hundred square miles either shave his head or wear a hat pulled down to his ears day and night so's he wouldn't get mistook and end up blasted for being 'Wild Red' Avril."

"Yeah, there's truth in all you say," agreed Tory. "Lot of foolhardy men—and plenty of professional bounty hunters, too—charged out after that blood money."

"And not a damn one of 'em has earned a red cent." Fletcher chuckled again. "Matter of fact, they all gotta be in the hole for the jobs they left and the money they spent on gear and extra cartridges."

"That don't mean a few of 'em didn't get a chance to burn some powder, though," said Sneed, his own mouth curving into a wry grin. "Way I heard, a couple different bunches found themselves stompin' over the same ground down Chadron way and ended up blastin' hell out of one another."

"Yeah, I heard that too," Tory snapped, frowning impatiently. "But you fellas are missin' the whole point I'm trying to make."

"Well, make it then," Fletcher told him. "If cookie calls out grub is ready, I'm gonna go eat no matter if you're still mumble-stumblin' around or not. And how the hell did you jump from this McGantry hombre you started out talkin' about to the bounty on Wade Avril, anyway?"

"That's just it! There's a connection between the two if you take time to think and remember." Tory paused long enough to toss a quick glance toward the men down in the common area, making sure none of them were starting to pay any attention, then lowered his voice a notch and continued. "When Avril first popped up again a few days ago—after disappearing last summer when he originally broke with the Grogan gang—it was in some pissant little town down near North Platte. Remember? Avril gunned down Granger Weems and a couple other Grogan men who just happened to wander in and recognize him. But the thing is, there was another fella in the joint that day who threw down and aided Avril in comin' out on top... and that fella was none other than Lone McGantry!"

Sneed, who had plopped down on the edge of his bunk to pull off his boots, now leaned forward in a show of increased interest. "Yeah, I recollect hearin' something about that, too. Seems McGantry has started up a small horse ranch or some such in the area. Like you said, he happened to be in the place where Weems and those other two braced Avril. Didn't like the lopsided odds, so he stepped in, to even 'em up some."

"Another case of Mr. Do-gooder stickin' his nose in," Fletcher spat. "Sounds like a bad habit he flat can't control."

"Call it what you will," Tory said. "Thing I can't help wondering is—what if McGantry is *continuing* not to like the odds stacked against Avril, what with the army of bounty hunters sicced on him and all, and is sticking with Wild Red to help him try and ride clear of 'em."

Fletcher scowled. "I thought you said McGantry stayed on the right side of the law. If that's the case, how could he square going to so much trouble to help a notorious character like Avril? Sidin' him in a spur of the moment situation is one thing. But after knowing the full story—meanin' how Avril, by all reports, was a desperado and killer second only to Grogan himself— that oughta color things a whole different shade, oughtn't it? Just 'cause the two of 'em had a falling out and Grogan is the one lookin' to settle the score with blood, don't make Avril cleansed of what he was or all the bad he did. You know damn well there's still a whole batch of law dogs over in Montana chompin' at the bit to get their paws on *any* of Grogan's outfit, ol' Wild Red bein' prime among 'em."

"There's salt in what you say, I can't deny it," Tory allowed. Yet, at the same time, his expression showed a stubborn refusal to leave it at that. "But while it's true McGantry ain't ever been branded an outlaw, some of the stories I've heard about him make it plain that neither is he above goin' against the grain of authority if he believes strongly enough he's in the right. In other words, I wouldn't rule out that, havin' saved Avril's bacon once, he might not still see the man as gettin' a raw deal where Grogan is concerned and so be willin' to help him get clear of that with a promise of getting square with the law later on."

Fletcher sliced a hand dismissively through the air. "Bah. That sounds way too far- fetched. You'd have to grease that chunk of gristle with a *lot* of gravy to get me to swallow it!"

"I don't know," Sneed muttered, looking somber, thoughtful. "I've heard some of those stories about

McGantry, too. How he was known to go kinda rogue, borderline insubordinate a time or two back when he was scoutin' for the Army...and you gotta wonder, if he has hisself a horse ranch clear down by North Platte, what in blazes brings him up here to our neck of the woods? Then there was that other fella, who we took for his partner, skulkin' around behind the wagon where we never got a good look at him..."

Fletcher's eyes grew wide and danced back and forth between the other two men. "Jesus Christ. I don't believe this. You mean both of you actually think there's a chance that other hombre might be Wade Avril...and you crazy fools are formulatin' the notion we oughta make a try for the bounty on him?"

CHAPTER TWENTY-SIX

THE STORM HAD PASSED ON BY MIDNIGHT, LEAVING IN ITS wake a clear sky hung with a fat, bright moon and filled with an array of particularly brilliant stars. It was as if the churning deluge from earlier had scoured and rinsed everything to a gleaming new sheen.

On the sodden expanse of rolling grassland, the hulk of the Hanes wagon stood out like a proud, stubborn survivor. Its canvas wrappings were wind-battered and sagging, here and there heavy with captured pockets of water, yet all remaining intact. The cluster of horses bunched tight along one side stood tall and steady, some with heads hanging low, nostrils expelling visible puffs of breath in the chill air. Their damp backs and rumps were shiny-looking in the silver-blue wash of star and moonlight.

A full three hours before daybreak, the shadowy, silently moving shape of a man slipped away from the wagon and began moving among the horses. He clucked softly, soothingly to all of them, even as he singled out one animal in particular.

And then, from elsewhere in the murkiness, a somewhat hushed but not nearly as soft voice said, "What the devil are you doing, Smith?"

The man so addressed hesitated only a moment before going ahead and finishing the act of slipping a bridle over the head of the horse that had been his mount for the past several days. Then, proceeding calmly to fasten the bridle in place, he answered over his shoulder, "What does it look like I'm doing? I'm pulling foot, Lone. I decided it's time and past time that I cut clear of you and the others and went on to take care of my business on my own."

Lone reverse melted out of the shadows of the wagon, scowling fiercely. "What the hell are you talkin' about? What's got into you?"

"Reality. Common sense. Call it what you want. All I know is that it's time for me to get away from anybody with a shred of decency in them. It all came to me clear last night—all of it, you understand? Like the thunder and lightning picked me up, then shook me and gouged into me until every one of the poisonous memories of who I really am got released. That little surface scratch that Bright Moon nudged loose before? That wasn't *shit*!" Smith's face turned ugly with torment. "Who I was as Wade 'Wild Red' Avril and the things I did...I deserve to be hunted down like a rabid dog!"

"Even by the likes of Pike Grogan?" Lone said icily.

"What difference does it make by who? A rabid dog has to be put down. Period."

"What about all that talk of ridin' to the bullet—the one that has your name on it—and rammin' it back at whoever's aimin' it your way?"

Smith shook his head in a hopeless way. "That was

before I realized the full truth about myself. Don't make no difference if you turn a rabid dog back loose with the rest of his mangy pack or put him in with a batch of cuddly little puppies—he can't change, can't be fixed. There's only one thing he deserves and that's to be cut down before he spreads more of his poison."

"Damn it," Lone snapped. "You want to talk deserves? I deserve more of an explanation than that before I let you just cut and run."

Smith's expression went hard, challenging. "Before you *let* me?"

Lone struggled visibly to hold himself in check. He tossed an uneasy glance back toward the wagon. Then, exhaling a ragged breath and keeping his voice low, he said, "Look, can you at least spare me a couple minutes to try and understand this more? And can we step off a little way so's not to disturb the others?"

Smith didn't move for a minute. Then, still glaring, he eased out away from the horses and tromped off a dozen paces. Lone followed after him.

"I'll tell you right now," Smith proclaimed at the outset, "all you're doing is losing sleep and wasting your breath. You're not gonna change my mind."

"Because you had a lousy bad dream?" Lone wanted to know.

"It wasn't a dream, goddammit! That's the problem," Smith groaned. "It was reality. The reality of who I truly am—all the memories that have been bottled up these past months suddenly busting loose and landing on me like a ton of bricks. Don't you get it? I'm outlaw scum who has robbed and killed and cheated and abused women...is that somebody you *want* to stick around and ride the river with?"

"What I want is to finish the job I set out to do with the fella I set out to do it with," said Lone. "And that fella was somebody lookin' to right his former wrongs and move on *past* 'em...not jump at the first chance he got to backslide and wallow in a puddle of self-pity."

"To hell with you!"

"Sure. To hell with me. And to hell with the Hallams. And to hell with all the other people back in Sarben who were willin' to give you the chance you now all of a sudden don't want to give yourself...oh yeah, I almost forgot to include Judith, the gal you left waitin'—".

Smith's fist shot out in a looping right hook. But Lone was ready. He leaned in, blocked the attempted punch with his left forearm, and brought his own right fist up in an uppercut that landed hard under the point of Smith's chin. The blow snapped Smith's head back. He staggered, slipped on the still-wet grass, and spilled to the ground.

Lone advanced to where he'd fallen, stood over him with feet planted wide and fists hanging at his sides. Ready if Smith showed signs of wanting to continue the fight, hoping that wouldn't be the case.

Smith looked up at him with what was becoming a too-familiar glare. "You keep Judith's name out of this, damn you, or I'll punch you again."

Lone spat to one side. "You didn't make it the first time, you horse's ass. What'd I do, jar your memory loose all over again?"

Smith backhanded blood away from his mouth. "Don't flatter yourself. You don't hit that hard."

They traded smoldering looks for a long count. Until Smith pushed to a sitting position, breathing out a ragged sigh of his own. He raised his knees and rested his forearms atop them. His glare faded, replaced once more by the tormented look. "I don't know what else to say, Lone...I feel all torn up inside. In my head, in my gut. All those clearer recollections of what I was, the things I did...it makes me sick. I don't see how I can—"

"Knock it off," Lone interrupted sharply. "Ain't we been through this already once before? That word once more—*was*. You're doing it again, dwellin' on what you was, things you did at another time under different circumstances. Comes down to it, it's mostly up to you whether you want to get over that or not. Some things a man can't run away from or ride around, he's gotta plow *through* and then live with what's on the other side."

"You really believe that?"

"You think you're the only hombre with some black deeds in his past who fought to break free of 'em and start over clean?" Lone's own expression turned grim. "After my folks were massacred by a pack of Pawnees when I was an infant, I grew up with a powerful Injun-hatin' chip on my shoulder. *All* Indians, you under-stand? I didn't care whether they was Pawnee, Crow, Ute, Sioux, any tribe you can name—I wanted to see every one of the red devils dead. And, since hostilities with several of the tribes was still goin' on when I was old enough to ride out with the Cavalry, I proceeded to do my damnedest to make that happen. Won't go into specifics, but I did things durin' that time that made me as much or more of a savage than those I set out after. I got my head straight in time and have moved on. But if I allowed it, I have plenty of bloody regrets I could keep beatin' myself up over."

Neither man said anything right away.

And then, faintly, from within the wagon, a baby's wailing drifted through the stillness.

Lone jabbed a thumb. "There. There, goddammit, is something good and decent we both had a hand in. No matter what else we've done or been, we came along and took the time to help this family and that little baby. I ain't discounting the important part Miss Sue played by any means, but *we* still allowed it. And the job ain't done. No matter what else we got goin' on, we need to take time to help get the wagon fixed and that mother and baby on into town and into a warm, clean bed with a roof over their heads. Or are you bound and determined to just chuck the whole good and decent try, and instead let the weight of that fella you once *was* go ahead and drag you down and away?"

Smith's eyes narrowed but never quite reached the glare from earlier. He exhaled loudly out through his nostrils. "You annoying pain in the ass. There you go, making sense and being right yet again." He reached up. "Give me a hand back to my feet. We still got a couple hours to daybreak. Not enough time to try going back to sleep and we've probably woke up everybody else by now anyway. There's adequate light to see for getting started on that blasted wheel, wouldn't you say? How about we get after it? The quicker we can get Mrs. Hanes and her little girl into town, the better."

CHAPTER TWENTY-SEVEN

"WELL, HELL. THEY DONE CLEARED OUT ALREADY." So declared Lefty Sneed from where he, Fletcher, and Tory sat their horses a hundred yards short of the spot occupied by the broken-down Hanes wagon the previous evening. The sun was barely an hour old above the eastern horizon, the morning air still crisp from last night's chill.

"You sure we got the right spot?" Tory questioned.

"Yeah, we got the right damned spot," Fletcher grunted. "Don't you see the smoke wisps rising up from where they made a morning campfire? That sure ain't left from yesterday, not after all the rain last night."

The three men gigged their mounts up closer to the ring of smoldering ashes. Frowning down at the sight, Sneed said, "Man, they must've rolled out at the first glimmer of light. Guess we put some almighty fear in 'em after all."

"That, I guess, and maybe some of what Hanes said about his wife and newborn," suggested Tory. "Mrs. Hanes had been all bellied out last time we saw her, remember? Could be there was some extra hurry for her needin' to get into town and see a doctor."

"Could be. Except there ain't no doctor in Russet no more—not since ol' Doc Fromier kicked the bucket last winter," said Sneed.

"Oh, yeah. I forgot about that."

Sneed rubbed his jaw. "Not that he was much of a sawbones to begin with. Leastways not by my reckoning. The way he wheezed and coughed all the time—how the hell could anybody trust a so-called doctor who couldn't even cure his own self?"

"Jesus Christ, you two!" Fletcher exclaimed. "Who gives a damn about doctors or knocked-up wives or any of that shit? I didn't listen to you blabber half the night, then drag my ass out here at the crack of dawn for that. We're supposed to be after the bounty on Wade Avril, remember? So why and where Hanes and his brood went don't matter squat. Where did this McGantry character and his partner, who *might* be Avril, go? That's what I want to know."

"Okay, okay," responded Sneed. "I don't claim to be no kind of big-time tracker, but I *can* read sign after a fashion. Especially when they're as fresh as the ones leading away from here." He jabbed a finger down at the ground. "Plain to see the wagon rolled off toward town. And five horses followed along with it."

Fletcher frowned. "*Five* horses? How does that fit with just two hombres—McGantry and the one we're figurin' to be Avril?"

"That I can't say. I'm just tellin' you what's there on the ground."

"When we were here yesterday," spoke up Tory, "there *was* five horses picketed off to the side. In addition to

Hanes' wagon nag, I'm sayin'. And I noticed some gear stacked on the ground that didn't look to be any part of Hanes' stuff. Must be those extra horses are pack animals."

"Three pack animals for two men? That'd be a bit much, don't you think?" Fletcher questioned.

"If one of 'em is Avril and McGantry's siding him for whatever reason, they could be planning a far run to get clear of Grogan and the bounty he's put out. Or maybe just going to ground for a long spell." Tory pursed his lips. "Either way, it could account for stocking up heavy, meaning to avoid any re-supply stops so's not to risk being spotted anywhere."

Sneed looked thoughtful. "Another possibility could be the old trick of owlhoots on the dodge sometimes bringing a spare horse so's they got a remount in case it comes to out-runnin' a posse—or, in this case, a pack of bounty hunters—tight on their heels."

"Okay," Fletcher said grudgingly. "I guess one of those explanations must fit. The thing now is being able to stick with the tracks until we catch up and find out for sure. Mainly, find out if any of 'em lead to Wade Avril."

"Followin' the fresh wagon marks shouldn't be hard at all, especially since we're pretty sure they're headed for town." Sneed paused, his forehead puckering some. "If the horses branch off and take to more broken ground, though, that could get a little trickier."

"Well, it's the horse riders we're after," said Tory. "And, for reasons I mentioned just a minute ago, it seems like Avril would want to steer clear of going into town for fear of being recognized."

"But remember him and McGantry seem bent on

playing do-gooder roles when it comes to helping the Haneses," Sneed pointed out. "Could be they'd risk it, briefly, just to make sure Mrs. Hanes and the baby and so forth got situated good and proper."

"Especially if they have any idea what a bunch of dreary old mossyhorns Russet is full of," snorted Fletcher. "Anybody there did recognize Avril, they wouldn't have the onions to do nothing about it. For sure not the law. Creaky ol' Marshal Philpot? He ain't worth shit for the few hours of the day he manages to be sober, and after about three each afternoon, he's sloshed to the gills." Fletcher gave another derisive snort. "Remember that time he tried to arrest us for disturbin' the peace and we pantsed him? Left him standing right there in the middle of the Cork 'N Bottle saloon with his britches, gun belt, and the wholes works puddled around his ankles?"

Sneed made a sour face. "Yeah, and I remember the royal ass-chewin' we got from Cotton over it, too."

Fletcher's expression clouded at the memory. "Well, if we haul in that twenty-five hundred dollar bounty for Wild Red, then we won't have to worry no more about ass-chewings from Cotton Thayer or anybody else, will we? We'll set ourselves up high and mighty and then *we'll* be the ones gnawing on the asses of jaspers hoppin' to do our bidding."

"Comes to that twenty-five hundred dollars," Tory said, eyebrows pinching together slightly, "I want it as bad as anybody. But what it's gonna take to claim it? Either of you besides me find that kinda disgustin'?"

"Delivering Avril's head in a sack, you mean?"

"Yeah."

"Hell," said Fletcher. "For twenty-five hundred dollars, I'd deliver his *sack* in a sack!"

Sneed grinned slyly. "We could aim for the big reward—the five grand—by delivering him alive."

"Never mind," said Tory. "I'd rather be disgusted and alive than take a bullet and end up dead for my trouble. Gonna be hard enough gettin' close enough to gun Avril down without trying to brace him. All reports say he's hellacious fast. And I don't know about McGantry's gun speed, but he damn sure knows how to use one plenty good."

"You leave that big square-faced bastard to me," Fletcher grated. "I don't care if there ain't no money ridin' on his ass, I still mean to leave him toes down somewhere."

"Well, we ain't gonna get nowhere or catch up with nobody by sittin' here jawin' about it," said Sneed. He wheeled his mount. "Come on, let's find out where these tracks take us."

———

THE TOWN of Russet lay in a shallow valley just off the western edge of the rolling grassland. Beyond, the land rose in higher hills with rocky ridges poking up through lines of thick tree growth. The community in between was modest in size, laid out in a fairly orderly pattern, mostly wood-frame houses with a half dozen tall, false fronts marking the buildings of the central business district. Two different church spires rose up a reasonable distance apart, and a meandering creek curved around the southern end of everything. All in all, it looked like a friendly, welcoming place.

But not for men on the run.

Lone called his party to a halt atop the long, gentle slope that led down into Russet. Reining Ironsides up alongside the wagon where Jeffrey and Mae sat in the driver's box, he said to them, "Okay, folks. You'll be able to make it fine from here. But me and my friends need to part ways with you now."

Hanes' forehead wrinkled. "I'm sorry to hear that. Can't you come on in the rest of the way and stay at least for a little while? Rest a bit, have a hot meal?"

"Please," Mae was quick to add.

Lone reached out and gently ruffled the girl's hair. "I'd like to, honey. I really would. But it ain't in the cards at this time. Not for me, Smith, and Bright Moon." His gaze returned to Hanes. "Miss Sue will be stayin' with you, though. But if you'll hold for just a couple minutes, I'd like a word with her before we head off."

Looking somewhat puzzled, Hanes replied, "Sure. Whatever you need."

Lone swung Ironsides to the rear of the wagon, where Sue was riding inside with Sara and the baby. He dismounted, left the gray ground-reined, stepped around and tapped on the tailgate, saying, "Like to speak with you, ma'am, if you'll step out for a minute."

She emerged and hopped down, wearing her own puzzled expression. Lone gestured, and they walked off a dozen or so yards, coming to a stop beside a low bush sprouting spring buds of some flower Lone didn't recognize. He could feel the eyes of Smith and Bright Moon looking on from where they sat their horses back by the wagon.

But the only eyes he cared about at the moment

were the soft brown ones of Sue Leonard looking up at him.

In a quiet voice, she said, "Is this where you put a bullet in my head to keep me from being able to testify against you?"

The question gave Lone a bit of a start. But the only outward response he showed was a flat, level gaze before saying, "Do you really think, for one second, there's any chance of that?"

She tried to hold his eyes but, once again, couldn't. Looking down, she said in an even quieter voice, "No, of course not. No matter how angry I felt toward you, or how much I loathed you for dragging me off the way you did, I-I somehow never felt fearful you would harm me." Now, her eyes lifted, and her voice grew stronger. "In fact, I not only sensed you wouldn't harm me, but I felt a certainty you would *prevent* any harm from befalling me."

A corner of Lone's mouth quirked up. "Kinda knocks the bottom out of me comin' across as a fearsome bad hombre, don't it?"

"I didn't say you *couldn't* be fearsome," Sue countered.

"Then why didn't you say something to the Haneses about me and Smith holdin' you as our captive, our hostage?"

"In case you didn't notice, I—and all the rest of us, for that matter—have been just a little bit busy ever since you took me to the Hanes wagon. Besides, what hope could they offer me when they had a whole plate filled to overflowing with their own hard luck?"

"What about those three proddy cowpokes who came callin' just before the storm? Didn't they strike you as possible saviors—hearty souls who'd jump at the chance to rescue a damsel in distress?"

Sue wrinkled her nose in disgust. "Apparently, you've never heard the old saying that goes, 'from the frying pan into the fire.' Any damsel who found herself in the hands of obvious pigs like those three would soon find herself anything *but* rescued."

"Guess stackin' up favorable against trash like them," Lone allowed, "sorta balances out not bein' took as all that fearsome."

Sue looked at him with a gaze suddenly softer than any before. "You want me to say it again? Trash like them represent exactly the kind of harm I knew you would keep me from."

Lone felt an unexpected tightening in his chest. He expelled a breath. "All the same, I know I've put you through a heap of unpleasantness. Lame as it probably sounds, I regret havin' to do it. But I want you to know it's over. I also want you to know, for whatever it's worth, that I think you're a damn fine woman. I'm sorry you were left a widow at such a young age. For the time you had together, I hope your husband was the kind of man you deserve. And goin' forward, though I know it ain't my place to say, I hope you don't waste the rest of your life tidyin' up after that no-account brother of yours."

"He wasn't always like that," Sue said defensively. "He lost someone too. Not to death, that might have been kinder. His wife—who was no good from the start, though no one could convince him of that—jilted him a year ago. Ran off with a bustle salesman, of all things. James started drinking then, and hasn't stopped. As sad as that is, what's even worse is that if the little rip came crawling back, I know he'd take her in a heartbeat." Sue set her jaw firmly. "After I blackened both of her roaming damn eyes, that is!"

Lone grinned. "Hell hath no fury like a big sister scorned, eh?"

"Something like that."

His grin fading, Lone said, "Well, big sister, we're turnin' you loose to go on into Russet with the Haneses. Me, Smith, and Bright Moon are movin' on. Hanes tells me there's a telegraph office in the town. You can contact your people back in Coraville from there."

He started to turn back toward the wagon but was stopped by Sue's hand on his arm. Those brown eyes probed into him. "There's something more I want to say. Last night...early this morning, I heard you and Smith talking. When he was planning to ride off on his own. I didn't understand all of it, the names Avril, Grogan, and so forth. But I understood enough to know this much— something Bright Moon has been assuring me all along —and that's that you and Smith are good men with troubled pasts who are bent on confronting this Grogan person to right some dreadful wrong."

"That might be kinda right. But don't go makin' us sound too noble and pure-hearted. We're the same hombres who kidnapped you and made you a hostage, remember?"

"Don't make light of what I'm trying to say—what I feel, what I know from the things I've witnessed. Your gentleness with little Mae, how much you went out of your way to protect and aid the Haneses, the kindness and respect you and Smith both show Bright Moon, and how you settled down and encouraged Smith last night when he was on the ragged edge. Yes, you've also displayed some roughness, even harshness, in ways I don't find particularly agreeable...but nevertheless—and to paraphrase your line from a minute ago—I think you're a darn fine man, Lone McGantry."

Lone felt that tightness in his chest again. He said, "Ma'am, that's one of the nicest things anybody ever said to me. I'll remember it and treasure it."

Sue eyed him earnestly. "Then why don't you come on into the town for a little while? Rest a bit, get cleaned up, have a hot meal. I know for a fact Bright Moon could use some new clothes, even though she's too shy to ask for herself. No tricks by me, if that's what you're thinking. I promise not to raise any kind of alarm or send off my telegram until you're back on the trail again."

It was a mighty tempting notion. Lone reached up involuntarily and rubbed his heavily whiskered jaw. Their back trail had been clear when he'd checked, and the rain had erased all sign for a wide swath since then. And how much risk would there be, really, if they made a quick stop in this sprinkling of a town out in the middle of nowhere?

"You could at least check with Smith and Bright Moon, see what they think of the idea," Sue suggested.

That turned out to be the clincher. When Lone put the question to Smith and Bright Moon, they both—for all the reasons and justifications that swept through Lone's head, and more—expressed an eagerness to make the stop.

And so it was they who accompanied the Hanes wagon on down into Russet.

CHAPTER TWENTY-EIGHT

GRANNY MAVIS, THE MIDWIFE WHO'D BEEN SCHEDULED TO help with Sara Hanes' delivery if the child hadn't come so unexpectedly early, turned out to be a stout, elderly widow lady who reminded Lone a great deal of Ma Sharples. So much so, in fact, the former scout had to do a double take when he first saw her.

Granny's home, a large single-story house with spare rooms set up for the service she provided to the community's mothers, was where the Haneses and those accompanying them went directly upon arriving in town. Learning the baby had already been born and hearing the complications involved, the old widow became very concerned and businesslike and promptly ushered Sara, the baby, and Sue into a large delivery/nursery room where mother and child were put to bed. Then Granny and Sue, the two of them instantly hitting it off—helped no doubt by the praise Sara heaped on Sue for all the help she'd been so far— combined their focus on further care and precautions to ensure continued good health for the patients.

While this was underway behind a closed door, another elderly lady who introduced herself as Beth and said she was Granny's assistant, informed the men it might take some time and so if they had other matters to tend to, then they might want to go ahead and pursue them. In the interim, she assured them, she would see to the comfort of Mae and Bright Moon.

Grinning sheepishly, Jeffrey Hanes said to Lone and Smith, "Guess it's plain enough us fellas ain't needed nor especially wanted hereabouts for a while. Speaking for myself, that's okay on account of I need to see a fella at the local hardware about a job offer now that I ain't got my spread no more." He slapped his injured leg. "Hope it's work I can do on the hobble until this doggone thing mends. While I'm there, hopefully I can at least find something in the way of a proper crutch—this pickax I been making do with sure ain't the most comfortable thing."

"Wishin' you luck on both counts—gettin' the job and findin' a crutch," Lone told him. "Don't reckon you need me and Smith taggin' along, so we'll find something for ourselves to do. We been pushin' our horses out on the trail for quite a spell, strikes me they deserve a good rubdown and curryin', the treat of some good, rich grain. There a decent livery stable in town you'd recommend?"

"Yeah, there is. We'll step outside, I can point it out to you."

Smith grunted. "I been out on the trail same as those horses—hope some over-eager liveryman don't take one look at my shabby condition and come after me with a curry comb too."

Outside, after Hanes had pointed them on their way,

Lone and Smith took their five horses and headed for the livery. It was still early, but the town's citizenry appeared up and about and busy with their various tasks. No one seemed to pay them any particular attention, even as they passed through a section of the central business district amid other horsemen, wagons, and buggies traversing back and forth.

The livery stable was off near the end of a quiet side street with the creek running close beside its corral. A stocky, balding, bow-legged gent who introduced himself as Driscoll greeted Lone and Smith out front of a sun-peeled but sturdy-looking barn and seemed pleased to have the business.

When Lone explained what they wanted done and asked if he could take care of them within a couple hours, Driscoll assured him it would be no problem. His charges for doing the work were quite reasonable. "I'll have to charge you a little extry for unloadin' your pack animal," he explained. "Less'n you want to do it yourselves 'fore you go. Either way, I'll be requirin' you to be the ones to load her back up. That way, you can keep your gear in the order you want and make sure it's all accounted for. But it *will* all be there, my guarantee."

"We trust in that," Lone told him.

"We'll get out of your hair and let you get to work," Smith added.

"Done and done," Driscoll declared.

Lone and Smith took their saddlebags and Winchesters and started to leave as Driscoll led the first pair of horses deeper back into the barn. They'd only gone a couple steps, though, before Smith touched Lone's arm and brought both of them to a halt. Using the muzzle of his rifle as a pointer, Smith said, "Lookie there."

What he indicated was a sign painted on a piece of one-by-twelve board nailed over the door to the tack room that neither man had noticed before. The lettering on the sign read:

- *Sleeping Loft – 25 cents per night*
- *Cold Bath – 25 cents*
- *Hot Bath – 50 cents*
- *Clean Towel – 5 cents*

"All kidding aside about me being shaggy enough to need a curry comb," Smith said, "I for sure *could* use a bath and a shave. How about you?"

"I'm plenty due for the same," allowed Lone.

"Yet I can't hardly go to a barber or a regular bath house with this boot blacking gunk in my hair. And it's probably too early for Driscoll to have a couple tubfuls of water heated up. A 'cold bath' likely means a trough of rainwater out back in the corral. Think that delicate pink behind of yours could stand a dip in some fresh, chilly rainwater?"

Lone chuffed. "This leathery ol' behind of mine has withstood bathing in icy mountain streams cold enough to shrivel the onions of a stud grizzly. I can sure as hell stand it if you can."

"Okay then." Smith grimaced. "Now I need a good bath even more—to try and scrub the image of shriveled griz onions outta my head."

———

Forty minutes later, after losing a coin toss for who got first turn in the water trough, Lone had emerged from taking seconds and was in the process of drying off and getting dressed again. He'd donned his pants and boots but was still shirtless. Same for Smith, who'd just finished shaving, as Lone had done while the coin toss winner was in the trough and was patting the last flecks of shaving suds off his face. Their gun belts were hanging on a nearby corral rail, and Winchesters leaned against the same.

The sun was warm on their bare backs and the two men were feeling refreshed and relaxed, their recent long hours in the saddle and the meager amount of sleep attained during the stormy night largely offset. The grim business that still lay ahead was never far from their minds, but for a little while, it wasn't crowding in quite as tight. What they were looking forward to next, before hitting the trail again, was rejoining Bright Moon and Sue Leonard for a planned sit-down meal at a local café.

As he pulled a rolled-up clean shirt out of his saddlebags and shook it loose, Lone said, "In accordance with something Sue mentioned to me, we need to be sure and take time to stop somewhere for Bright Moon to pick up some new clothes before we head out. Don't let me forget."

Raising a flap on his own saddlebags and rummaging into the pocket, Smith replied, "Got it. I'll remind you."

That was when a loud voice barked out sharply from the livery barn behind them, saying just two words. "Wade Avril!"

Smith's head snapped part way around in response.

Lone didn't turn. He knew instantly what the

shouting of the name meant and what was going to happen next.

"It's him, alright!" confirmed a second voice.

That one second's hesitation, the time it took to get a reaction for the sake of confirming the target, was all Lone had for calling on reflexes honed to a keen edge over many years when survival meant being able to respond in the blink of an eye to life-threatening strikes that came equally as fast. Without pause or conscious thought, he lowered his head and instantly flung himself into Smith, taking them both off their feet and flat to the ground. While they were still in the air, dropping down, two tightly spaced gunshots crashed from separate barn windows and the slugs they hurled, sizzled mere inches above the entangled falling bodies before chewing into the corral rail right where Smith had been standing.

Lone's quick action saved them from those first two bullets. But that didn't mean it was over. By an additional dose of sheer luck, however, where he and Smith landed was directly in front of their leaning rifles and hanging gun belts. Both men instantly realized this and neither wasted a moment—Smith now propelling himself as swiftly as Lone—before snatching a repeater and rolling in the opposite direction. More bullets hammered into the spot they had just vacated, gouging dirt and chipping away corral wood.

Smith belly-scrambled frantically behind the water trough/bathtub.

But, rolling the other way, Lone found himself with much leaner pickings when it came to finding cover. His only option was a large iron cauldron suspended from a tripod over a cold fire pit—Driscoll's set-up for heating bath water. It wasn't much, but better than being caught totally out in the open. And, on the plus side, the cast iron skin of the cauldron would turn anything short of a cannon ball. If only the damn thing was larger! All Lone could do was work with what he had and do his best to keep it between him and any more incoming rounds.

And come they did, hot and heavy. Ripping through the air, slashing at Smith's water trough and bonging like a dull church bell off Lone's cauldron. Somewhat to his advantage, despite Lone's less thorough cover, was the unmistakable fact that the main target of the ambushers, and therefore, the heaviest concentration of fire was on Smith—who, as Wade Avril, represented the bounty pay they obviously were out for. The advance shout of that name was what had given Lone his scant warning of what was going to come next. And now, as he crouched to cover with his mind racing, it told him something more: The shooters were amateurs. A professional killer or manhunter would have opened fire cold. That didn't mean these bastards out for blood money weren't still a dangerous threat, but knowing it wasn't the kind of thing they were accustomed to and maybe not entirely comfortable with, could make a difference.

Still, Lone told himself, he couldn't simply rely on speculation about the inexperience of the ambushers to result in a difference that would get him and Smith out of this fix before one of those bullets found its mark—a counter move of some kind, in spite of their desperate, pinned-down positions, would have to be launched.

———

INSIDE THE LIVERY BARN, positioned at windows twenty feet apart, Lefty Sneed and Art Tory were experiencing the sting of powder smoke drifting back into their eyes, along with knots of anxiety tightening in their guts from the ambush failing to go as smoothly as intended. Luck seemed to have been running their way when, upon first arriving in town, they'd come to the livery checking for any newly stabled animals and not only found the mounts they were looking for but, amazingly, learned the very man they sought was out back taking a bath. An eager scramble to take advantage of this was in process now, but their luck seemed to be faltering.

"Goddamn it, we should have waited for Fletcher to get in position!" Tory wailed, even as he triggered another round from his Henry repeater at the water tank behind which Smith—*Wade Avril*, in Tory's mind—was hugging the ground.

"We had 'em dead to rights—smack plain in front of us without their guns," Sneed snarled in response. "It was too sweet of a chance to pass up!"

"If it was so sweet, then why ain't Wild Red laying out there dead? I never saw anybody move as fast as that goddamn McGantry!"

"He got lucky, that's all," Sneed insisted, cranking out another shot and then immediately chambering a fresh round. "But ain't neither one of 'em going nowhere, we got 'em pinned like bugs under a rock. Just keep pouring it on—Fletcher will be joining in any second and then we damn sure will be able to finish them!"

"I hope to hell he hurries up."

As if on cue, both of them caught the thud of

hurried footfalls on the floor of the loft directly over their heads. And then, a moment later, a third source of rifle fire began to make itself heard.

CHAPTER TWENTY-NINE

LONE SAW THE CHUNKY VENT DOOR SWING OPEN AT LOFT level, centered above the two low windows already spewing lead. Once again, he knew what was going to follow. "Watch out high!" he hollered over to Smith. Being pinned down by horizontal fire was smothering enough, but rounds angling down from elevation presented an even narrower chance to gain cover; especially behind a low barrier like the water trough. Lone's risk wasn't changed that much due to the height of the suspended cauldron. And, as with the opening rounds from the two ground-floor windows, the first shots blasting down from the rifle barrel poking out the loft opening were concentrated on Smith.

Lone could see that by pressing skin tight to the side of the trough and hunkering as low as possible at its base, Smith managed to stay temporarily unscathed. The downward angling slugs sliced away the lip of the trough wall directly over him, spraying him with wood splinters and skimming mere inches above his shoulder and hip before burrowing into the dirt. But it would be impossible to hold in that cramped position for very long, and while he was, Smith was completely frozen from attempting any return fire.

Lone wasn't a hell of a lot better off, but he at least had a small degree of movement, plus he was enduring only about thirty percent of the fire Smith was taking. If they were going to have any chance at all, it fell on the former scout to make something happen, to find a way to break the log jam of lead piling up from just one direction. It would only get worse if he or Smith, either one, took a hit, leaving whoever was left to face the full focus of all three ambushers.

Lone was damned if he was going to let that happen, at least not without costing the bushwhacking bastards *some* measure of payment in return.

He decided what he had to do. It was crazy, desperate. But he couldn't see where he had any other choice. If he timed it right...

There were about twenty yards of open ground between where he was and the nearest inside corner of the corral. A few feet beyond that was a corner of the livery barn. If Lone could cover that distance without getting cut down and make it around the end of the barn, he not only would be out of all lines of fire but would also have the freedom to maneuver *against* the ambushers.

He waited, crouching slightly lower, leg muscles bunching like coiled springs. When the next sporadic flurry of slugs came his way, bonging off the cauldron and gouging into the rim of the fire pit—all meant to keep him pinned in place—he was ready. He gauged what would come next. If it followed the pattern he anticipated, attention would swing back away from him, and a renewed heavier volley would again hammer Smith.

It happened just that way. And, when it did, he sprang from cover and bolted for the corner of the corral. As he ran, he held his Winchester Yellowboy out in front of him, waist high, aimed at an angle back toward the side of the barn. He fired blindly without breaking stride. Once, twice, three times—as fast as he could jack home fresh rounds between trigger pulls. He had no idea if he hit anywhere close to the windows with ambushers in them, but it just felt damn good to be throwing some lead back in their general direction.

The unexpectedness of his move succeeded in taking him quite a ways before he started drawing fire from the surprised ambushers. Then the reaction came like a swarm of angry .44 caliber hornets. They buzzed ahead and behind him. One streaked so close to the back of his neck that he felt the heat of its passing. Miniature geysers of dirt spurted up from the ground directly in front of him, and splinters of wood flew from a corral post.

Lone reached the corner of the corral. He threw his Yellowboy ahead, leaped to plant one foot on a middle rail, then launched himself up and over. A bullet skimmed the bottom of his right boot heel, sending a momentary shiver down the length of his leg as he nosedived to the ground outside the corral. He landed in a none too graceful roll, retrieved the Yellowboy as he scrambled to his feet, then went racing around the corner of the barn. Bullets continued to whine and scrape wood behind him.

Once in the clear, Lone stopped and leaned heavily against the end of the structure. His breath was coming in rapid puffs, and his heart was hammering. *By God, he'd made it!* No time to ease up, though—now he had to keep pressing, even harder, make it count all the more. Get the ambushers off Smith's back and then work on sending them to hell, wishing they'd never come to play for blood.

An instant after this thought crossed Lone's mind, another rifle report sounded. Only this one came *from* out in the corral, not issued by one of the guns that had been so relentlessly shooting *into* it. And then, punctuating the shot, came a man's agonized cry.

Recognizing what had just happened, Lone bared his teeth in a wide wolf's smile. His run from cover had not only gained him the freedom to maneuver, but it had also given Smith relief from being so hopelessly pinned down. Amateurs that they were, *all* of the ambushers had diverted their attention to chasing Lone with their bullets in an attempt to bring him down. This gave the savvy Smith an opening to pop up from behind the trough long enough to deliver a bullet of his own— one that blew Art Tory, it would soon be revealed, clean out of his window. When return fire poured his way again, Smith dropped back to cover.

Confirming all of this, Lone heard a voice that he thought he recognized as belonging to the CT wrangler called Lefty wail mournfully, "Jesus Christ, he got Tory!"

From up in the loft, a slightly more muffled voice— Fletcher's, Lone now felt certain—responded, "If there's nothing you can do for him, then pour it back even harder! Make the bastard pay—I gotta go find out what that big square-faced sonofabitch is up to!"

Lone barked out a quick, harsh laugh. *Come right ahead, mister. Be glad to accommodate you.*

But no, that could wait a minute. He thought of something else. His first inclination had been to swing around and rush into the barn, meet Fletcher coming down from the loft. Have it out then and there.

But that's what Fletcher would be expecting, be ready for. Lone had gotten the tables turned around this far by doing the unexpected. Why not throw in another dose of that before being in a hurry to confront Fletcher? The rap of Lefty's rifle starting in again, pouring a fresh rain of lead at Smith, made up Lone's mind and identified his next unexpected move for him.

Be with you directly, Fletch buddy. Just hold your horses.

Lone turned back to the corner of the building and eased up to it. He held the Yellowboy up and ready, knowing he'd chambered a fresh round after his last shot. Around the corner, Lefty was continuing to shoot steadily, cursing with each trigger pull. Lone took a deep breath, held it.

Then, leaning out and bringing the butt of the Yellowboy to his shoulder in a smooth motion, he took careful aim. Just as he'd hoped/expected, the barrel of Lefty's rifle was extended out his window far enough to present a decent target. Lone stroked the trigger of his Yellowboy. His aim was true; the rifle was ripped from Lefty's grasp and sent windmilling away to end up clattering onto the corral dirt. Inside the window, unseen from Lone's vantage, Lefty fell away howling and cursing in pain.

Lone dropped back, grinning. He hollered over toward the water trough, "The way should be mostly clear if you're done layin' down on the job, Smith! I got business inside...meet you there!"

But the trouble with what he'd just done, Lone came

to realize, while it had diminished and maybe even eliminated any further threat from Lefty, it had also allowed Fletcher more time to descend from the loft and get set for dealing with "that big square-faced sono-fabitch." Nor did it help that Lone found the interior of the livery barn damned dim and murky as his eyes tried to transition from the contrasting bright sunshine outside. To counter, he ducked quickly through the open double doors at the front and cut hard to his left. This placed him in a shadowy corner where he froze, allowing his vision to adjust while at the same time listening tight for any sounds that might indicate movement by Fletcher from deeper in.

Whatever chance he had to hear anything else was drowned out by the pained caterwauling of Lefty from somewhere up ahead, bemoaning the damage done to his hands by having the rifle shot out of them. "Oh, god, they're stinging like fire all up through my arms," he wailed. "And my trigger finger is twisted and busted to hell and gone!"

Then you shouldn't have had it stuck through a trigger guard squeezing off shots at my friend, you wretch!

The remorseless response passed through Lone's mind, but he stayed quiet. He'd made it through the door and into this pocket of shadows, and now wasn't the time to give away *his* position. That's what he was biding his time in hopes of Fletcher being over-eager enough to do.

As his vision adjusted more to the interior dimness, Lone saw that the corner he'd ducked into was only a short ways down from the tack room that had the sign over its door advertising sleeping lofts and baths. Then he saw something else. Lying on the ground in front of the door was the bulky, bound and gagged form of Driscoll, the liveryman. Lone realized the ambushers must have done this to him when they first showed up, to keep him from getting involved and try warning Lone and Smith. The fact they'd gagged him and tied him up indicated they at least hadn't killed him or they wouldn't have gone to the extra trouble.

Driscoll lying motionless meant they *had* clubbed him unconscious, though. Probably a gun barrel rapped across the back of the head, Lone guessed. But then, looking more closely, his vision still adjusting, Lone saw that the liveryman *wasn't* unconscious. At least not now, not any longer.

He was lying partially on his right side, at a forty-five-degree angle to the tack room door, his legs extended out toward the barn's center aisle. That meant his face, one cheek flattened tight to the hard-packed dirt floor, was turned almost directly to Lone. And his eyes were wide open! While the rest of him stayed motionless, those eyes—staring straight at Lone—were moving frantically. That's what had caught Lone's attention in the first place and was continuing to hold him nearly mesmerized.

Repeatedly, Driscoll's eyes would roll down as far as they could within their sockets, then suddenly jerk up and back to the other extreme. His shaggy eyebrows would jerk on the uproll, too. He did this over and over. Watching, Lone could only conclude the poor bastard must be suffering some kind of nervous seizure or spasm brought on by the blow to the head.

Edging forward now, skirting up along the front of the tack room, Lone passed close to the bound man and whispered softly, "Hang on, mister. I'll get you some help as soon as I can."

He moved slowly, silently past the tack room, which was essentially a structure within a structure, a twelve-foot by twelve-foot box whose door and walls were of newer lumber utilizing the floor of the loft running along this side of the main barn for its ceiling. Lone's aim was to work his way along the row of stalls that lay ahead, ducking in and out of each recess, until he got some indication of where Fletcher was lurking. There was also the matter of the still whimpering Lefty. Though his moaning had quieted down some, if he was still at it when Lone reached him, it would present an opportunity to shut him up the rest of the way.

It turned out, however, that the quieter noise coming out of Lefty was enough to finally allow Lone to hear another sound. It was that of wood creaking under a shifting weight, like perhaps from a man stepping on it. It seemed to have come from just behind and somewhere above where Lone suddenly halted.

And then, piecing it together with something else, Lone all at once understood. Damn near too late, but he finally got it...Driscoll had been trying to warn him with his jerky eye movement: *Look out! Watch out overhead!*

Lone spun in a hundred-eighty-degree turn, sweeping both his eyes and the Yellowboy's muzzle upward. There was Fletcher, leaning out from the crawl space over the tack room with a six-gun in his hand. The sneaky bastard had never come *down* from the loft at all—but rather had merely shifted to a different elevated position from which to try and gun Lone.

As Fletcher's arm extended, aiming the hogleg, Lone kicked backward and simultaneously triggered his

Yellowboy. Both guns roared. Lone hit the ground flat on his back, feeling Fletcher's bullet tear through the thick trapezius muscle just above his left shoulder. The burning pain was nothing, though, compared to the satisfaction he got from seeing the bottom half of Fletcher's face disappear in a burst of scarlet salted with white flecks of shattered jawbone and teeth.

Lone lay still for a moment and allowed himself a weary groan. Then he sat up, automatically levering a fresh round into the Yellowboy. He didn't look, but he could feel warm blood dribbling down over his chest and over his shoulder blade in the back.

He wondered where Smith was.

He wondered, too, why Lefty had now gone totally quiet. Unfortunately, he didn't have to wonder about that for very long. Lefty quit being quiet.

"Now, you sonofabitch. You might have ruined my gun hand, but that don't mean I can't still find a way to slice out your goddamn liver!"

Lone slowly turned his head and looked over his bloody shoulder. Lefty was about ten feet away, moving toward him in short, shuffling steps. There was a wild look in his eyes and in his hands was a three-tined hay fork, held in a threatening manner, ready to make a sudden, savage thrust. Lefty's hands might be hurting, and his trigger finger was visibly mangled, but that didn't make his grip on the long handle of the hay fork appear very damned weakened. He was close enough now to make a damaging lunge—those wild eyes conveying he was more than ready to do it—and Lone was in an almost impossible position to block or evade...

Strangely, the crack of the rifle being fired from

somewhere deeper in the barn sounded much louder than the closer exchange just completed between Lone and Fletcher. Maybe that had to do with it being so welcome a sound to Lone's ears. Even more welcome was the sight of the bullet it hurled, striking Lefty and knocking him off his feet before he could make good on his intentions. He toppled face down, dead, with the hay fork clattering to the floor beside him.

Smith came strolling unhurriedly down the barn aisle, his Winchester resting on his shoulder. When Lone looked up at him questioningly, he said, "I decided I should cover the back in case your pal Fletcher tried to make a run for it rather than a fight of it."

Lone sneered, "He didn't do either one. He didn't run and the yellow cur sure as hell didn't fight...appears he only ever had the stones to strike from ambush."

"I saw. That was mighty close. I was too far back to try a shot before you got yours off."

"That's okay. I'll settle for you takin' care of pitchfork boy," said Lone.

Smith shrugged. Then, gesturing to the bullet burn on Lone's shoulder, he remarked dryly, "I didn't notice before—but did you cut yourself shaving or something?"

CHAPTER THIRTY

NEEDLESS TO SAY, THE EVENTS THAT MORNING AT
Driscoll's livery greatly hastened the departure of Lone,
Smith, and Bright Moon from the town of Russet. A
gaggle of citizens naturally came flocking to see what all
the shooting was about, but Driscoll handled most of
them with his increasingly animated telling and re-
telling of what had happened. There was also a blustery,
pot-bellied old marshal named Philpot who showed up
and tried to take charge with talk of investigations and
inquests and so forth. But Lone and Smith politely
disarmed him, explaining they didn't have time for any
of what he was spouting, then proceeded to gather up
their horses, gear, and Bright Moon and make ready to
leave.

They did take time to say goodbye to the Haneses
and Sue, who insisted on cleaning and bandaging
Lone's wound before she'd let him go, and to make a
stop at the general store where Bright Moon picked out
a couple new blouses and some personal items; then
they were on the trail well before noon. The planned sit-

down meal at a café was abandoned without comment. Their alternative combination breakfast/lunch was day-old biscuits and jerky eaten in the saddle while they kept on the move.

Lone pushed them hard and steady through the balance of the day, until finally stopping for night camp on a flat, grassy rise within a cluster of cedars and willows overlooking a small lake. They tended the horses, cooked and ate a good supper, then sat talking around the fire as darkness thickened and the clear sky overhead began to fill with a wash of early stars.

To her surprise and initial discomfort, Lone made it a point to encourage Bright Moon's participation in their discussion. While the Cheyenne were known to treat their womenfolk better than most Indian tribes, it was nevertheless unheard of for a female to ever have a voice in male-dominated council sessions or group meetings of any sort.

"In case you ain't figured it out by now," Lone explained to Bright Moon, "you ridin' in the company of me and Smith puts you in more danger than what you had a right to expect for this trip back to your people in the north. From the git-go, that alone shaped up to be tough enough on its own. Now, the trouble attached to us only adds to what you're facin'. I want to make sure you understand, and I want to hear if you got any ideas on how best to make it still turn out okay for you."

The girl's smooth brow wrinkled, and her eyes went back and forth between Lone and Smith. Then she asked, "Is it that you wish for me to no longer travel with you?"

"That's not it at all. Not the way you make it sound," Smith was quick to assure her. "We're pleased and honored to have you traveling with us. Our concern is that you may be harmed because of it. By being in our presence if more trouble comes our way—which it most likely will."

Bright Moon frowned. "I do not understand. Being with you and Lone makes me feel...safe. More so than at any time since I was taken from Flat Falls."

This statement surprised and touched both Smith and Lone. The reaction showed on their faces and in the look they exchanged with one another.

Bright Moon continued, "The reservation in Oklahoma was crowded and untidy. Those of us brought down from the north were not made to feel welcome. We were looked upon mostly as only more mouths to be fed and more bodies requiring space and blankets and other provisions already in short supply. When the two men, Curtis and O'Greary, came to take me back north, I thought it was a good thing. They treated me well enough, but to them, I was just...what you say...a task. A job.

"Then O'Greary left, and Curtis found the Tate brothers to continue on with us. That was when things turned very bad. They frightened me...and Curtis, too, I think. In the end, they all fought to protect me, especially Curtis, so perhaps I should think more favorably of them because of that. But when the two of you arrived, I somehow knew from the first that you were different. Troubled men, yes, but with good hearts. Men who would also protect me, yet not for the purpose of wanting to claim me for yourselves, like the Tate brothers. Everything I have seen since has only convinced me more. You would stand up for any who are vulnerable. But now you tell me I may come to harm being with you...I do not understand."

Lone and Smith exchanged looks again, each clearly unsure how to respond. After a beat, Smith went ahead. "Think back to when I first showed up at Flat Falls, in the company of several other men. Back when you thought of me as Sad Eyes," he said. "One of those other men, the leader of our outfit, was a man named Grogan. Pike Grogan. Remember him at all?"

Bright Moon nodded. "Yes. I do. He, like the other men who rode with you, had a hard look. Hard and greedy. They looked at the people of our tribe, especially the women, in a way that was not good. The same way the Tate brothers looked at me. I remember, even back then, noticing and wondering why it was the look in your eyes was so different."

"I'm not so sure," Smith said ruefully, "you were quite seeing the straight of it, gal. For sure not then. Maybe not even so much now."

"Maybe you're the stubborn blockhead refusin' to see the straight of it. Others besides Bright Moon—the Hallams, the rest of the folks back in and around Sarben—all picked up on something similar," Lone reminded him.

Smith made a dismissive gesture. "That's an argument for another time. The point we're trying to impress on Bright Moon now has to do with Grogan. How that hard look of his has plenty of genuine menace and danger behind it, and how a big dose of all that is aimed at me—which is why being around me puts her at risk for getting caught in the line of fire."

"So since I saw you and him together in Flat Falls,

you and this man Grogan have become enemies?"
Bright Moon asked.

"Yeah. In a big way. Big to the point he is offering to
pay money to anyone who hunts me down and kills me
for him."

"But those men who caused the trouble this
morning in Russet, they were not from Grogan. They
were the same cowboys who appeared at the wagon
yesterday, threatening the Hokes family."

Smith nodded grimly. "That's right. But somewhere,
somehow between then and this morning, they figured
out I'm Wade Avril—that's my real name in case you
haven't picked up on it by now, the one I went by when
you saw me as Sad Eyes—the man Grogan is now
offering money to have killed. That was enough to turn
those cowboys into bounty hunters looking to earn the
payoff."

Bright Moon's expression turned intense, thoughtful. "Yes," she said, partly as if to herself. "I did not know
of this bounty hunting matter. But the name Wade
Avril, yes, that I am familiar with. During the time I was
at the Oklahoma reservation, you see, through a trusted
confidant, I was able to carry on a correspondence with
Eagle Soaring back at Flat Falls. He and I learned to
speak English and read and write from an old
missionary couple who lived on our reservation until
they died. Eagle and I have been promised to one
another in marriage since we were children. When I
was part of the group selected to be sent away but he
was not, we vowed to find a way to stay in touch until we
could be together once again."

Lone nodded. "Uh-huh. We're familiar with your
story. It was Eagle's father, Iron Wolf, behind the

arrangement to get you returned to Flat Falls, was it not?"

"That is so." Bright Moon's expression clouded somewhat. "I am grateful to Iron Wolf for that. Because he is a sub chief of our tribe and Eagle Soaring's father, I have always had to outwardly show him respect. But, in truth, I have long seen that within him, there was a hardness and a kind of greed not too different from men like Grogan. It was true the arrangement he made with Grogan and his men to find a safe haven on our land in return for food and clothing we were not getting in sufficient quantities from the agency, was of much benefit to our people. But it was also a benefit to Iron Wolf. It elevated him and made him popular with the people even though many of the old chiefs had reservations about him much like my own."

"How does Eagle Soaring look upon his father?" Lone wanted to know.

"He looks upon him with much respect and love, the way any good son should," Bright Moon replied, rather tersely at first. Then, after only a faint hesitation, she added, "Yet, as he has confided in only me, Eagle also recognizes a strong ambition and personal drive in his father that may not be directed toward the best long-term interests of our whole tribe."

"Iron Wolf is a warrior at heart," said Smith. "I saw that right away. Even though he knows it is a guaranteed lost cause in the end, he wants nothing more than a taste of glory like from the old days. A daring sweep of raiding and killing, a final strike back at the hated White Eyes."

"Yes. Sadly, it is so."

"Guns," Smith said, spitting the words from his

mouth like it was a dirty taste. "I recall it all now, the sharpest part of the memories knifing through me out of last night's storm. A part I never got around to telling you about, Lone. The talk and the planning between Grogan and Iron Wolf. The sickening realization growing inside me of what it would mean if we went ahead and helped make it come true."

Lone scowled, looking thoroughly puzzled. "What guns? Make what come true? What in hell are you talking about?"

Smith's smile had a ghastly, haunted quality to it. "Maybe nobody had it clearly in mind, but I can't help wonder if that's not where it was headed right from the start. Yeah, at first it was a pretty slick deal between Grogan and Iron Wolf, greased by that snake Weems, that had benefits both ways. We—who Iron Wolf could tolerate because, as outlaws, we were fighting our own kind of battle against the white authorities he hated—got a damned effective hideout, and he got food and supplies to help his people and at the same time help his personal status.

"But then some other motives started to enter in. Possibly, I always had a hunch, greased along some more by Weems. There were hints that Iron Wolf knew the location of some previously undiscovered gold deposits on rez property. When the question got put to him, he revealed that, yeah, that was the case. He showed proof. It was almost like he was waiting for the right time. And then came the rest of what he was waiting for...he was willing to part with some of the gold. Plenty, in fact—what Indian ever gave a damn about gold except for the grief it caused them from white men who came to rape their land for it? But what

Iron Wolf wanted in return for gold was no longer just blankets and flour and the like."

"I can fill in the rest," muttered Lone. "He wanted guns to finally make his glory ride against the White Eyes."

"I was gone from Flat Falls by this time," Bright Moon said. "But Eagle Soaring wrote me about it. He was greatly distressed by his father's intentions. The only hope he saw came from one of Grogan's men." Here, her eyes fell to rest on Smith. "That is how I am familiar with the name Wade Avril. Within the tribe, just a few young hotbloods were aware—and wildly in favor—of what Iron Wolf was seeking. Eagle dared not speak out against them or his father. But Grogan's man, this Wade Avril, showed no fear to speak out against all."

"But still," Smith intoned dully, "the robbery of guns took place. Grogan got wind, I don't know how, of a wagon shipment of a hundred rifles on the way north out of Bismark. To be distributed fifty-fifty to forts Tyrone and Cormyer, two of the most outlying posts still active for ensuring compliance by reservation Indians. Because of the remoteness of the forts and the vast lands they're watching over, this shipment of arms was something a bit special seven-shot Spencer repeating carbines chambered for .56-60 cartridges."

Lone emitted a low whistle. "Wheeoo. Not even Custer's slaughter at the Little Big Horn was enough cause for the tight-assed Army brass to make the switch from continuing to issue their tried-and-true Springfield trapdoors for the Cavalry boys to fight the balance of the Indian hostilities with. The Springfield is a powerful knock-downer, I won't argue that, but it ain't no Winchester or Henry repeater. I heard something about a smattering of those seven-shot Spencers being made available as a sort of 'in-between' gun. Never had call to try one myself, but from what I understand, they perform pretty good. Though in the wrong hands—like a pack of hotbloods led by a renegade sub-chief seeking a final run at past glory—I reckon you'd have to say there wasn't much good about what they was aimed at performin'."

"That's why," Smith said offhandedly, "I blew the goddamn things up."

Lone fought to keep his jaw from dropping too far. "You *what*, you crazy bastard?"

"It was sorta my resignation letter from the Pike Grogan gang."

Bright Moon was looking at Smith with a pleased and proud smile. "Eagle wrote me all about it," she said. "He was overjoyed by the act, but of course, had to mask his feelings. His father and Grogan were furious beyond words—as were Grogan's men and the young hotbloods ready to follow Iron Wolf. The rest of the people in our village did not fully understand, they only knew there was a bad accident at the cavern where the outlaws had been staying, a large explosion that caved in the entrance and buried whatever was inside. They thought it a blessing that only one man, someone named Wade Avril, was reported killed in the explosion."

"Kind of a premature proclamation, that business about me being killed," Smith remarked wryly. "But, boy howdy, don't think that Pike and the boys—not to mention a handful of Iron Wolf's braves too, for a while —didn't try their damnedest to make it come true in the days and weeks that followed. I hid practically under their noses at first, then lit out for Texas, maybe Old Mexico. I figure that's where I'd be right about now if that Nebraska thunderstorm hadn't stalled me and left me for that damn Granger Weems to stumble on."

"I guess that explains, once and for all," said Lone, "his instant fury at the sight of you even after months had passed. Not a much surer way to rile a fella and keep him that way than to get between him and some gold."

Smith wagged his head. "I just couldn't let 'em go through with it. Not put those Spencers in the hands of Iron Wolf and what he intended to do once he had 'em. The suffering and bloodshed it would mean for unsuspecting folks. Indians, too, when the cavalry started hitting back; you know how ruthless some of those retaliation strikes have turned in the past...I was already growing pretty disenchanted with the whole outlaw thing, the way we were living, and the stuff we were doing. Stuff I'm not claiming I wasn't right in the thick of...but serving up rifles to renegades in return for a handful of gold? No, that was too much. The last straw. I knew I not only had to cut the cord for myself, but I had to do it in a way that removed any chance of leaving those rifles still up for grabs. We had some dynamite stored in the cavern that we used now and then on bank vaults, and Pike had shown me a thing or two about setting charges...so my parting message included a demonstration of how good I'd been paying attention to his lessons."

CHAPTER THIRTY-ONE

"WELL, I RECKON WE'VE MADE CLEAR ENOUGH OUR concerns for you continuin' to stick with us. I don't know what more to add," Lone said to Bright Moon. "Hell, I got some things made clearer to me, too, in the process. But none of it changes the risk we're all ridin' under."

Bright Moon looked thoughtful. "The risk you speak of for me being with you...may I ask how it is, if all of this reaches back to the guns and the falling out between Smith and Pike Grogan, you are so willing to ride with Smith and share in the risk, Big Lone?"

The question caught Lone off guard and pushed his eyebrows up a few notches. Bright Moon's thoughtful look turned into a probing gaze waiting for an answer.

Smith also chimed in, saying, "Tell her, *Big Lone*. I'd kinda like to hear the answer myself."

Lone shot him a quick sideways scowl before turning back to Bright Moon's question. "Well, little gal," he said, "all I know is that sometimes a fella happens on a thing that kinda sticks in his craw as not bein' quite right. Lopsided odds, somebody bein' bullied or cheated, different things...dogged if I don't seem to have a knack for runnin' into situations like that. Some might call such matters other folks' business or problems. I try to do that, too. Every time. Sometimes I can walk away, sometimes I can't. In the case of this trouble magnet," a thumb jab toward Smith, "I couldn't. It started out as three-to-one odds I wasn't willin' to let slide. After that, some more things happened quickly that grabbed my shirttail and pulled me deeper in until my own hide was partly on the line. So I saw it as havin' no choice but to stick."

Bright Moon smiled faintly. "Same as with the Hanes family. You did not walk away from their troubles, including standing up to those rude cowboys who showed up to bother them."

"Yeah, and look what it got me."

"Got *us*," Smith was quick to add.

"I was answerin' the question about my knack for takin' on the risk of other folks' problems. You were there only because you're already at the top of that list."

Smith smiled. "No good deed goes unpunished, eh?"

"I ain't so sure you rate as a good deed," Lone grunted.

"Please," Bright Moon interrupted. "I believe my question has been answered. I also believe," with a faint smile again, "part of the answer is that you two are more alike than you realize or may ever be willing to admit."

Lone grunted again. "Well, here's something we all need to admit and think about dealin' with—that bein' how our little shindig this morning in Russet is only gonna add fuel to the fire already breathin' hot on our behinds."

Smith frowned. "How so? You don't mean you're worried about that old Marshal Philpot coming after us, are you?"

"No. Hell no." Lone waved a hand dismissively. "For all his bluster and talk, I doubt that old rumpot could find his way out of town without somebody leadin' him by the hand. But the talkin' part—from the marshal, Driscoll, even Sue when she sends her telegram back to Coraville—that's for damn sure gonna come after us. The name Wade Avril was heard enough, so it's gonna spread like a wildfire sparkin' up all over again. And a new swarm of bounty hunters—like those that flocked to the Sarben and Ogallala area where you first resurfaced, only to be left empty back there—are now gonna rise up, fast, with Russet as a new startin' point to try and pick up a fresh scent."

"There's a lovely picture to take into our dreams tonight. But I guess what you say makes sense. Again," allowed Smith.

"The good part about the picture," Lone said, "is that we got a wild, wide open stretch of canvas spreadin' ahead of us for it to be painted on. We set a steady pace. Keep to rough country. Mask our trail where we can, stay outta sight from towns and ranches...we do that, no reason we can't outdistance the hounds up in all this wild as easy or easier than we did down in Nebraska. Hell, if Grogan hears you're already in Dakota headed in his direction, maybe he'll decide to try and save himself some money by comin' to meet you part way and take care of you himself."

"That would be real accommodating of him." Smith appeared to savor the thought. "I haven't quite figured out why him and the boys didn't head out on the hunt straight off as soon as I was spotted in Sarben. They sure as blazes were keen on getting their own hands on me in the beginning. Whatever new scheme him and Iron Wolf are cooking up seems too important for him to take a break from. And if it's something he's got that tight a grip on, it must be big and that'll mean bad news when he pulls it off."

"It is the digging that is keeping them all so busy," Bright Moon remarked, in a tone that sounded surprised they were overlooking something so obvious.

"What digging?" Lone and Smith said in unison.

"In the holes."

"What holes?"

"The ones in the back side of the mountain. The ones the old tribal medicine man reminded Iron Wolf about last winter." A look of sudden realization came over Bright Moon. "Eagle wrote me about this, about how excited Iron Wolf and Grogan became and how they immediately started sending men into the holes. But neither of you, of course, would have any way to have heard these things, would you?"

"No. But I sure want to hear more now," Smith responded. "Tell us about the holes."

"I am not saying it right." Bright Moon scowled. "Not just holes, but...stretched out, like worms."

"Tunnels, you mean?"

"Yes! That is the word—tunnels. Natural tunnels," Bright Moon said, "running from smaller caves on the back side of the mountain. They are the reason many elders call the place 'Grief Mountain,' because of a time when some children went exploring in them and were never found. They reach deep into the mountain, maybe all the way through, some believe. Iron Wolf and

Grogan are counting on the right tunnel, if dug deeper, leading through to reach the great cavern from which the guns might still be salvaged."

"How could that be?" Lone cut his eyes over to Smith. "You blew up the cavern, right? The Spencers have to be buried and crushed under rubble."

Smith rubbed his jaw. "Not necessarily. That was a big-ass cavern. Like I told you before, easily able to fit all our gang members, horses, and a heap of supplies. The rifles were stacked at the back, all the way in. Waiting for Iron Wolf to show up with the gold and take posses- sion. The charge I set was in the cliff face over the entrance, sealing everything off. But those rifles, in as deep as they were, could possibly be found unscathed. If somebody was able to burrow to 'em."

"I'll be damned," Lone muttered.

"Grogan believes that to be the case and has convinced Iron Wolf the same," said Bright Moon. "They have teams of men digging in the tunnels every day."

"Like I mentioned, Grogan knows how to set charges, make things blow a certain way." Smith grimaced. "He'd recognize how I brought the cliff down over the entrance. It'd be enough to make him think there was a chance for the guns to still be intact deeper in."

Nobody said anything for a minute. The only sound was the crackling of the fire.

Until Lone spoke in a determined growl. "Alright. Let's look at it as things havin' just been made simpler. Everything we're aimin' to do when we reach the Flat Falls territory is now right there in one spot—on the rez. We drop off Bright Moon and then you and me, Smith, go pay our visit to Grogan. Ride to the bullet, remember? Ain't like we're gonna have to poke around wonderin' where to find him. You remember how to get back to that mountain where the big cavern is, don't you?"

It took a second for Smith's mouth to spread in a rake-hell grin. "Damn betcha."

Lone spread his hands. "Then there you have it. We sashay in, dodge a few hotblooded braves and ex-gang pals of yours, drag Grogan's ass out of whichever hole he's crawled in, then you finish what you set out for. Hell, come to think of it, maybe I oughta turn you in and claim the bounty money first. You know, just to make ourselves a profit. *Then* we'll do the rest. Whatya think?"

"I think you're crazy. But there's nothing new in that," Smith told him. "Just like there's nothing new in me agreeing to the plans you lay out. Including this one."

"What about me?" asked Bright Moon. "Do you still want to get rid of me, or am I included too?"

"Damn betcha you're included!" came the simultaneous response from both men.

CHAPTER THIRTY-TWO

FOR THE NEXT THREE DAYS, THEY PUSHED STEADILY NORTH in accordance with the plan Lone had outlined. They stuck to ruggeder ground, leaving minimal signs, following low, twisty gullies and dry washes that kept them off the skyline, swinging wide around any hint of a ranch or a town. They neither saw—nor were seen by—another living soul. Periodically, Lone would loop to the rear to check their back trail, always relieved to spot nothing of concern.

A cold, misty rain clung to them for most of one afternoon before finally lifting. Otherwise, the days were sunny and hot, though not punishingly so; the nights were brisk under cloudless skies.

The pack horse was well stocked, so their necessities were adequately served. Each evening, Bright Moon would change the dressing on the bullet burn to Lone's shoulder, applying some of the salve Sue Leonard had sent along. Their meals were hearty, if somewhat redundant. Bacon, beans, biscuits. Tins of fruit, most commonly peaches, sometimes embalmed beef. They saw wild game on more than one occasion, but always in an open area where Lone cautioned against a rifle shot that could be heard for miles and might, therefore, draw unwanted attention. Twice, however, Bright Moon had luck in nearby streams and presented catches of fish that fried up as a welcome change.

By their fourth night out from Russet, they had crossed into North Dakota. They camped that night in a grassy, shallow depression rimmed to the west and north by jagged rocks interspersed with pine brush and a few spindly trees. This served as a partial block to the chilly wind that had arisen at sunset and now sighed through the pines like a mournful whisper. The depression had plenty of graze but no fresh water for the horses. They carried sufficient water, though, in their canteens and two large water bags on the packhorse. It was from one of these bags that Lone had watered all of the animals before graining them against the chill and then picketing them for the night.

He and the others sat around the fire now, sipping from post-meal cups of coffee and talking some before getting ready to turn in. The flames of the fire snapped and guttered in the wind gusts that swirled down over the rocks and brush. Overhead, the stars shone like ice chips against the dark canopy of the sky.

"I ain't been up this way but once, a long time back," Lone was saying. "I figure by mid-day tomorrow we oughta be on the front edge of the Flat Falls rez. That should put us in territory as familiar to you two— maybe more—than it is to me."

"Most likely. Since we've both spent more recent time in the area," agreed Smith.

"Way I recall," Lone went on, "between here and

there is a stretch of badlands. Nowhere near as big as the better-known sprawl down in South Dakota, but formidable all the same."

"Uh-huh. They're there. Nothing like the ones down south, true," said Smith, "but mighty barren and empty. That line of bare, jagged rocks we could see to the north as the sun was going down? That's them. I oughta know, they're where I hid out that first week or so after I blew the cavern and made my split from Grogan."

"I figure we'll be passing along the eastern edge of 'em. Not too far in."

"Sounds right. If things turn too hot after we have our run-in with Grogan, be worth keeping in mind they could make a good fall-back spot where we could lay low for a spell if need be. Like I did before."

Lone nodded. "Good to know. Definitely worth keepin' in mind." He took a drink of coffee then turned his attention to Bright Moon. "Now, little gal, if we get you onto rez property, are you gonna be able to connect back up with your people okay, while me and Smith go 'front Grogan like we planned?"

"Yes. I will be fine," Bright Moon assured him.

"How are you going to explain how you got back?" asked Smith. "You'll need to be careful not to connect yourself to us. After we get done doing what we have in mind, you understand, we're going to be a couple of mighty unpopular hombres."

"Maybe not as unpopular as you think," said Bright Moon. "Maybe it is time more members of my tribe knew about the foolishly reckless scheming of Iron Wolf."

Lone winced. "That sounds like awful dangerous talk, little gal. Like Smith said, you need to be careful.

Me and him can make a run for it. You have to keep livin' here."

"It is time for Eagle Soaring to become a stronger voice in our tribe. He will look out for me. And, for me, he will even take a stand against his father." Bright Moon smiled disarmingly, first at Lone and then Smith. "Do not worry, I won't do anything foolish. You two need to worry about yourselves, not keep being so concerned about me. As far as explaining how I got back, I will very innocently plead how was I supposed to know that the two men who brought me—men I believed to be arranged by none other than Iron Wolf—would turn out to be such trouble-making scoundrels?"

Lone and Smith exchanged looks.

"Now I'm worried about something else," said Smith.

"What's that?"

"Poor Eagle Soaring. I wonder if he has any idea what a devious gal he's about to take as his wife?"

"Don't you dare tell him," said Bright Moon. "The joy of marriage, remember, is a man and woman learning things about one another they might otherwise never know."

"Uh-huh. But what if they're better off *not* knowing?" Smith teased.

"I suggest you leave it at that," cut in Lone. "You two keep goin', we'll end up none of us gettin' any shuteye. And I need my beauty sleep."

"There's a statement *nobody's* going to argue with," Smith quipped, and then barely managed to duck Lone's empty coffee cup.

A handful of minutes later, the weariness from another long day in the saddle started to take hold.

That, combined with the sharpening bite of the chill wind, made the thought of wrapping up in a warm bedroll all the harder to resist. While Bright Moon and Smith did exactly that, Lone went to make a final check on the horses.

When he returned, they were both seemingly already asleep. He stoked up the fire so it would give their closely bundled forms a thorough toasting before it started to die back down. Then he retrieved the cup he'd tossed at Smith earlier and filled it with the last of the coffee left in the pot. This, along with his Yellowboy and a sheepskin-lined jacket he pulled from his possibles pack, he carried to a notch in the higher rocks about twenty yards from the fire and his two sleeping companions. He settled back into the notch, out of the wind, with the jacket draped over him and the warm cup between his palms.

Without making a production of it, each night after the others had gone to sleep, Lone had taken watch for a few hours. He was near certain no one was close on their trail, but a dose of precaution never hurt. He would get comfortable, keep vigil, maybe doze an eye blink or three, then sometime after midnight take to his bedroll for four hours of hard, deep sleep. Yeah, something could still happen in those wee hours. A skilled night stalker, in fact, knew that hour just before dawn was when an encampment or an individual was most deeply lulled, most vulnerable. But no roaming bandits were apt to have that kind of skill or training. And Indians, which would mean reservation-jumpers under these circumstances, disliked night conflict unless forced into it. Finally, a posse or pack of bounty hunters, Lone figured, would be too anxious, too impatient to hold off making their move so late.

So he reckoned the wee hours to be relatively safe, and it was important for him to get *some* amount of decent sleep or risk letting his senses become too dulled to rely on in case a problem broke sudden-like. Besides, his backup—Ironsides—had proven time and again to be about as good a guard dog as any he'd seen. If the big gray sensed a hint of trouble or danger, he'd make some noise about it.

So Lone sat, watching and listening. Sipping rapidly cooling coffee. Thinking. Thinking about the matter at hand and, naturally, about his beloved but tragically lost Velda. No matter where he was or what he was doing, she was never far from his thoughts. Tonight, at times, it seemed like the mournfully sighing wind was whispering her name.

Lone dozed and then came out of it with a jerk, cursing himself. *If you're going to stand watch, damn it, then do it right!* Even though the wind seemed to have abated some, it felt suddenly colder. He set aside the empty coffee cup and shrugged into the sheepskin jacket. He blew on his hands, wishing he'd thought to grab a pair of gloves. Christ, they hadn't ridden *that* far north!

And then Ironsides chuffed.

It was so faint that for a moment, Lone thought it might have been a rogue gust of the fading wind. But no, there it was again. Another faint chuff accompanied by a hoof pawing tentatively at the grass. The gray was definitely picking up on something, yet at the same time didn't seem overly agitated by it. That was damned odd. Frowning, Lone quietly lifted his Yellowboy from where it was leaning against a wall of the notch and laid it across his lap.

Lone listened harder, more intently. He swept his eyes in a wide, slow scan, avoiding the glow of the campfire so as not to affect his acclimated night vision to the wider, non-illuminated expanse around him. He had a poor line of sight to where the horses were picketed, but from what he could see, all appeared to be stirring somewhat. He peeled out of his notch and ghosted silently closer to them.

That's when he spotted the tall, slender form of a person moving within the line of animals. Lone froze. Watching, he saw the person reach out and gently pat Ironsides' neck—and the big gray actually *leaned into* the caress! Lone was stunned. What the hell...

Then the person stepped out from the mass of shadows thrown by the animals, and Lone was stunned again. But at least now he understood. Knew *why* Ironsides had responded so docilely.

Lone stepped forward and said in a low, measured tone, "Sue?"

In the murky starlight, Sue Leonard went momentarily rigid. Then Lone saw her shoulders relax, and she smiled. "Lone. You move like a ghost...you startled me."

"*I* startled *you*? What in blazes are you doing here?"

The smile titled. "If you offer me some hot coffee against this bitter night air, I'll tell you. Believe me, I've got plenty you'll find worth hearing."

CHAPTER THIRTY-THREE

THE CAMPFIRE WAS STOKED BACK HIGH AND HOT, A FRESH pot of coffee had been brewed, and a surprised Bright Moon and Smith were awakened to the sound of Lone speaking with someone who turned out to be Sue Leonard once again in their midst. The four of them now sat huddled close around the snapping, popping flames, each holding a steaming cup between their palms, listening to Sue relate how and why she came to be there.

"Only a couple hours after you three rode out of Russet," she was saying, "the posse from Coraville showed up. Not an official posse, mind you, not a group of men properly sanctioned and deputized. Fred Kurtz honored the agreement he made to hold off twenty-four hours before forming a posse. This bunch came at the demand of Twin V cattle boss Vance Veldon, who refused to believe Lone and Smith didn't play a more direct part in the shootout that killed so many of his men. One of them being his nephew."

"Seems to me that high-handed cattle bosses are

gettin' thicker than fleas wherever you turn," grumbled Lone. "And just about as annoying."

Sue replied, "You don't know the half of it. But more about that in a minute. First, let me tell you about the make-up of this so-called posse. It's led by Veldon's ranch foreman, a man named Tobe Medford; a decent enough fellow from what I know, just aiming to do the job his boss sent him out on. He's got three other Twin V wranglers with him—one of them, Chico Racone—is supposedly a pretty good tracker."

"He must have something on the ball if they were that tight on our tails," Lone admitted grudgingly. "I sure never saw no sign of any hounds when I did my back trail check."

"If they pushed through part of that storm and then kept coming while we were stopped helping the Haneses, they' d've had the chance to close a lot of gap between them and us," Smith pointed out. Then, with a sarcastic twist to his mouth, he added, "No good deed goes unpunished. Remember?"

Lone swore under his breath.

"Also in the posse," Sue continued, "is Johnny Case, Kurtz's former deputy. He went against the marshal's will and was so determined to join the chase that he even turned in his badge."

"He had the stink-eye for us right from the git-go," muttered Smith.

"And he also had an eye for someone else," Bright Moon said quietly, aiming a sly smile toward Sue.

Sue heaved a weary sigh. "Yes, it's true Johnny has been in love with me for years. At least, he thinks he is. But I've never felt anything in return, and he's never had the courage to come right out and...I guess I should be somewhat flattered that him standing up to Marshal Kurtz and even being willing to give up his badge was largely because of me, but—doggone it, why are we even talking about such a thing when there are so much bigger matters at hand?"

"That's a good question," Lone grumbled, wondering why he found the talk about Sue and Johnny Case so particularly annoying.

"One more thing about the Coraville posse," Sue said after taking a sip of her coffee. "The final member is none other than my brother James."

"You've got to be kidding!" Smith blurted. Then he quickly added, "Sorry. No offense meant."

Sue gave a faint shake of her head. "No need to apologize. My first reaction was pretty much the same. But you wouldn't believe how much he's changed in only a few days. He's sober, for one thing. But, more than that, he's...he's been hardened. By being on the trail for those days and nights, I guess. Out in the wind and sun. Among men used to and totally accepting of such conditions. In the time I've been riding with them, this side of him has only deepened. For the first time since his wife jilted him, I feel like he can finally start taking care of himself again—maybe even me a little bit, if the need arose."

Lone grinned. "As capable and self-sufficient as you've shown yourself to be, it's hard to see that need arisin'."

"I'll take that as a compliment. But everybody needs somebody, sooner or later."

Lone and Sue held each other's eyes for a long beat. Until Smith said, "This business about you riding with your brother and the rest of that bunch...how did that happen? And how is it you're separated from them now?"

"Me riding with them happened because I insisted on it when they left Russet," Sue responded. "I can be rather forceful when I need to be."

Lone said nothing. Just smiled a little and made a *"see what I mean?"* gesture.

"Before we get to what I'm doing here now," Sue continued, "let's back up to Russet for a minute. You can imagine the chaos you left in your wake there. I hadn't even sent my telegram yet when the men from Coraville showed up. I'd been back in with Sara Hanes and Granny Mavis most of the time before then. I was still trying to sort out all the details I was hearing about everything that had happened."

Smith cocked an eyebrow. "I can imagine all of the 'facts' that were swirling hot and heavy."

"One fact staying consistent was that the three dead men all rode for Cotton Thayer's CT brand. And when a messenger was sent out to notify him, he responded with all haste, tearing into town with a pack of hard-looking hombres strung out behind him."

"Swell," said Lone. "Yet another high-handed cattle boss out for our hides."

Sue's brows pinched together. "It gets even better. Ironically, on the way in, the CT outfit crossed paths with the posse from Coraville. They all came pouring into town together and, yes, the 'hides'—to keep it in polite terms—of you and Smith were very much a point of discussion that soon became a common goal for all of them."

"So have we now got *two* packs of bloodhounds after

our...er, hides...or are they lumped together into a sort of small army?" Smith queried.

"One lump. And only eight men. Plus me."

Smith looked at Lone. "Only eight. Four apiece. I was worried for nothing. They'll make a good warm-up for Pike and the boys when we get to 'em...*if* we ever get to 'em, the way a parade is starting to be strung out behind us!"

"Who's headin' this parade?" Lone asked Sue. "Did Thayer himself saddle up, or is he another general who just points and then leads from the rear?"

"Only a pointer. His ramrod is a man named Connors. He reminds me a lot of Tobe Medford from the Twin V. They're of a type and seem to be getting along pretty well, at least so far. I guess they're sort of co-leaders of the group. Two members of the original Coraville posse—Ikes and somebody they called the Kid—dropped out and turned back," Sue explained. "That leaves a group made up of four and four. Medford, Racone, Johnny, and my brother—that's four from Coraville. Then Connors, Reed, Barkley, and Calder from the CT." She paused, eyeing Lone. "The one named Calder, Grif Calder, has taken over from Racone as lead tracker. He claims he used to scout for the Army...and claims also to know you."

Lone pursed his lips in thought. "Grif Calder. Sure, I know him. Or *knew* him. We scouted together out of Fort Morgan in Colorado for a spell. Good scout, always seemed an okay fella. Leastways he was back then."

"Don't know how good a fella he still might be," said Smith, "but apparently, he remains a pretty good scout. Good enough, anyhow, to have tracked us all this way."

Sue shook her head. "No. He didn't track you. Not really. He didn't have to."

Lone looked puzzled. "What do you mean?"

"I mean nobody had to do any tracking because the parade, as you call it, has known right where you're headed ever since leaving Russet. Flat Falls Indian reservation, to return Bright Moon. Right?" Sue paused, her expression turning somewhat grim. "And then, somewhere in the same vicinity, to confront this Grogan person who's behind the bounty on Smith...or should I say 'Wade Avril'?"

Smith eyed her flatly. "Keep it, Smith. I'm parting ways with that other fella. And when I'm done with Grogan, I'll also be done with Avril. Once and for good."

"How is it," Lone wanted to know, "this parade of hounds know all this? And, if they do, why have they waited all this time—since we left Russet—to make a move on us?"

"They know so much about your intentions," Sue answered, "because you apparently talked a little too freely in front of Jeffrey Hanes. As soon as he heard mention of Wade Avril and the big bounty on his head, he started chattering like a magpie. Thinking if he gave enough information, I guess, it might earn him a piece of the pay-off."

"That ungrateful little bastard," Lone growled.

Smith sneered. "Like I keep telling you, no good deed goes—"

"Don't say it again," Lone warned him, "or I'll chuck another cup at you, this one with hot coffee still in it."

"Anyway," Sue continued, "armed with this informa-tion—and more added by liveryman Driscoll, mainly the Wade Avril part—the new, joint posse was formed, and in short order, was outfitted and ready to ride. Knowing what they knew, their plan was not to try tracking and following and hoping to catch up with you on the trail, but rather to ride hard with the aim of outdistancing you and then be waiting to catch you by surprise when you got to the Flat Falls area. I won my demands to join them by playing up outrage over the way I'd been treated as a hostage and arguing I deserved to be on hand when they confronted you."

Lone regarded her for a moment, then asked, "And your real motive?"

"None of your business. I'm not even sure myself."

Smith gave it a beat before saying, somewhat impatiently, "So where does all that bring us to in the here and now? Where is this joint posse at the moment? And, with all due respect, Miss Sue, what are you doing here?"

A tolerant smile played across Sue's lips. Pointing, she said, "The posse is about a mile and a half that way, to the east and a bit north. Their plans have now changed. That's what I'm doing here...I came to warn you."

"Warn us about what? What are they plannin'?" asked Lone.

"An ambush. About mid-morning tomorrow, in a stretch of broken land that Calder and Racone rode ahead and identified as a good spot."

"More pissant ambushers," Lone growled. "They're gettin' to be about as thick as high-minded cattle bosses. And, since they have a habit of throwin' hot lead instead of just hot air, even a bigger concern."

"Each day, Calder has been riding ahead on scout," Sue related. "Today, from a high crest, he just happened to catch sight of you three. It was unexpected. Neither him nor any of the others figured our group had caught up that much. They also recognized that we had been inadvertently running on a course parallel to yours—like I said, about a mile or two to the east.

"Faced with all of this, Medford and Connors sent both scouts, Calder and Racone, out once more to see if they could find any land feature that presented itself as a good spot to intercept you and end the chase earlier than originally planned. The scouts came back describing what they called a stretch of badlands up ahead that your current course would be taking you through—including a narrow passage you'd have to use, which would be ideal for an ambush."

Smith brooded for a minute and then said, "If we packed up and lit a shuck out of here right away, we could outfox 'em. Be gone and through the edge of those badlands practically before they got saddled up in the morning." He paused, his brows pinching tight. "*Or*...we could hold up on the sides of that pass and wait to do a little ambushing of our own."

"My brother is riding with those men," Sue was quick to remind him.

"That's by *his* choice!" Smith snapped back. "We gave him every opportunity to keep his drunken ass back in Coraville."

"That's a mean thing to say!"

"Sorry if my feelings toward anybody who's part of a pack out to hunt me down and nail my hide to the wall for blood money ain't real charitable."

Lone slashed a hand through the air. "Everybody pull in your horns and take it easy for a minute. Sue has brought us warnin' so—"

"I brought you more than just a warning," Sue cut him off. "I brought you the means to keep the posse off your backs while you proceed to do what you set out for."

"How?"

"It's right in front of you," Sue stated with a bit of a smirk. "I'm your hostage again. Come daylight, you tie me up with a gun held to my head, march me out where they can plainly see. Order them to back off and stay that way until you've finished your business with Grogan. Only then will you set conditions for releasing me unharmed."

There was a span of stunned silence.

Until Lone said, "You mean you'd actually be willin' to—"

Sue cut him off again. "It's already done. I slipped away after everyone was asleep. Left my bedroll messed up as if I'd been taken by force. Left a note behind that read: *We've got her again. Don't do anything stupid. Will meet with you in the morning.* No signature, but I've little doubt they'll figure out who it's supposed to be from. Before the sun went down, Calder and Racone had pointed out to all of us where you were camped. I memorized some distinct features of this overlooking rocky rim. When there was enough starlight for me to make them out from a distance, I started walking this way."

Smith was shaking his head as if in amazement even before she was done speaking. "That's incredible thinking on your part. Gutsy, definitely a little crazy. But still, just maybe..."

"Maybe hell," Lone declared. "It's damned clever

and brave. And now that Sue has stuck her neck out for us, it's our job to make it work."

"Agreed," said Smith. "But something to consider... four of the men in that posse have no real tie to Sue. She's basically a stranger, giving them not quite as much reason to be swayed by whether or not harm comes to her."

"I thought of that, too," Sue countered. "But I'm confident my brother and Johnny—Medford, too, if it came down to it—will not allow that kind of cold indifference."

Lone considered a minute. Then said, "I got to go with that, too. I'd even toss in Grif Calder. Unless he's changed one hell of a lot since I knew him, he ain't the kind of man who'd be any part of leavin' a woman to harm if he could help it."

Smith exhaled a deep breath. "All right. I guess we've got ourselves a plan then." He swept his eyes skyward. "What else we got is a precious two or three hours 'til daybreak. Don't expect any of us is gonna sleep real sound, but we ought to try and get some rest all the same. One way or another, tomorrow is shaping up to be a mighty full day."

———

Despite Smith's prediction, Lone, for one, was able to eke out some meaningful slumber. It was something he'd trained himself to do years past during his scouting days. There'd been times when he found himself deep in hostile Indian territory, with redskins out for his scalp swarming close on all sides, yet he'd make do with even the most uncomfortable concealment and catch some sleep within it. In order to endure and keep going, a body had to sleep for whatever amounts they could grab whenever possible.

On this night, however, Lone did do some churning in his bedroll at first. There was much to consider. This time, he wasn't alone in hostile territory. There were other lives riding on the line as well. Sue Leonard; what an amazing woman she was proving more and more to be... Bright Moon; merely wanting to get back home, back to the young man she'd been betrothed to since childhood yet caught up in the turmoil of white men she had no stake in...Smith; haunted by the specter of "Wild Red" Avril and wanting desperately to bury that ghost along with its still-living link in the form of Pike Grogan...Velda; always there, always close in his mind yet tragically gone from reach...Sue again; crowding thoughts of Velda, making Lone feel disloyal and ashamed...

Then, the sleep came. And then Sue returned. Not in churning, restless thoughts, though. Nor in a dream. But for real.

"Lone..." Her breath was warm on his cheek, her voice a husky whisper. "If you want me to go, say so fast and firm and I'll leave. Otherwise..."

He was wide awake now, gazing deep into her eyes, shining in the starlight only inches from his face.

"Are you sure?" he husked softly.

"I haven't been sure about anything where you're concerned since you first stood in my doorway back in Coraville, you big galoot...how about helping me make up my mind?"

Lone peeled back his bedroll and held it open. "Be my great honor and privilege, ma'am."

CHAPTER THIRTY-FOUR

"YOU ROTTEN SONSABITCHES." JOHNNY CASE'S LIPS curled apart, baring his teeth like a snarling dog as he spoke. "I could tell right from the first you were nothing but lowlife scum. Now you're proving it yet again."

Lone let his gaze sweep slowly over the eight horsemen bunched before him, purposely skimming past the former deputy as a sign of what little significance he counted him to be. There were only two other faces he recognized. One was that of Dr. James Risen; Sue's brother. Lone could see right away what she meant about him having changed. Indeed, he looked harder, grimmer, his formerly lean face now hollower-cheeked and haggard. He was in need of a shave, his hair was uncombed and windblown, and his once crisp, white shirt was sweat-stained and streaked with dust. All of which made the borrowed six-gun holstered on his hip look not quite so incongruous. Sitting his horse farther back in the assemblage, the beefy, bearded mug of Grif Calder appeared little changed from what Lone remembered. Some flecks of gray that hadn't been present before in the beard, blue eyes washed out a little paler, fringed buckskin shirt and feather-adorned slouch hat traded for wrangler garb and a John B Stetson—otherwise not much different.

The rest of the men returning Lone's gaze had a commonality to their appearance that could be fitted to ranch crews most anywhere. Unshaven, sun-browned and wind-burned faces, perpetually squinted eyes bracketed by deep crow's feet, colorful neckerchiefs, tobacco lumps in some cheeks, cigarettes dangling from the corners of some mouths. The notable difference here being that this collection was more heavily armed than a random gathering of standard wranglers was apt to be.

The face-off in progress was occurring on a flat plain of stubbly grass about halfway between what had been the night camps of those involved. There were a few clumps of brush and some nests of wind-blunted boulders scattered about. The sun had been up just a little more than an hour. The air was totally still.

Two of the men before Lone sat their mounts slightly ahead of the others, marking them as most likely being the ramrods Sue had spoken of. Both were broad-shouldered six-footers and both conveyed an added air of competence and self-assurance.

"Which one of you is Tobe Medford?" Lone asked.

"That'd be me," answered the husky gent to the left of the other one. He had strong, even features with a touch of flintiness to his eyes. He gave the impression of being a reasonable sort but with boundaries that, when crossed, would turn loose a not-so-reasonable side.

"If you're one of the he-coons leadin' this pack," Lone told him, "then tell that chatterin' chipmunk off behind you there to keep his mouth shut while we're conductin' business."

Medford's jaw muscles bulged visibly for a second. Then they relaxed and, without looking around, he said, "Consider him told." Johnny Case's eyes blazed at Lone but he clamped his mouth into a tight, straight line and said nothing.

The hombre to Medford's right spoke up, saying, "What about me? You got no orders for me?" His eyes were cold, colorless slits under bristly, bone-white brows, and he had a thin-lipped slash of a mouth. There was a definite edge to his tone that warned Lone to stay on guard with this one.

Lone met the stare from those cold slits, and he said, "You Connors?"

"That's right."

"Then my general orders, if you want to call 'em that, got contained pretty clear in the note that was left...don't nobody do nothing stupid. That'll make for the best chance to keep this thing from boilin' over and scaldin' more folks than necessary."

A corner of Connors's mouth twitched. "So you calculate two bracing eight as something that falls inside the boundaries of *not* doing something stupid. I got that right?"

"The way we calculate," responded Smith from where he sat his horse a couple yards behind and off to one side of Lone, "is that this Greener I'm holding, and what's on the other end of it, tallies up to being not so lopsided. Leastways not leaning in your favor." The references Smith was making had to do with the double-barreled Greener shotgun resting across his saddle pommel. The gaping twin bores of its muzzles were mere inches from the head of Sue Leonard, who stood on the ground next to Smith with her wrists bound together and her arms pulled chin high and held that way by a short leather thong tied to his saddle horn. Her appearance, in keeping with the role she herself had concocted, was disheveled and plaintive.

Connors eyed Smith. "So you're the famous Wild Red Avril, eh?"

"Some call me that. Some other things."

"Uh-huh. Say...where's the Injun squaw been travelin' with you all along? I don't see no sign of her this mornin'."

"We cooked her and ate her for breakfast. Got tired of having her underfoot," Smith answered, deadpan.

Connors grinned. "Real funny. Easy to see where the 'Red' comes from, and I've heard a God's plenty about your 'wild' side. Never figured you for havin' a sense of humor, though."

"Sorta depends on what a body finds amusing, don't it?"

As a matter of fact, early that morning, Smith had reached a decision on something that no longer seemed amusing—or necessary—to him. Rising ahead of everybody else, he'd proceeded to take a bar of strong lye soap and a pan of hot water and furiously scrub every trace of boot blacking from his hair. "Don't seem to be fooling much of anybody anyway," he'd declared, "and I'm damned sick of it. Besides, when I face Pike and the boys, I want to make sure before I put their lights out permanent-like that they see goddamn good and well who's pinching the wick." And so it was, for the first time in days and purposely minus any kind of hat, his mane of fiery hair was on full display in this morning's bright sunlight.

"Alright," Medford said, scowling, bringing an end to the exchange between Smith and Connors. "Now that we've traded names and tossed around some numbers and whatnot, let's get back to conducting the business as was mentioned. What's it gonna take to get Mrs. Leonard safely returned?"

"The same thing—the only thing—we've been wantin' from the get-go," Lone told him in an exasperated snarl. "And that's for people to stay off our backs long enough to let us take care of a pest control matter that, in the long run, everybody will be better off for."

Medford grunted. "Ever occur to you not to leave dead and shot-up bodies in your wake if you really want to go unbothered?"

"The only bodies we left laying were yellow ambushing skunks who came gunning for us and got what they asked for," said Smith.

"How about the woman?" sneered Connors. "You kidnap her again only on account of she came askin' for it too?"

Lone almost had to laugh at the irony of the question.

But before he could say anything, Johnny Case piped up again. "That sounded like a half-assed dirty remark, Connors. And not for the first time. I'm warning you, I'm damned sick of it and—"

James Risen, reined up right beside the former

deputy, cut him short. "Shut up, Johnny! This isn't the time and you're only making things worse." Then the doc swung a mournful gaze toward his sister, as if he wanted to say more, but all he got out was a strained, "Sue..."

Lone spoke out clear and sharp, saying, "If you want to throw around blame for us takin' a hostage—again—then look to yourselves. Stubborn asses like Deputy Johnny refusin' to believe we had nothing to do with that shootout outside of Coraville, even though we explained otherwise seven ways from Sunday, is what forced our hand to begin with. Then, even after we kept our end of the bargain and released her back at Russet, you pack of idiots got together and decided it would be a good idea to drag her along and try to corner us yet again...which brings us here to what we've got before us this morning."

"And that," said Medford, "brings us back around to my question...what's it going to take to get Mrs. Leonard released safely back to us?"

Lone felt the weight of everybody's eyes on him. He raised a hand and pointed. "Half a day's ride from here, to the north and some east, there's a town called Steadfast. Not much of a place, though maybe it's built up some since I was here a long while back. At any rate, it oughta have a café of some kind where you fellas can relax, have a nice meal, maybe a piece of pie and some coffee. Then there'll no doubt be a saloon you can wander over to and wet your whistles on something a little stronger than coffee...then, along about four or five in the afternoon I expect, things should have worked out so Mrs. Leonard will be delivered back to you there."

"And then what? What comes after that?" Medford wanted to know.

Lone eyed him. "I reckon that depends on you and those around you. For starters, if there's a brain among you, the first thing you oughta do is get this woman back to the safety of her home. After that, if any or all of you want to continue this with me and Smith...well, then come ahead on. But I warn you, all restraints will be off as far as we're concerned. No more talk, no more deals, no dodging. We see any of you in our gunsights, we'll burn you down without hesitation."

"Mighty sure of yourselves, ain't you?" drawled Connors.

"No brag, but we figure we got cause to be," Smith replied flatly.

Everything hung quiet for several beats.

Until Medford finally expelled a ragged breath and said, "Looks like we're gonna be spending the day in Steadfast, men. Waiting."

"Not so fast!" barked Connors, glaring at Medford. "You forgettin', *amigo*, you ain't got the whole say for everybody here?"

"Damn it, we talked about this!"

"We talked, but nothing got set in stone. To me and my boys, that woman don't mean shit as a bargainin' chip." Connors' slash of a mouth twisted cruelly. "Who's to say they won't go ahead and blow her head off anyway—or that she might catch a stray bullet if she's anywhere near when they 'front Grogan? Then all we'd be left with is knowing we pissed away a golden opportunity when we had the varmints right here in front of us!"

"Yeah, right here in front of us with a Greener

shotgun three inches from Sue Leonard's head, you cold-hearted bastard! You think they're bluffing?" Medford demanded.

"Yeah, I do! And I think we'd be damn fools to—"

The booming voice of Grif Calder broke in as he gigged his horse forward through the pack. "You can fire me right here on the spot or wait 'til we get back to the CT, Connors," he declared. "But either way, I ain't gonna stand by and let you or anybody else risk that gal's life no more than we've already done. McGantry's right— we were jackasses for draggin' her into this in the first place. Now, we need to not be bigger ones when it comes to gettin' her back safe."

Connors's nostrils flared, and fire blazed in the normally cold slits that were his eyes. "You're goddamned right about bein' fired, you ungrateful, disloyal old sonofabitch," he said through gritted teeth. "And the rest of you willin' to give in to the big bluff bein' pulled on you, can all kiss my ass. Me, Reed, and Barkley are pullin' out."

"Not necessarily," spoke up one of the other CT riders. "You see, me and Barkley feel the same as Grif. We think you're wrong, Mr. Connors. What's more, we came this far so kinda want to stick around and see how things finish playing out."

"To hell with all of you then! And you're both fired, too! The three of you had better figure on never returnin' to Russet, 'cause if you do, you'll be treated like dirt after I spread word how you turned yellow when we had the killers right under our noses. Me, I'm still cuttin' out."

"No, I don't think that'd be such a good idea," Calder drawled, pulling a long-barreled Navy Colt and aiming it casually at Connors. "The het-up condition you're in, you might go tearin' off and do something even jack-assier. I think it'd be best if you stuck with us, leastways until you get calmed down some...we reach Steadfast, we'll even let you buy us a drink."

CHAPTER THIRTY-FIVE

"ALL I'M SAYING IS THAT IT COULD HAVE GONE smoother," Sue persisted.

Lone gave a shrug. "Few things ever go perfect. I don't see your scheme as missin' all that far, though. We're shed of 'em, ain't we? Leastways for now. And we got it done without havin' to blow holes in each other. I'd call that a pretty good start to the day."

"Same here," Smith agreed. "Your plan worked fine, Miss Sue."

"I keep thinking about that mournful look on my brother's face. I wish there'd been a way I could have—"

"But there wasn't," Lone halted her. "He'll be okay when he sees you safe again. Just stick with recallin' how good your plan worked."

"Maybe so. But it might not have succeeded all the way if not for Lone's old friend, Grif Calder." Sue shook her head in dismay. "I sure made a bad read on that louse, Connors. Not to mention doing a dreadful disservice to Tobe Medford, at one time judging him and Connors to be cut from similar cloth."

Lone grinned. "Well, since he didn't hear you say it, we'll keep your secret. And as far as my old pal, Grif, I really had no way of knowin' what to expect out of him. But he by God came through a-shinin', didn't he?"

They were proceeding north, coming up on the southeast fringe of the badlands they were going to have to skim through. The eight-man posse they had recently faced down was faded from sight by now, having angled more to the east. Lone nevertheless kept scanning off in that direction, wanting to make sure none of them tried peeling back in an attempt at some trickery. He doubted such a thing—what with Medford, Calder, and Sue's brother holding Sue's safety as paramount—but it never hurt to be a little extra cautious.

As they entered into the badlands, even at its edges, grass and trees and shrubbery except for a few sparse, thorny clumps disappeared. Thrusting, tilting, jaggedly crested rock formations, all sun-bleached to a narrow spectrum of color between pale brown and tan, sprawled in a jumble on all sides. The horses' hooves, with no grass carpeting underneath them, clacked loudly on the hardpan and rock slab flooring.

"One thing about the start to the day that's still bothersome, though," Smith said, "remains the question of where Bright Moon ran off to?"

"I keep wondering about that, too," agreed Sue. "We haven't had time to really even discuss any possibilities. I just hope she's all right."

When they woke earlier, they had discovered Bright Moon and all her personal effects gone from camp. Smith hadn't noticed it in the semi-dark when he got up to wash the blackout of his hair, but as day started to break and the others began rising, that's when they realized the Indian girl was absent.

"I'm not too worried," Lone said now. "This close to her reservation, I'm sure she's fine. Knowin' how near she was and all the other business we had facin' us first thing could be why she took off—not wantin' to be no more of a burden or in the way, that's how she might've seen it."

"Yeah, that could explain it," Smith allowed. "Be like her to be thoughtful in such a manner, getting out of our way so we could concentrate on other stuff. Dang, I got to like that little gal. Sure would hate it if she met with any misfortune."

Lone drew rein on Ironsides and pointed just ahead. "Speakin' of misfortune, I'd guess that narrow twist up yonder, how it reaches in through those higher rocks to either side, is where we were supposed to meet some of our own—misfortune, that is, by way of the ambush that posse was plannin'."

Smith made a sour face. "Looks like a damn near ideal spot for one...gotta give 'em credit for that much. There's where your buddy Calder's savvy, since he helped pick it out, would *not* have been in our best interest."

"Yeah. If we run across him again," Lone muttered, "remind me to give the old rascal a swift kick over that."

"The thing I'd like to do swiftly," said Sue, "is go ahead and get on through that pass. Now that we're in sight of it, it makes me squeamish even though I know there's no ambushers in there. I just want to get it behind us."

"I know what you mean. I wouldn't mind puttin' it behind us neither," Lone told her. Then, smiling and gesturing to her still-bound wrists, which they'd kept that way as a guard against possibly being monitored via field glasses even after the posse was seemingly out of sight, he added, "But you think we got time to first take those ropes off you? We're deep enough in these rocks now to where not even field glasses can see us. That is, unless you're enjoyin' your play-actin' at bein' a helpless hostage all over again?"

Sue arched a brow. "I was never all *that* helpless as a hostage, even when it was for real, mister." She held up her wrists. "But yes, I'm ready to say goodbye to these ropes—and even more ready to be done looking down the double-barreled canyons of that doggone shotgun."

Now it was Smith's turn to smile as he lifted the Greener and rested it on a shoulder. "Now, now. No need to hurt this old girl's feelings. She was just doing her job. Besides, you're the one who staged all the pieces of our little sideshow. Remember?"

"I remember. But now the show is over so the stage props can be put away." Once the ropes had been severed, Sue rubbed absently at the minor chafing they'd done to her wrists. Then she reached down and undid the leather thong tethering her to Smith, releasing it off the saddle horn it had been tied to after they got her mount back from the posse. "Now let's get on through that doggone pass or canyon or whatever you want to call it."

Lone led the way, Sue behind him, Smith and the pack horse bringing up the rear. The morning sun was rising higher and hotter and beating down on the bare, pale rocks that crowded in ever closer, only reflected it back and amplified its heat. By the middle of the day, moving about in this broken land would be brutal. But

Lone couldn't help thinking, if things went as expected, then this day had been marked for some time to see a measure of brutality before it was over.

Even riding single file, it was clear as they drew nearer that the upcoming passage was going to be mighty tight. Like Smith had noted—and what caused Calder and Racone to choose it for such—a damn near ideal spot for an ambush. But that, thankfully, had been averted...

Until, suddenly, it no longer was!

If the ambush partly planned by Grif Calder had gone ahead under his direction—him having the savvy and cold-blooded, firsthand experience to know how to do it right—it likely would have suited the ideal setting. But in the hands of booze-fueled, over-eager amateurs, even the best set-up can be bungled. Which, in this case, meant bad results for the ambushers and more fortunate ones for the intended victims.

The problem for the ambushers was that they started shooting too soon. They should have waited until both Lone and Smith were in the cut and bottled there at each end, with nowhere to go on either side. That was, in fact, the plan devised and agreed on by the two men fixing to implement it—said men being Bishop Ikes and Kid Memphis, the pair of Twin V riders who allegedly "turned back" when the joint posse forming at Russet got too crowded for their tastes. In truth, their real reason for separating from the others had been formed upon hearing that one of the men they'd initially started after was none other than Wade Avril; and the fat bounty riding on him made a far better reason to give chase than anything the others seemed interested in. Furthermore, that bounty split only two ways sounded a hell of a lot juicier than too many fingers gouging out pieces for themselves.

So Ikes and the Kid had fogged the trail of the posse, unseen, as they rode hard to cut off the flight of Lone and Smith/Avril. And neither of the "scouts" riding with the posse, though both sharp-eyed, were any the wiser. What reason did *they* have to consider checking their back trail? The bounty-minded pair counted on this. Their intent all along, once the gap on the fugitives had been closed, was to slip in at an opportune moment and snatch the prize of Avril strictly for themselves. A fortunately timed skulk by the Kid of the posse's pre-dawn camp this very morning, right as panic was erupting over the discovery of Sue's staged abduction, gave every indication of that opportune moment being at hand. Since the posse's own ambush plan, which the Kid had overheard during a previous skulk of their camp, now appeared blocked, what was to stop Ikes and the Kid from filling in for them? And then riding away, either with Avril their prisoner—or his head in a sack?

So that's what was coming to fruition as Lone, Sue, and Smith had now reached the ambush site. Trouble was, the newly discovered skulking skills of Jerome "Kid Memphis" Darrold far outweighed his much bragged about—but never really proven beyond fast-draw displays and target shooting—skills at actual gun work. When the time came, he got nervous, over-anxious, and made a downright stupid move. Him and his double-holstered Colts were in low concealment off to the right of the cut's entrance. Ikes was a hundred yards deeper into the passage, crouched in high rocks with a Winchester. Two corks ready to plug each end of the bottle as soon as the riders had made their way inside.

But as Lone was starting into the cut, three-quarters past where the Kid was positioned, the latter shifted ever so slightly to ease a cramp in his leg. This caused the butt of one of his Colts to scrape softly against rock. It wasn't much of a sound—but enough to alert Lone. It was a sound that didn't belong, causing Lone's head to snap around and his eyes to go raking for the source.

He's looking right at me! the Kid's brain screamed. And that was enough to throw him into full panic. He thrust to a standing position, clawing for his guns and hollering, "They're onto us, Ikes! We gotta blast the sonsabitches!"

Lone saw the Kid pop up and heard him holler. The rest was all too clear. Another goddamn ambush! He had little doubt Smith could also see and hear what was happening, but he bellowed it over his shoulder anyway. "Bushwhackers! Get Sue down and take to cover!"

At the same time, he was palming his own Colt, even as the Kid's twin cutters came flashing into sight. Whoever the little bastard was, he was fast. But that didn't change the fact he was also panicky, his movements quick but frantic and half-wild. He triggered both guns at once, the slugs they hurled sizzling wide to either side of Lone and then ricocheting off the rocks in sharp, empty whines.

Lone fired a half second later, but his shot was hurried, too. It came close, though, spanging off a rocky spur just inches from the Kid's head, spitting dust and stony shards against his cheek and causing him to jerk away as he triggered two, even more, off-target rounds. But Lone couldn't count on the Kid's shooting to continue being so wild, especially not at such close quarters and with him having some concealment while Lone was caught more or less in the open.

Lone was too far into the narrow confines of the cut to be able to wheel Ironsides. That left two choices. He could either quit the saddle and try to find some concealment of his own in the jaggedness on the opposite side, or he could spur the big gray ahead, past the Kid's line of vision, and charge deeper into the cut where he expected a second ambusher to be waiting. It wasn't hard to make his selection. He sure as hell didn't like the idea of abandoning Ironsides and leaving him between Lone and the Kid trading fire—and whoever that other skunk up ahead was, he needed to be dealt with anyway.

Lone dug his heels into Ironsides and they surged forward, beyond the Kid's line of vision, even though the determined dumb ass wasted more powder and lead, killing additional rocks behind them. Any minute now, the Kid was about to have his trigger-happy hands full of a highly pissed-off Smith, and although he might not know it yet, he would be sorely in need of all the firepower he could muster.

For his part, though, Lone had to re-focus all his attention on whoever and whatever lay ahead for him and Ironsides.

It didn't take long to find out.

It was true the passage was damn narrow, but it was also relatively straight and short. That meant that when the second ambusher, Bishop Ikes—though Lone had no idea of his identity at the time—leaned out from a high crevice to take aim with his rifle, became just as exposed as Lone was down on the floor of the passage. And, with Lone coming fast and the exit of the cut less than thirty yards beyond, he'd have to shoot fast and accurately. Ikes had been set to open up on targets coming along at a leisurely pace, not this. And though he was a veteran of more than a few gun scrapes and not prone to panicking like the Kid, he was nevertheless a bit rattled by the sudden turn all of this was taking. Plus, it is difficult to accurately shoot at a downward angle.

All of these might have been excuses made by Ikes for missing that first shot. He possibly could have found some satisfaction in knowing how close he came, the bullet passing between Lone's left earlobe and shoulder, its hot breath felt on Lone's neck. But Bishop Ikes never had a chance for any of those things—no excuses, no satisfaction for coming close, no opportunity for a second try. Because little more than one second after he fired that errant shot, three .44 slugs fanned rapid-fire by Lone from astride a galloping Ironsides, were pounding into his chest and making him jerk and spin in a brief, grotesque dance even as they were killing him.

———

By THE TIME Lone rode out of the cut, turned, and quickly rode back through again to the entrance—with barely a sidelong glance as he went by Ikes' riddled body drooped partly over the edge of his ambush crevice—it was all over for Kid Memphis too. When he'd finally gotten around to turning his attention to Smith after Lone disappeared, the Kid only had the chance to say hello to a bullet from Smith's Winchester planting itself just above the bridge of his nose.

A safe but moderately shaken Sue was able to provide identities for the pair as the Twin V riders who had—falsely, it was obvious now—"turned back" to go home. The why behind their deception—to try instead for the bounty on Wade Avril—was also obvious. The details of how they'd shadowed behind and managed to be here, making their desperate play in this desolate place, would never be fully known. But to the survivors, it was of little consequence now. It was a grim piece of business over with...yet plenty more remained.

CHAPTER THIRTY-SIX

THE NEXT ENCOUNTER FOR LONE, SUE, AND SMITH WAS considerably more pleasant. It came as they were about an hour across the boundary of the Flat Falls rez, angling toward the bald dome rising up in the near distance out of scant trees and a jumble of broken, lesser rocks. Grief Mountain, as identified by Smith. Where waited Iron Wolf with his dream of guns and glory...and Pike Grogan with his greed for accessing heretofore untapped gold.

Whatever else happened, Smith/Avril—backed by Lone—was here this day to kill Grogan and put an end to his ruthless greed.

How Iron Wolf reacted would likely determine the fates of Smith and Lone—and perhaps his own.

But, before any of that, came the intervening sight of Bright Moon riding out to greet her former traveling companions. She looked more lovely than ever, clad in traditional Cheyenne maiden buckskins, though notably minus any brightly colored beads or feathers. Her hair was combed and braided to a glossy black sheen. Her smile was warm and genuine, but her eyes seemed troubled. She was astride the same horse as when she'd been traveling with Lone and the others, and riding beside her on a gleaming white stallion was a sinewy, bare-chested, handsome young brave Lone promptly figured to be Eagle Soaring, her betrothed. His expression was fixed and stern, though not necessarily unfriendly. Walking behind the pair, wearing similarly somber expressions, were about twenty other tribe members, a mix of young and old men and women.

"Welcome, my friends," greeted Bright Moon. "I am glad to see you made it safely."

"And we're glad to see *you* are safe," Lone replied. "We were a little worried by your absence when we woke this morning."

"I regret any undue concern I caused," Bright Moon said earnestly. "But a dream, a vision, woke me from my sleep and demanded I come to my people with all haste. There was not time to try and explain."

"Is everything okay?" Sue asked.

Bright Moon took a moment to answer, clearly seeking to choose the right words. Then she stated, "Both a great sadness and yet the lifting of a dark weight has occurred. Iron Wolf has perished, killed late last night, along with several braves and some of Pike Grogan's men, in a cave-in of one of the tunnels. That tragedy, that disturbance of so many lives passing between worlds, happening so near, is what somehow reached out and called to me. Our people are naturally in mourning, but in the hearts of many, there also is a sense of relief in the hope that this tragic thing will once and for all end the plans to recover the rifles and stage the futile uprising Iron Wolf insisted on pursuing." She then made a gesture toward the youth mounted beside her. "This is Eagle Soaring, my betrothed, and the son of Iron Wolf."

Lone's eyes went to the lad. "I am sorry for your loss," he said simply.

Eagle met his gaze. "It is as Bright Moon says...my heart is heavy, yet my spirit is strengthened by the belief that the misguided goals of my father and the man Grogan are now ended."

"What of Grogan?" asked Smith. "What has become of him?"

"He remains on the mountain. Waiting...for you." Now Eagle's gaze came to rest directly on Smith. "He knows you are coming and sought to flee with the small handful of men he has left. But my people—those who he lorded it over and treated disrespectfully after mollifying them with a few bags of grain and some blankets while, in truth, only craving the yellow ore that twists the minds of all Whites—will not allow him to leave. The mountain made my father pay for his poor choices. We will now give you, Smith, he who already once made a brave effort to eliminate the evil of the rifles, the chance to finish making Gro-gan pay."

Smith gave a solemn nod. "I thank you."

"My future wife assures me that you and the one she calls Big Lone are men of conflicted yet strong hearts. She says you each have the wolves of darkness and light often tearing at one another inside of you, but mostly, you keep the dark wolf at bay. I have faith in her judgment."

A wry smile tugged at one corner of Smith's mouth. "I can't speak for Big Lone here, but I'm afraid there've been times past when I didn't do a very good job of keeping that dark wolf at bay. I'm working hard on doing better, though, and this chance to exact payment out of Grogan is another step in the right direction... either way, your future wife is a wise young lady."

Bright Moon flashed a shy smile. "I have to be if I am to wed a man who will one day be a great chief of our tribe."

Eagle Soaring raised an arm and pointed toward Grief Mountain, saying, "Go then, Smith and Big Lone. Go do what you came here for...and may the right wolves within you prevail."

———

AFTER THE MANY hard miles and all the talk and anticipation, Pike Grogan in person at first looked to Lone like nothing much different from any other lean, lanky specimen of a man, unwashed and unshaven, you could find drifting most anywhere throughout the west. Until you got to the eyes. Two bottomless, soulless black things they were, staring out at the world as cold and unfeeling as two chips of coal. Any emotion displayed on his long, narrow face came from the wide, thin-lipped mouth that stretched nearly from one jaw hinge to the other.

Those eyes held steady on Smith as he and Lone rode slowly up to the rugged camp on the back slope of Grief Mountain. Grogan sat on a wooden crate in front of a sagging, dust-streaked canvas tent. A cigarette dangled from one corner of his mouth, and a tin cup was balanced on one knee. Half a dozen feet out from one corner of the tent smoldered a small campfire with a coffee pot dangling from a tripod over it. Another half dozen feet past the campfire, two men, heavily armed hard cases not too dissimilar in appearance from Grogan, leaned insolently against the sloping face of a large boulder. Their eyes also followed Smith's approach with no sign of emotion.

These were the only white men in sight. Thirty yards down slope, two dozen or so Cheyenne braves were spread out in a semi-circle facing up at the camp. They sat on pieces of broken rock or cross-legged on the ground, faces impassive, silently looking on. An array of war clubs and hatchets rested not so subtly across their laps or on the ground beside them.

Some of the braves stood and made an opening for Lone and Smith to pass through. Sue had remained behind with Bright Moon.

When the two horsemen reined up in the camp clearing, Grogan snapped away his cigarette butt and sneered up at Smith. "Well, well, well. The lost sheep returns...you double-crossing, back-stabbing sono-fabitch."

Smith and Lone dismounted slow and careful, one at a time, so one or the other always had his gun hand unoccupied, ready. When both were standing clear of their mounts, Smith responded to Grogan, saying, "I expected a warmer welcome than that, Pike. After all the trouble you been going to to get me back."

"*Pieces* of you back," Grogan corrected icily.

Smith's smile only widened. "There you go, continuing to be downright unfriendly. You might want to consider being more careful. Number one, I ain't no sheep. Number two, Granger Weems didn't call me near as many nasty names...yet I still killed him for what he did say."

"How? By talking him to death?"

"Sort of. I let a borrowed .44 speak for me."

"Uh-huh. I heard about that. Heard you had a little help, too. That'd be this big lug"—Grogan flicked a finger lazily toward Lone—"I take it?"

Smith nodded. "That's right. He cleans up around the edges, you might say...like he'll do with Shorty and Hechler holding up that boulder over yonder if they try sticking their noses in today."

"And I'm strictly yours?"

"How I figure it."

"'Wild Red' rides again, eh?"

"The name's Smith. I figure to bury that other fella along with you."

Geogan's sneer stretched so wide it nearly split his face. "You big feeling piece of shit. Best day you ever had, by any name you choose, you could never take me."

"*Worst* day I ever had, which was every one I wasted riding with you, I could have. Easy enough to find out for sure. All you got to do is stand up."

"You ain't worth the bother."

"Thanks for reminding me about my worth. From what I've been hearing, if delivered alive, it's five thousand dollars. So here I am," Smith grated. "I prefer cash."

"You'll take lead, damn you!" bellowed Grogan, thrusting up off the wooden crate and raising a handgun he'd been holding down out of sight. His arm swung around in a flat arc, aiming at Smith.

But fast as Grogan was with his already-drawn weapon, Smith cleared leather with equal speed. Both men fired at the same time. Grogan's slug—the bullet Smith had purposely ridden to—tore a furrow on the outer edge of the redhead's left bicep. Smith's bullet, the one he'd come to deliver as a counterpoint, slammed slightly off center into Grogan's chest, knocking the gang leader backward until he toppled onto and collapsed the canvas tent.

While that exchange was taking place, the two hard cases at the boulder, Shorty and Hechler, also made their play. Whatever past success they'd had with their guns—back-shooting and bushwhacking, apparently—clearly hadn't depended on speed. Because they had none. By the time they pushed off the boulder and slapped leather, Lone's .44 was already in his fist spitting tongues of red flame and a spray of lead. His slugs hammered the pair back against the boulder where they again leaned briefly before sliding slowly down, leaving streaks of gore on the sun-bleached rock.

It was over. That fast.

A couple of the braves rose from the semi-circle and trotted back down the slope, presumably to spread the word on what had just happened. The others remained looking on. The stink and visible wisps of powder smoke hung in the still air.

Lone and Smith stood together, hands automatically replacing spent cartridges into their gun wheels.

Lone said, "Well. You rode to the bullet."

"*We* rode to the bullet, friend," Smith countered. "And, all in all, a hell of a lot more than just one. In case you didn't notice."

"Uh-huh. But the one that counted, that's the thing to remember."

Smith's gaze drifted to the collapsed tent with Grogan's feet sticking out of the canvas folds. Quietly, he said, "But did it count for enough? Was it sufficient for me to have a right to consider myself purged? Clean? Fit to go back to Judith?"

"Only you can decide that. And her," Lone told him.

"What about you? You headed back to the Busted Spur?"

They could hear voices approaching and, turning to look, could see a group of people coming up the slope. Bright Moon, Eagle Soaring, and Sue were among them. Sue...Lone wondered if Smith's query stemmed partly from an awareness of her visit to Lone's bedroll the previous night. Or was Lone reading into it his own questions about that visit? *What to make of a few fleeting but wonderful moments with Sue...and the contrasting memory and now guilt-ridden ache over Velda...* Too often, the inner conflicts of a man were harder to come to grips with than those on the outside. Simple matters that could be settled with fists or guns.

"Yeah, I expect I'll have a couple new foals waitin' for me when I get back," Lone responded to Smith, even as his gaze lingered on Sue coming up the slope. Then, cutting his eyes over and dropping them to the bullet burn on the redhead's arm, he said, "Say...you cut yourself shaving or something?"

A LOOK AT BOOK ELEVEN:
RUTHLESS VALLEY

Wayne D. Dundee's rough 'n' tough fan favorite is back in the saddle, ridin' tall and hell-bent on delivering justice.

Lone McGantry is no stranger to danger. But when a favor for a friend embroils him in treachery, he finds himself at a crossroads.

After a man's belief in his runaway wife's innocence drives him to chase her into the heart of danger, Lone is called upon to aid in the search, risking everything to save him from the clutches of those with malicious intent. Standing in their path is attorney Niles Lavin and his ruthless investigator, both determined to seize control of a valley rich with untapped resources.

As loyalties are tested, Lone realizes that fulfilling his obligation may demand more than he ever imagined—and force him to confront the true depths of his resolve in a battle full of ruthless enemies.

AVAILABLE JUNE 2024

ABOUT THE AUTHOR

Wayne D. Dundee is an American author of popular genre fiction. His writing has primarily been detective mysteries (the Joe Hannibal PI series) and Western adventures. To date, he has written four dozen novels and forty-plus short stories, also ranging into horror, fantasy, erotica, and several "house name" books under bylines other than his own.

Dundee was born March 24, 1948, in Freeport, Illinois. He graduated from high school in Clinton, Wisconsin, 1966. Later that same year he married Pamela Daum and they had one daughter, Michelle. For the first fifty years of his life, Dundee lived and worked in the state line area of northern Illinois and southern Wisconsin. During most of that time he was employed by Arnold Engineering/Group Arnold out of Marengo, Illinois, where he worked his way up from factory laborer through several managerial positions. In his spare time, starting in high school, he was always writing. He sold his first short story in 1982.

In 1998, Dundee relocated to Ogallala, Nebraska, where he assumed the general manager position for a small Arnold facility there. The setting and rich history of the area inspired him to turn his efforts more toward the Western genre. In 2009, following the passing of his wife a year earlier, Dundee retired from Arnold and began to concentrate full time on his writing.

Dundee was the founder and original editor of Hardboiled Magazine.

His work in the mystery field has been nominated for an Edgar, an Anthony, and six Shamus Awards from the Private Eye Writers of America.